CHILD *of* GOD

A NOVEL

LOLITA FILES

SCRIBNER PAPERBACK FICTION
Published by Simon & Schuster
NEW YORK LONDON TORONTO SYDNEY SINGAPORE

SCRIBNER PAPERBACK FICTION
Simon & Schuster, Inc.
Rockefeller Center
1230 Avenue of the Americas
New York, NY 10020

First Scribner Paperback Fiction edition 2002

For information regarding special discounts for bulk purchases, please contact Simon & Schuster Special Sales at 1-800-456-6798 or *business@simonandschuster.com*

Designed by Charles Hames
Manufactured in the United States of America

1 3 5 7 9 10 8 6 4 2

The Library of Congress has cataloged the Simon & Schuster edition as follows:
Files, Lolita.
Child of God : a novel / Lolita Files.
p. cm.
1. African-American families—Fiction. 2. Tennessee—Fiction. I. Title.
PS3556.I4257 C48 2001
813'.54—dc21   2001032832

ISBN 0-684-84143-6
0-7432-2591-0 (Pbk)

CHILD *of* GOD

A NOVEL

LOLITA FILES

SCRIBNER PAPERBACK FICTION
Published by Simon & Schuster
NEW YORK LONDON TORONTO SYDNEY SINGAPORE

SCRIBNER PAPERBACK FICTION
Simon & Schuster, Inc.
Rockefeller Center
1230 Avenue of the Americas
New York, NY 10020

First Scribner Paperback Fiction edition 2002

SCRIBNER PAPERBACK FICTION and design are trademarks of
Macmillan Library Reference USA, Inc., used under license by
Simon & Schuster, the publisher of this work.

For information regarding special discounts for bulk purchases,
please contact Simon & Schuster Special Sales at 1-800-456-6798 or
business@simonandschuster.com

Designed by Charles Hames
Manufactured in the United States of America

1 3 5 7 9 10 8 6 4 2

The Library of Congress has cataloged the Simon & Schuster
edition as follows:
Files, Lolita.
Child of God : a novel / Lolita Files.
p. cm.
1. African-American families—Fiction. 2. Tennessee—Fiction. I. Title.
PS3556.I4257 C48 2001
813'.54—dc21   2001032832

ISBN 0-684-84143-6
0-7432-2591-0 (Pbk)

This book is dedicated to my
extraordinary mother,
Lillie B. Files,
to the first person I ever considered my hero,
my brother,
Arthur James Files, Jr.,
and to the loving memory of my father,
Arthur James Files, Sr.

CHILD *of* GOD

PROLOGUE

In all things there is a law of cycles.

—TACITUS

CHAPTER ONE

There's no sweeter stench than the scent of a burning baby.

Grace raced across the yard, her steps hastened by the cries upon the wind.

"Somebody help me," she cried. "My grandbaby's trapped inside the house."

She grabbed a large branch and began to beat against a window. It broke away and released a menacing gust of fire that licked the edges of her hair and sent her reeling backward in a choking fit.

The anguished cries from inside the house escaped through the broken pane, hanging upon the wind.

"*Waaaaaaaaaaaaaaaaaaaaaaaaaaaaaaaaaaaaaaaaaaaaaaaaaaa aaaaaa...*"

It was a wild and airy sound, a wailing that trailed off into a whirlwind of echoes. In the midst of the biting-cold night, the house was engulfed in a blizzard of flames.

Polo stood out front, drenched in sweat, flinging buckets of water. The fire became more savage with each bucket he threw. Grace found her footing again and began beating her house with another tree branch.

"Mama, it's not slowing down," Polo said, out of breath. "It's getting bigger. The water's making it worse."

"Just keep trying. It's got to be stopped."

"*Waaaaaaaaaaaaaaaaaaaaaaaaaaaaaaaaaaaaaaaaaaaaaaaaaaa aaaaaa...*"

The cries of the baby were deafening.

Polo threw away the bucket and grabbed a tree branch. He followed his mother's lead and began to swat at the fire.

Grace lifted her nose, catching the scent of the wind.

"Oh my God. Oh my God. Oh my God." She fell to her knees in exhaustion.

"Waaaaaaaaaaaaaaaaaaaaaaaaaaaaaaaaaaaaaaaaaaaaaaaaa aaaaaa . . ."

The haunting cry was like a lingering note in a dirge. Then it faded into the night and was never heard by Grace or Polo again.

Grace raised her head and listened to the sound as it waned. Silent tears fell onto the dusty earth. If not for the gentle shaking of her shoulders as she dropped her head into her hands, Polo would not have known she was crying.

"My grandbaby is dead."

Polo dropped on his knees in the dirt beside her, trying to make out her words as she sobbed into her soot-stained palms. He thought she was asking about his sister. He wrapped his arms around her in a tight embrace.

"Mama, Ophelia's all right," he said. "She's out there by them fir trees."

Ophelia stood in the shadows of the woods, watching the fire gut the house. In the dazzling glow of the flames, she had seen her mother and brother trying to get to the baby and calm the blaze.

Grace's sobs grew heavy as the soot from her hands now covered her face. Her long black satiny hair hung loose and tangled around her head. Polo held his mother close, rocking her in his arms.

The fire raged on before them, consuming the house.

"Mama, we couldn't do nuthin'," said Polo. "The baby was 'sleep when we went next door. It wasn't nothing burning in the house. The stove wasn't even on. The baby was 'sleep."

"How we gon' tell Ophelia about the baby?"

The look of terror and questioning in his mother's eyes frightened him.

"I think she already know. Look like she came from out by the barn. That's why she standing by them trees."

"What was she doing over there?" Grace asked. She was almost hysterical.

"I'on know, Mama. She always be in the barn." He rocked

Adams shoes. He strutted back and forth across the
shooting the shit," as he put it, with the patrons.

wore the same outfit every day. Folks figured he either
whole lot of black pants and white cotton shirts with
black stripes, or he had a woman stashed away who
ed them every single night. No one knew. Caesar could
the Lucky Star at five A.M. after juking all night and return
even A.M. to reopen the liquor store, and the shiny black
ts and white cotton shirt with broad black stripes would still
intact, pants creased, shirt crisp. He was never musky.

No matter what time of day it was, he always had a peach
Nehi in hand. And he never had a stain on his shirt.

As he paraded around the store, not even sweating in the afternoon heat, he sucked on a cold bottle.

"Y'all done heard 'bout that Boten baby and the fire?" he
said to no one in particular. He belched a bouquet of peaches as
he turned a chair around and sat down.

"Yeah, but you know who baby that was, don't you?"

A short, fat red woman with moles all over her face and neck
talked out of the side of her mouth as she chawed on a chicken
leg. Caesar nodded at her, gulping the soda.

"Uh-huh. I done heard it's that boy Lay's baby. That's why
they done shipped him off to Dee-troit like that, tryna to be
slick. Them folks ain't foolin' nobody. They think folks don't
know 'bout him and his sister."

He belched again. This time it was loud.

The fat red woman was sucking the marrow out of her
chicken bone. The suction noises of the marrow coming up
from inside the bone were audible throughout the room.

"All them Botens got something wrong with 'em," she said.
"I'on know what it is, but they's all a little quirky."

"Not all of 'em. Just Grace and her family."

Caesar and the fat woman stopped talking and turned
around toward the back of the room. In the corner sat Sukie,
hidden in the shadows. There was a warm glass of gin in front of
her and a half-empty bottle. Her burnt-orange hair was wound
in a big ball and piled high atop her head.

his mother faster. "She ain't crying or even coming over here to
ask 'bout the baby. I'on know, maybe she in shock. I guess she
already knows he's dead."

At those words, Grace fell onto her son's chest and began to
cry again.

As the two held each other, the wooden porch collapsed,
and the entire house folded in on itself.

Polo's girlfriend came running from across the field.

"I could see it from my house," she said. "I could see the
flames just shooting up into the sky."

Polo ignored her, rocking his mother. Coolie ran next door
to Polo's uncle's house for more water. She returned, hurling
the bucket so hard, the entire thing flew into the flames.

"What are you doing?" Polo cried. "The house can't be
saved, it's already gone."

"We gotta put the fire out," she said. She ran next door for
more water. Her short, curly hair was sticking to her face and
neck in sweaty ringlets, and her peach-colored skin was flushed
from the heat. She ran closer to the house. The fire licked at her,
rushing up the front of her skirt.

She screamed and danced around in a frenzy.

Polo let go of his mother and leaped upon his girlfriend,
throwing her to the ground. The fire on her skirt was extinguished as they rolled in the dust. Smoke rose from the hem in a
funky puff.

A car approached in the distance. Grace's husband, Big
Daddy, sped toward them in his bright yellow '59 Ford. Before
he had turned the engine off, Big Daddy and Grace's brother,
Walter, were dashing out of the car, running to the house.
Within seconds they realized there was nothing either of them
could do to save it.

Big Daddy rushed over to Grace. Walter stood rooted, staring at the fantastic flames.

"What happened, baby?" Big Daddy said in his booming
voice.

Grace's sobbing grew louder.

"We was all next door just sittin' around, like we've done a hundred times before. Hamlet was in there. We didn't want to disturb him since he was 'sleep. The next thing you know, it's this fire. My baby's little boy done died in there."

Big Daddy grabbed his head and dropped to his knees beside her. He wrapped his tree-trunk arms around her and released his muffled cries deep within the security of her shoulder.

Walter stood above them. "Ain't nuthin' we can do but let it burn out," he said. "It's too far gone now."

He wanted to hug and comfort his sister, but Big Daddy and his overpowering strength were in the way.

"Where's Ophelia?" Big Daddy asked, choking back tears.

He looked around for his daughter amid the fire and smoke. Polo and Coolie pointed in the direction of the trees. Big Daddy turned to see Ophelia facedown in the dirt, her hands digging deep into the earth. Her body was wracked with sobs as they all watched her, alone in her pain.

From the porch next door, Sukie looked out. She glanced at her husband, Walter, who was still staring down at Grace and Big Daddy. She looked at the burning house, now a frame shrouded in the brilliance of the fire. She noticed Ophelia in the thicket of trees, covered with dirt and leaves as she grieved in the darkness.

Sukie shook her head.

With a slow turn, she sucked her tongue and went into the house to mop up all the water Polo and Coolie had wasted.

CHAPTER TWO

Downtown, Tennessee, was about eighty miles north of Columbia, right square in the middle of the route to Nashville. It was hard to get folks to drop in for a spell. There wasn't much there for anybody to see.

Downtown was a dustbowl. There were four main buildings: the Green Goods Grocery Store, Kleinstein's Feed and Seed, the All-County Bank, and the Lucky Star Liquor Joint.

All the black folks lived arou... what was called Downtown's o... ther out, on the vestiges of wha... farms. They came into town to stop... shop for food, or to get supplies for t... stein's.

Downtown had been Downtown for ... Billy Varnessy went to New York with his co... weekend his cousins would go downtown in ... Billy Varnessy was from up in the hills of Tenne... that downtown New York was called downtown ... flat. He remained in New York for five years, ma... chunk of money in land development, and returne... nessee. He married Betty Carbunkle from Hohenwald a... settled a little town. His wife wanted to name it Varness... Billy decided to call it Downtown, because he hoped th... would one day become his version of New York. There was ... area of land in that part of Tennessee that was flat. Billy Varnessy's Downtown was very hilly.

During the week, many of the black folks worked the farms and homes of white landowners in the surrounding areas, and hung out in the evenings at the Lucky Star Liquor Joint. The Lucky Star was perched on top of one of the four hills that made up Downtown. At the top of the inclined dirt road, there was a big green house with a makeshift sign of Christmas lights in the shape of a star. More Christmas lights adorned a sign with the words LUCKY STAR LIQUOR JOINT painted in bright red letters. It flashed on and off twenty-four hours a day. Over the years someone had painted an F over the L in LUCKY, and someone else had tried to take it off with paint thinner. It never came all the way off, so to a stranger passing through town, it looked like the FUCKY STAR LIQUOR JOINT. Caesar Bucksport was the owner.

Caesar, with his big, greasy, processed pompadour, would walk around the Lucky Star drinking peach Nehi, dressed in shiny black pants, a crisp white cotton shirt with broad black stripes that was always too tight over his very potbelly, and

The natives in general were terrified of Sukie. People had heard talk for years that she was into roots. No one ever saw her do them, but they knew she was capable of laying down a serious mojo. It was obvious that once she had been very beautiful. Her hair was long and silky, her skin soft and smooth. And her eyes were an exotic blue-green-gray. No one had ever seen eyes like hers on a Negro in Downtown. A number of men made attempts to seduce her when she first arrived, even though she was married to Walter Martin. They knew she was from Louisiana. The men were excited to have a Creole in their midst.

Not long after she married Walter, Sukie caught him cheating with an eighteen-year-old girl from a neighboring town. The next day Walter's eyes swelled up big and red, then closed shut for a week. The doctor was called in, but he could offer no clear explanation. Walter worked with Big Daddy as a ranch hand. He was unable to work for days until the swelling just up and went away on its own. The girl he was caught with met a similar fate. Word spread that her breasts turned hard as rocks. Everyone concluded this was the work of Sukie. The cryptic smile she wore gave it all away.

None of the people in town could understand why Walter stayed married to her. It was as though he were under her spell.

"Y'all ain't got to stop talking just 'cause I'm here," Sukie said to Caesar and the woman.

She picked up the glass of gin and sipped it. Sukie drank like a man but never showed her liquor. Caesar eased up with his peach Nehi and went back to the bar. The woman kept chewing on her chicken bone.

"Just as well that baby died," Sukie said. "Couldn't no good come from a child like that. God took it. Got his reasons, too. He don't reco'nize sin. Won't stand for it. That baby dyin' was the best thing that could happen. That baby was the devil, he wasn't no child of God."

She picked up the bottle of gin and poured more into the glass.

"You want some ice in that, Miss Sukie?" Caesar asked.

He high-stepped over from the bar with a chilled lowball glass filled with ice. Sukie cocked a blue-green-gray eye at him like a parrot. She watched as he put the glass down on the table and filled it with the gin from the other warm glass.

"That baby wasn't no child of God," she repeated.

Caesar raced around the rest of the bar while everybody acted as though Sukie wasn't there. No one wanted to say anything more to set her off. A tall black boy with a clubfoot and nappy hair got up and put some money in the jukebox. The sounds of Dinah Washington filled the room as he cripped over to the pool table and started a game.

Sukie finished her gin and pushed her chair back from the table.

"Y'all ain't had to stop talking 'cause of me. Ain't my family you talking 'bout nohow. She the one got them fool chillun."

Caesar was doing his best impression of a barnyard rooster trying to be a gamecock. He rushed across the room, grinning with yellow teeth.

"You sho' you don't want nuthin' else, Miss Sukie?"

Sukie got up and gave him an evil eye. He turned around and stepped over to the next table.

"They ain't my chillun. They ain't none of mine," she said and left the Lucky Star, still mumbling under her breath. Everyone watched from the windows as she made her way down the winding dirt road to the bottom of the hill. When she was way out of earshot, the tall black boy with the clubfoot and nappy hair began to dance.

So did everyone else.

his mother faster. "She ain't crying or even coming over here to ask 'bout the baby. I'on know, maybe she in shock. I guess she already knows he's dead."

At those words, Grace fell onto her son's chest and began to cry again.

As the two held each other, the wooden porch collapsed, and the entire house folded in on itself.

Polo's girlfriend came running from across the field.

"I could see it from my house," she said. "I could see the flames just shooting up into the sky."

Polo ignored her, rocking his mother. Coolie ran next door to Polo's uncle's house for more water. She returned, hurling the bucket so hard, the entire thing flew into the flames.

"What are you doing?" Polo cried. "The house can't be saved, it's already gone."

"We gotta put the fire out," she said. She ran next door for more water. Her short, curly hair was sticking to her face and neck in sweaty ringlets, and her peach-colored skin was flushed from the heat. She ran closer to the house. The fire licked at her, rushing up the front of her skirt.

She screamed and danced around in a frenzy.

Polo let go of his mother and leaped upon his girlfriend, throwing her to the ground. The fire on her skirt was extinguished as they rolled in the dust. Smoke rose from the hem in a funky puff.

A car approached in the distance. Grace's husband, Big Daddy, sped toward them in his bright yellow '59 Ford. Before he had turned the engine off, Big Daddy and Grace's brother, Walter, were dashing out of the car, running to the house. Within seconds they realized there was nothing either of them could do to save it.

Big Daddy rushed over to Grace. Walter stood rooted, staring at the fantastic flames.

"What happened, baby?" Big Daddy said in his booming voice.

Grace's sobbing grew louder.

"We was all next door just sittin' around, like we've done a hundred times before. Hamlet was in there. We didn't want to disturb him since he was 'sleep. The next thing you know, it's this fire. My baby's little boy done died in there."

Big Daddy grabbed his head and dropped to his knees beside her. He wrapped his tree-trunk arms around her and released his muffled cries deep within the security of her shoulder.

Walter stood above them. "Ain't nuthin' we can do but let it burn out," he said. "It's too far gone now."

He wanted to hug and comfort his sister, but Big Daddy and his overpowering strength were in the way.

"Where's Ophelia?" Big Daddy asked, choking back tears.

He looked around for his daughter amid the fire and smoke. Polo and Coolie pointed in the direction of the trees. Big Daddy turned to see Ophelia facedown in the dirt, her hands digging deep into the earth. Her body was wracked with sobs as they all watched her, alone in her pain.

From the porch next door, Sukie looked out. She glanced at her husband, Walter, who was still staring down at Grace and Big Daddy. She looked at the burning house, now a frame shrouded in the brilliance of the fire. She noticed Ophelia in the thicket of trees, covered with dirt and leaves as she grieved in the darkness.

Sukie shook her head.

With a slow turn, she sucked her tongue and went into the house to mop up all the water Polo and Coolie had wasted.

CHAPTER TWO

Downtown, Tennessee, was about eighty miles north of Columbia, right square in the middle of the route to Nashville. It was hard to get folks to drop in for a spell. There wasn't much there for anybody to see.

Downtown was a dustbowl. There were four main buildings: the Green Goods Grocery Store, Kleinstein's Feed and Seed, the All-County Bank, and the Lucky Star Liquor Joint.

All the black folks lived around the inner edges of town in what was called Downtown's downtown. The whites lived farther out, on the vestiges of what used to be plantations and farms. They came into town to stop at the All-County Bank, to shop for food, or to get supplies for their livestock from Kleinstein's.

Downtown had been Downtown for over a hundred years. Billy Varnessy went to New York with his cousins in 1854. Every weekend his cousins would go downtown in the big city. Since Billy Varnessy was from up in the hills of Tennessee, he figured that downtown New York was called downtown because it was flat. He remained in New York for five years, made a decent chunk of money in land development, and returned to Tennessee. He married Betty Carbunkle from Hohenwald and they settled a little town. His wife wanted to name it Varnessyville. Billy decided to call it Downtown, because he hoped that it would one day become his version of New York. There was no area of land in that part of Tennessee that was flat. Billy Varnessy's Downtown was very hilly.

During the week, many of the black folks worked the farms and homes of white landowners in the surrounding areas, and hung out in the evenings at the Lucky Star Liquor Joint. The Lucky Star was perched on top of one of the four hills that made up Downtown. At the top of the inclined dirt road, there was a big green house with a makeshift sign of Christmas lights in the shape of a star. More Christmas lights adorned a sign with the words LUCKY STAR LIQUOR JOINT painted in bright red letters. It flashed on and off twenty-four hours a day. Over the years someone had painted an F over the L in LUCKY, and someone else had tried to take it off with paint thinner. It never came all the way off, so to a stranger passing through town, it looked like the FUCKY STAR LIQUOR JOINT. Caesar Bucksport was the owner.

Caesar, with his big, greasy, processed pompadour, would walk around the Lucky Star drinking peach Nehi, dressed in shiny black pants, a crisp white cotton shirt with broad black stripes that was always too tight over his very potbelly, and white Stacy Adams shoes. He strutted back and forth across the room "shooting the shit," as he put it, with the patrons.

He wore the same outfit every day. Folks figured he either had a whole lot of black pants and white cotton shirts with broad black stripes, or he had a woman stashed away who washed them every single night. No one knew. Caesar could leave the Lucky Star at five A.M. after juking all night and return at seven A.M. to reopen the liquor store, and the shiny black pants and white cotton shirt with broad black stripes would still be intact, pants creased, shirt crisp. He was never musky.

No matter what time of day it was, he always had a peach Nehi in hand. And he never had a stain on his shirt.

As he paraded around the store, not even sweating in the afternoon heat, he sucked on a cold bottle.

"Y'all done heard 'bout that Boten baby and the fire?" he said to no one in particular. He belched a bouquet of peaches as he turned a chair around and sat down.

"Yeah, but you know who baby that was, don't you?"

A short, fat red woman with moles all over her face and neck talked out of the side of her mouth as she chawed on a chicken leg. Caesar nodded at her, gulping the soda.

"Uh-huh. I done heard it's that boy Lay's baby. That's why they done shipped him off to Dee-troit like that, tryna to be slick. Them folks ain't foolin' nobody. They think folks don't know 'bout him and his sister."

He belched again. This time it was loud.

The fat red woman was sucking the marrow out of her chicken bone. The suction noises of the marrow coming up from inside the bone were audible throughout the room.

"All them Botens got something wrong with 'em," she said. "I'on know what it is, but they's all a little quirky."

"Not all of 'em. Just Grace and her family."

Caesar and the fat woman stopped talking and turned around toward the back of the room. In the corner sat Sukie, hidden in the shadows. There was a warm glass of gin in front of her and a half-empty bottle. Her burnt-orange hair was wound in a big ball and piled high atop her head.

The natives in general were terrified of Sukie. People had heard talk for years that she was into roots. No one ever saw her do them, but they knew she was capable of laying down a serious mojo. It was obvious that once she had been very beautiful. Her hair was long and silky, her skin soft and smooth. And her eyes were an exotic blue-green-gray. No one had ever seen eyes like hers on a Negro in Downtown. A number of men made attempts to seduce her when she first arrived, even though she was married to Walter Martin. They knew she was from Louisiana. The men were excited to have a Creole in their midst.

Not long after she married Walter, Sukie caught him cheating with an eighteen-year-old girl from a neighboring town. The next day Walter's eyes swelled up big and red, then closed shut for a week. The doctor was called in, but he could offer no clear explanation. Walter worked with Big Daddy as a ranch hand. He was unable to work for days until the swelling just up and went away on its own. The girl he was caught with met a similar fate. Word spread that her breasts turned hard as rocks. Everyone concluded this was the work of Sukie. The cryptic smile she wore gave it all away.

None of the people in town could understand why Walter stayed married to her. It was as though he were under her spell.

"Y'all ain't got to stop talking just 'cause I'm here," Sukie said to Caesar and the woman.

She picked up the glass of gin and sipped it. Sukie drank like a man but never showed her liquor. Caesar eased up with his peach Nehi and went back to the bar. The woman kept chawing on her chicken bone.

"Just as well that baby died," Sukie said. "Couldn't no good come from a child like that. God took it. Got his reasons, too. He don't reco'nize sin. Won't stand for it. That baby dyin' was the best thing that could happen. That baby was the devil, he wasn't no child of God."

She picked up the bottle of gin and poured more into the glass.

"You want some ice in that, Miss Sukie?" Caesar asked.

He high-stepped over from the bar with a chilled lowball glass filled with ice. Sukie cocked a blue-green-gray eye at him like a parrot. She watched as he put the glass down on the table and filled it with the gin from the other warm glass.

"That baby wasn't no child of God," she repeated.

Caesar raced around the rest of the bar while everybody acted as though Sukie wasn't there. No one wanted to say anything more to set her off. A tall black boy with a clubfoot and nappy hair got up and put some money in the jukebox. The sounds of Dinah Washington filled the room as he cripped over to the pool table and started a game.

Sukie finished her gin and pushed her chair back from the table.

"Y'all ain't had to stop talking 'cause of me. Ain't my family you talking 'bout nohow. She the one got them fool chillun."

Caesar was doing his best impression of a barnyard rooster trying to be a gamecock. He rushed across the room, grinning with yellow teeth.

"You sho' you don't want nuthin' else, Miss Sukie?"

Sukie got up and gave him an evil eye. He turned around and stepped over to the next table.

"They ain't my chillun. They ain't none of mine," she said and left the Lucky Star, still mumbling under her breath. Everyone watched from the windows as she made her way down the winding dirt road to the bottom of the hill. When she was way out of earshot, the tall black boy with the clubfoot and nappy hair began to dance.

So did everyone else.

PART II

1945–1949

SUKIE

*Woe to the house where the hen crows
and the rooster keeps still.*

—SPANISH PROVERB

CHAPTER THREE

Grace's children were fascinated with Aunt Sukie. She was a mystery to them, with her beautiful burnt-orange hair and her strange blue-green-gray eyes.

When they were very young, they didn't know to fear her. Sukie's ways seemed magical, as did the air around her. Every morning after breakfast, before they headed to school, they rushed across the yard to her house to eat the thick slices of cake and fresh cookies she would leave for them.

Sukie was always making something in her kitchen. If it wasn't food, she was boiling and drying leaves for the strange, fragrant concoctions that crowded her cabinets and countertops. The house always smelled of cinnamon. The spice's keen scent matched the color of her hair.

Lay adored her. From the moment he could speak, his first words were "Susu." It became his pet name for her.

Even though Lay was the middle child, his older sister Ophelia and kid brother Polo deferred to his authority. He was a wiry, athletic boy with strong features and a confident, aggressive bearing. His eyes were dark and penetrating, and when he stared at folks, often they couldn't hold his gaze without being unnerved. He was a natural bully. He reveled in taunting the other children in town. He took toys, bikes, candy. He didn't steal them. Kids surrendered when he asked. No one ever challenged him. That always disappointed him, because Lay relished a good fight.

He had a penchant for things dark, often dragging his brother and sister down to the banks of the creek to hunt small animals and fish for the sheer thrill of dissecting them. Ophelia never enjoyed these jaunts. She preferred hanging back, away from the water's edge, reading books as her brothers toyed with their kill.

She was a soft-spoken girl with a delicate demeanor, smooth brown skin, and thick plaits that hung past her shoulders.

Grace was very protective of the girl, sheltering her from the other children in town. Ophelia began school late, when Lay was big enough to go. She was two years older than her brother, but Grace didn't want her to attend school alone.

"What do you get out of doing that?" Ophelia asked her brothers as they gutted a small squirrel near the bank. "Why you want to kill innocent animals? It's not like we're taking them home to eat."

"I wanna know what's inside," Lay said. "I like knowing what makes things tick."

"Those animals have families. You shouldn't be murdering just for fun."

"That's dumb," Polo said to his sister. "What other reason is there for us to do it?"

Polo didn't believe his own words, but he wanted Lay to think he did. The killings sickened him at first, but over time he'd developed a thicker skin. He admired his older brother. Where Lay was fearless, Polo was hesitant and, at times, afraid. He was a lean boy, dark, rugged, almost pretty, with short legs, a long waist, and an even, sometimes excitable temperament. He was his father's favorite.

While having his father's approval was important to him, Polo envied his brother's confidence and daring even more. He longed for his brother's attention. Polo and Lay had as good a relationship as two brothers could, but Lay and Ophelia had the stronger bond. Lay was curious about Ophelia and what went on in her head. She looked and behaved so differently from him and Polo. That alone was enough to keep his attention fixed.

One day Lay called Ophelia out to the front of the house.

"What?" she said.

"Come with me," he answered, beckoning her with a crooked finger as he raced through the trees toward the creek. "I wanna show you something."

Ophelia ran behind him, clutching a worn copy of Hans Christian Andersen's fairy tales. When she reached the water's edge, her brother was standing beside a small brown dog that was lying on its side.

"Whose dog is this?"

"It belonged to that boy named Booty," Lay said. "I asked him if I could have it and he said no."

Ophelia stooped to stroke the dog but saw that the underside was covered with blood. Flies had begun to gather and swarm.

She screamed, dropping the book she had been clutching. She moved away, stumbling back onto the muddy bank.

"It's dead," she whispered.

"I know," he said with a grin. "I killed it. I wanted you to see it first. Look."

He pulled a bloody knife out of his pocket. He held it out for her to admire.

Tears fell from Ophelia's eyes as she scrambled from the creek bank and ran to the house.

The three children were as different from one another as could be, living in the shadows of Sukie and Walter's strange presence across the yard.

As they grew older, two of them became more united in one area of thought.

Polo and Ophelia realized that neither of them liked their aunt very much.

All three of the children knew Sukie didn't like their mother. They never saw any proof of this, other than Sukie's obvious indifference. Sukie didn't talk to Grace. She spoke around or about Grace even in her presence. On rare occasions Sukie would address her, and Grace would give a quiet response, appreciative of the scrap of attention. She wanted Sukie to like her, but she knew this was something that could never be.

Of all the children, Sukie was closest to Lay. She seemed

taken with him from the moment he was born, and while she
didn't communicate much with Grace, she was more than willing to offer her assistance when her first son was born.

"Why she like you so much?" Ophelia asked.

The two were sitting by the creek bank. Lay skipped rocks
off the surface of the water.

"She say we kindred spirits."

"What does that mean?"

"It means I understand her, and she understand me."

Sukie and Lay would sometimes sit for hours in her kitchen.
She would share with him dark tales of New Orleans, her Creole people, and voodoo. He savored his words, enchanted by
the power of chemicals and spirits over the mind. Lay's attach-
ment to her was so strong, he felt more affection for her than for
his own mother.

As a child, he picked up cursing from one of the boys in
town. It upset Grace a great deal, but he would not stop, no
matter how she protested and threatened to punish him.

The first time Sukie heard him swear, she delivered a re-
sounding slap to his face, a gesture that numbed his right cheek
and produced a shrill ringing in his ears.

"Don't let me catch you doing that again."

"Why?" he asked, his face stinging. "I hear you cuss sometimes. If you can do it—"

She slapped him again. Lay stared up at her, his dark eyes
glistening.

"You let me catch you doing it again," she said, "and it'll be
the last time you ever say a word to anybody."

Lay threw his arms around her waist.

"I'm sorry, Susu," he said, his words muffled in her dress.

While Lay went on to a life rich with profanity, Sukie never
heard another curse word from him again.

Lay followed Sukie's every suggestion save one.

"You shouldn't be spending so much time with that gal," she
said.

"But she's my sister. I love Ophelia."

"She ain't like you and Polo. You ain't never notice how different she look?"

"Yeah," said Lay, "but that don't mean nuthin'."

She pinched him on the arm.

"Ow," he cried.

"Don't give me no lip," Sukie said with a frown. "I'm telling you she different. You need to leave her alone 'cause I say so."

No one knew why Sukie and Walter had no children of their own. People said it was because Sukie was evil and messed with roots. That God had cursed her womb because of the way she treated folks. She didn't associate with anyone in town. No one dared to speak to her. Some had tried when she first moved to Downtown. She greeted them with a dark flash of her eyes and a cold turn of her shoulder. Yet every Sunday she was in church, her loud exaltations of prayer for a child rising up to the heavens. No one joined in her desperate pleas. Half the town hoped that her prayers would fail.

There was talk that maybe Walter was sterile. He'd had his share of venereal diseases and doctor visits from his days of whoring before marrying Sukie. Some of the town gossips disagreed with this. It was rumored that he had a secret baby with someone not long before he and Sukie were married.

"Oh, you talkin' 'bout that gal . . . what was her name?" Caesar scratched his belly. "I can't think of her name right off. Anyway, that baby was born dead."

"No," said Mrs. Betty, a grayed woman with a curved spine and a taste for whiskey. "That ain't the one we talkin' 'bout."

"Well, I heard it's another one out there somewhere," Caesar said. "Much as that boy cut up, I'm surprised there ain't more."

"I heard the baby was 'flicted," said Caroline Hixton. She worked at the Green Goods Grocery and sometimes cooked for the Lucky Star Liquor Joint. "If I had a 'flicted baby, I'd hide it, too."

"Naw, see, that's not what happened," said Caesar. "The

baby got the droplip. Lip hang down long as my arm. It's just ugly, is all."

Folks in the Lucky Star nodded and grunted as they listened to the talk. And while no one could agree on just what was wrong with the baby, they all agreed that the baby was alive somewhere and that it wasn't normal. It was anyone's guess which version of the story was true.

Mrs. Betty read dreams and tarot.

"Unnatural things come to unnatural people," she said. "Something 'bout Walter Martin is real unnatural. An unnatural man can't help but have an unnatural baby."

When Polo was still a newborn, Grace walked in on Sukie and Big Daddy in the big four-poster bed, fucking. She could hear them as she walked down the hallway, and when she reached the doorway, she could see Big Daddy's strong, tar-colored back pumping up and down.

She could hear Sukie's moans and screams and see her wrapping thick honey-brown legs around Big Daddy's back. Grace stood at the door and watched. The room smelled of warm cinnamon and musk. She watched her husband as he grabbed on to hunks of Sukie's thick burnt-orange hair. Sukie was the first to see her. She kept fucking as her gaze remained fixed on Grace.

Big Daddy noticed that Sukie's attention had shifted. Still pumping, he glanced over his shoulder, following the direction of her eyes. He saw Grace in the doorway, tears streaked down her face. He jumped up, his dark towering nakedness filling the room. As he stuffed himself into his pants, Grace turned and made her way to the kitchen. Big Daddy came in a few moments later, sitting down at the table across from his wife.

She was picking collards, separating the leaves from the stems, cutting them into ribbony strands to be boiled.

"Seem like I done throwed 'way more leaves with worms on 'em than I done cut up good ones."

Big Daddy watched the movements of her hand as she rolled

the leaves and cut them toward her body with the sharp edge of the knife.

"I started to get mustards," she rambled, "but I know you like collards better. Mustards stank the whole house up."

"Grace . . . I'm sorry."

She looked up at him, her face bare of expression. She examined him, his eyes, his torso, the unfastened belt. She bit down on the inside of her lip as the taste of bile rose to the top of her throat. She coughed.

"I don't know why you still wear them navy blue pants," she said, still clearing her throat. "The hems done fell out, and the waist is unraveling. Every time I put 'em aside to make into rags, you manage to find a way to dig 'em out again."

Big Daddy fidgeted, his dread heightened all the more by her calm.

"Grace, baby, she came in here, and I was by myself, and she just started touching me. I couldn't get her offa me. I couldn't stop touching her back."

"Some people just like that," Grace said. "They defenseless against people like her. Sukie's pretty, Big Daddy. You ain't got to apologize for being a man and seeing what a man see when he look at her."

She looked over at him sitting across the table from her. She felt sorry for her husband. She knew his strength was no match for her sister-in-law's.

Big Daddy let out a deep moan, tears dropping onto his cheeks. "But I let it happen," he said, shaking his head. "I betrayed you. I made a vow 'fore God to be true to you. I don't love nuthin' more than I love you, Grace. She's just a woman. I shoulda been stronger than that."

"She's not just a woman," Grace said. "There was nuthin' you could do."

"I shoulda been stronger."

"Just hush, baby," she said. "Sukie's got a power none of us ain't gon' ever understand. All we can do is just live 'longside it, and do our best not to stir it up. Wasn't nuthin' you could do."

Big Daddy's mouth hung open, a trail of saliva dripping out as his body heaved with silent sobs.

"You think this enough greens?" Grace asked.

Big Daddy sat before her, wringing his hands.

"It won't never happen no more. I promise. I love you, Grace. I swear 'fore God I love you."

"I think this'll be enough," she said. "I'ma put four hamhocks in the pot. We shouldn't eat more than that."

Big Daddy reached over and touched Grace on the arm. He looked her in the eye. She smiled at him as though she understood.

"She shole got some pretty hair, don't she?"

"You got pretty hair, too," he said.

"Mine don't smell like cinnamon, though. And it ain't that color, neither."

Sukie sauntered in the kitchen, pulling her clothes together. She walked toward the back door. She looked into Grace's eyes as she walked by.

"I guess we even now," she said. "Time'll tell how even we gon' be."

Big Daddy hung his head.

"I'll send Lay over in a while with some greens," Grace said. "He probly gon' want some of that pie you made anyway." Her tone was soft. Big Daddy glanced sidelong at his wife, terrified by her even demeanor.

Sukie smirked and opened the screen door. "Don't want no greens. I done ate already." She glanced over at Big Daddy. His head hung to his chest.

"We'll send some anyhow," Grace persisted. "Walter might be hungry."

At that remark, Sukie's eyes narrowed. She slammed the door behind her. In the back room, baby Polo awakened and started to cry.

"I'll go get him," Big Daddy said.

"No, you better go wash up. That cinnamon smell might make him sick. We'll be eating after awhile."

Grace pushed her chair back and wiped her hands on her

apron. Big Daddy pulled her to him, his tree-trunk arms locked tight.

"It won't never happen no more," he whispered. "I promise."

Grace could smell cinnamon all around her. She couldn't breathe in his arms. She was spinning. When he let her go, she smiled at him and kissed his lips.

"Now go wash up," she said to her husband.

Big Daddy grabbed a heavy pot of hot water from the stove and rushed from the kitchen.

Grace leaned over the sink, her mouth a tight line. She waited until she could hear him pouring the water into the washtub behind the curtain in their bedroom. After a short while, she heard him climb in.

She opened her mouth and threw up. When she felt she could not throw up anymore, she grabbed the dipper from the bucket of water beside the sink and drank. She sloshed the water around in her mouth. She spit it into the sink.

In a rare moment of rage, she yanked open her kitchen cabinets, sorting through the contents. With her right arm, she swept everything onto the floor, dropped to her knees, and rifled through the pile. When she found the cinnamon, she threw it into the sink. Fumbling for a match, she set the cardboard box of spice aflame. A red burst of smoke shot straight into the air, filling the room with its powerful sweet odor. The kitchen was filled with Sukie's presence.

Grace sank back onto the floor, her head in her hands. Polo's hysterical cries from the bedroom resonated throughout the house.

The kitchen smelled of warm cinnamon and musk.

CHAPTER FOUR

Walter met his wife, Sukie, the first day he was in New Orleans.

He left Tennessee in a hurry, when Ophelia was still a baby, and landed at a graying, portentous boardinghouse just off Dauphine in the French Quarter.

The Chateau le Lux, a grand and luminous name for such a

dilapidated place, was governed by Madame Lucien, a small Creole woman with a shock of coarse, flaming red hair and penetrating green eyes. Her accent rolled with a syrupy thickness, at once very French and very southern, resonant with the dark mystery of dank tropical forests, primal poisons and panaceas, warm winds, and midnight rituals.

Around Madame Lucien's neck hung a dried chicken foot curled tight around a twig. The ominous claw was nestled between the leathery curves of her yellow bosom, highlighting the harsh delicacy of the claw and the woman herself. She lived in the Chateau le Lux with her two sons, her daughter, Sukie, and an assortment of transient tenants—faceless people who faded into and out of the house during the hazy shadows of dusk and dawn.

Her sons were twenty and twenty-one, big, rusty-haired boys who towered over everyone in the house. There had been another daughter, Celine, the eldest of the children and very beautiful. She died in a tragic fall from the window of one of the rooms on the third floor. It had been a sitting room when Celine fell to her death.

Madame Lucien's husband, a mortician, died in that same sitting room a few months after Celine's death. He had been having a vigorous debate with Sukie when his chair fell back into the exposed blades of a window fan. The fan was installed in the window the day after Celine fell.

François Lucien was decapitated at once, the sharp blades shearing off his head in swift, clean strokes. His blood stained the staid pattern of the carpeting in an odd design of everwidening circles. The head rolled over into a corner, resting upright next to an African fern. Blood formed a pool around the base of the fern's pot and was absorbed into the texture of the clay. Within the week, the fern had doubled in size.

François's eyes were stunned wide by the shock of death. At the funeral, he was buried in a blindfold, his head perched snug atop the body. Behind the blindfold the eyes pressed, bareballed, against the cloth. Not even the mortician who prepared his body could get the eyelids to shut.

The room had been closed off from boarders ever since. It was now Sukie's bedroom. She had been the sole witness of her father's death. She never spoke of it to anyone. Not even the police.

Walter studied the pictures on the mantel as he waited for Madame Lucien to show him to his room. He picked up the frame that held the smoldering image of Celine. Her eyes were a penetrating green, and the bounteous mane of reddish hair cascaded over her shoulders. Her smile was sweet and generous. Walter traced her face with his finger.

"C'mon. I'll show you your room," crackled the twisted Creole drawl.

Walter looked up. Madame Lucien stood before him. Her eyes were on his hand as it clutched the picture of Celine. She glared at the finger that had been tracing her daughter's face. A fury danced behind the green lights of Madame Lucien's gaze.

Walter hurried to place the photo back on the mantel. In his haste, it fell over and crashed to the floor, glass shattering against the stone hearth and flying in shards around the room.

Madame Lucien's face turned several shades of red. Her fists clenched and unclenched as she stepped closer to him.

"We've got your room all ready," the daughter, Sukie, said, materializing from the gloom and breaking the bitter silence that hung between Walter and her mother.

Madame Lucien turned to look at her daughter, her eyes narrowing in anger. Walter saw what appeared to be a wry smile as the corner of Sukie's lips curled upward. She faced off, eye to eye, with her mother.

Placing her hand in his, Sukie led Walter up the stairs to the third floor.

Walter followed the girl in silence. From behind her, he watched the thick tresses of silky red hair bouncing free upon her shoulders. He admired the firm turn of her calves as she led the way through the shadows of the hall. The seductive swing of her hips pulled him in. The faint scent of cinnamon toyed with his nostrils. Walter could feel his nature swell, despite the anxious beating of his heart.

Sukie stopped in front of a door and, with hesitation, turned the knob. She glanced over her shoulder at him, her hand still clasping his, her eyes beckoning him to follow.

Walter did, the swell pressing tighter against his pants as he gazed into the mysterious blue-green-gray eyes of the girl. Her skin was beautiful and smooth. In the darkness of the doorway, he imagined she smiled at him.

The room was spacious but dim and gave off both a seductive warmth and a dusty chill. A large canopy bed dominated it. Candles adorned every open area of space, including the floor. Shadowy pieces of filtered light broke through the darkness, giving greater outline to the furniture, the candles, and the figure of Sukie, who had released his hand and walked on farther, deep into the room.

Walter placed his suitcase on the floor and stood just inside the doorway.

"When was the last time this room was used?"

Sukie walked over to the dark, heavy drapes and tied them back. Gossamer curtains lay behind them. More light sifted into the room, but it was dimming as dusk faded into darkness.

"A long time ago," she answered, her voice magical and spicy, not as patois-thick as her mother's, but a distinct southern flavor with a pronounced, provocative drawl.

He could smell Sukie's cinnamon scent as it enveloped the room, despite the dusty funk that hung over everything.

"This used to be my nana's room," Sukie said. She sauntered away from the window, over to the bed. "Me and Nana used to lie in this bed and share all kinds of secrets." She sat on the edge of the mattress, stroking the covers with a reverent hand.

Walter couldn't make out the details of her face, but he could see the penetrating eyes peering at him from the shadows.

He sat down in a chair near the door, making a discreet tent with his palms over his crotch to conceal the bulge.

"Who is Nana?" he asked, his voice quivering against his will.

Sukie fell back on the bed, her arms outstretched like wings.

"Na-na was my grand-ma," she sang, her arms moving in swift motions over the covers, as though she were flying.

"Oh."

"Umm-hmm. Nana talks to me sometimes. She tells me what to do."

A strange feeling began to wash over him as he sat in the chair, his member paining him, watching her lying so carefree on the bed. He wanted her to leave him alone in the room. At the same time, he wanted her there. Walter was both afraid of her and aroused by her beauty, her mystery, and the cinnamon smell.

"Do you have a nana?" she asked. Her voice zinged around the room with a sharp resonance.

"Huh?"

"Do you have a nana?"

Walter didn't answer as his palms made anxious movements across the fabric covering his crotch. "What's the matter with you? You can't talk or somethin'?"

"I only saw my grandma one time," he said. "When I was little. At my daddy's funeral."

The room grew dimmer as Walter listened to the sounds of Sukie's arms flapping against the bed mingled with the sound of his palms moving across the rough cloth of his pants.

"Close the door," she said, her voice breaking the darkness.

"What?"

"Shut the door and come here."

Walter sat frozen in the chair.

"Shut the door," she demanded.

Walter pushed the door with his palm.

"Now come over here," Sukie said, her voice charged with electricity.

Walter didn't get up from the chair. He didn't know what the girl wanted. And he was afraid. Of what, he wasn't sure.

"Don't make me come over there."

Walter rose from the chair and walked with slow steps across the room. Sukie patted the bed beside her, gesturing for him to sit down, and peered into his face.

"You scared of me, ain't you?" Her spicy breath was hot against his cheeks. "Yeah," she whispered, "you scared of me. Everybody's scared of me. Even my mama."

As she said this, her hand touched Walter's thigh, sending a charge through him that wracked his body. Her hand snaked its way up his thigh to the tight spot in his groin that had been troubling him. She held his gaze as she found the spot and squeezed it.

"You shouldn't be scared of me," Sukie said, her hand massaging the area. She unzipped his pants and pulled his hardness through the opening in his boxer shorts. Walter's heart beat an erratic rhythm; his face broke out in a cold sweat that blended with the hot mist of Sukie's breath.

Sukie held him in her hand, her grip tight. She jerked him a few times, then stopped, her face closer to his, her lips a hair away from the flesh of his own.

"You still scared of me?" she asked, the softness of her voice disintegrating around him.

Walter was overpowered by her presence.

"Uh-uh," he said, the sound escaping him as a high-pitched, closed-lipped groan.

She pushed him back onto the bed, sliding down his body, her mouth hovering above the tight swell of his groin. Her mouth encircled him.

Walter closed his eyes and leaned his head back. His blood raced through him, hot like lava, building thick and rapid, until he erupted, filling the receptive mouth of the girl.

She smiled, snaking her way up onto his chest. She moved close to his face, her breath still cinnamony, but now coupled with a gamy, musty smell.

"I told you you shouldn't be scared of me." She smiled.

Walter stared at her with wonder.

She grinned, laying her head down on his chest.

"Just wait," she said. "I'm a different kinda woman. I can show you some things."

· · ·

Walter awakened to cold air rushing over his naked body. The covers were on the floor and the sheets were tangled.

He sat up in the bed, his limbs sore, his mouth dry. He squinted in the darkness of the room.

"Hey," he called out. "Hey."

The chill wind whipped through the open window, flapping the curtains like elephant ears.

"Hey," he called out again.

No one answered.

Walter stared into the pitch dark of the room, afraid. When he tried to move, his groin hurt. His arms felt as though he had been lifting something heavy. He rubbed his eyes and peered into the darkness.

He stood from the bed with slow, meticulous effort. As his legs adjusted to the weight of his body, a sharp cramp pierced the back of his thigh.

He sat down on the cold floor.

"Where are you?"

His words ricocheted off the walls. He patted the floor in search of his clothes.

Sukie sat in a corner of the room, near an open window at a point where the walls met, her knees tight against her chest.

The cold air blended with the faint smell of cinnamon and sent a chill through him that made his teeth chatter.

Sukie crawled forward, then sprang upon him naked, her weight pushing him back against the floor. She mounted him like an animal, her arms raised high above her head as she thrashed against him. Walter watched her, his arousal divorced from his conscious mind. His eyes were wide as he lay beneath the girl. She bucked and lurched above him, uttering obscenities and words he'd never heard before. Her hair was a maze of red ropes in orbit around her head.

Walter felt his pelvis swell. The swelling mounted with her thrashing until Walter thought his bladder, or whatever it was that was filling up, would burst.

He squirmed, surprised to find that he was pushing back

and moving with a desperation that matched the girl's. He squeezed his eyes shut as the tightness in his groin became unbearable.

Sukie fell forward on his torso, her lips close to his ear. Her hair fell heavy on his face. Walter's groin exploded, and the starburst radiated outward until it reached his very fingertips.

He opened his mouth to speak. She hushed him with her hand. And even though his body was no longer being physically moved, Walter felt as though he were being taken hostage and spirited away.

"You ain't got but one nut."

She was leaning over him. The blue-green-gray eyes shone with a magical light, even in the darkness.

"I ain't never heard of nobody with one nut."

"Don't matter," he said. "Everything else still work."

Sukie laughed, shaking her hair. "I like it. It makes you different. Just like me."

"What are you?" Walter asked.

"I'm just what you see."

"I'm not sure I know what that is. I ain't never met nobody like you before."

"I'm just what you see," she repeated. "I tasted you. Just as you tasted me."

The odd cadence of her words mixed with the eerie glow of her eyes made Walter nervous. He sensed trouble. It excited him. Something inside told him he should leave that house, right then, and get as far away from the woman as he could. He remained beside her, compelled by her very presence.

"If you want to, you can leave," she said, as though reading his thoughts.

Walter reached out and touched her face.

"I know."

When dawn began to break through the shadows of the room, Walter and Sukie were still entangled on the floor.

Careful not to disturb her, Walter sat up, rubbing his eyes. He glanced down at the sleeping girl. As she stirred under his gaze, her mouth opening, her eyes making erratic movements beneath the lids, a realization as bizarre as the moment descended upon him.

It the midst of fear and desire, he had fallen in love with this girl.

Sukie and Walter were married by a local preacher, and then they left New Orleans.

Madame Lucien went missing not long after Walter's arrival in New Orleans. It was said that no one saw her leave. No one ever saw her return.

When Sukie left town with her husband, she never even told her brothers goodbye.

PART III

1928–1932

GRACE

*We find things beautiful because we
recognize them and contrariwise we
find things beautiful because their
novelty surprises us.*

—W. Somerset Maugham

CHAPTER FIVE

Grace was born in Downtown, Tennessee, on March 18, 1928. She was the second child of two. Her parents, Benny and Amalie Martin, raised chickens and grew squash and collards to sell to the Green Goods Grocery.

Walter came first. He was a quiet boy, full of dreams. Too many dreams, Benny Martin thought. Walter was always looking for something different than what anybody else had.

"That's gon' get you in trouble one day, boy," Benny would say. "Don't you know ain't nuthin' new and different under the sun? You ain't gon' never have nuthin' nobody else ain't done already had befo'."

Grace was Walter's joy. He thought she looked like a doll, with her head full of jet-black curls. She was a smooth pecan-tan color and had eyes that danced like jumping beans. Her smile was beautiful. Big, brilliant teeth. Teeth too big for words. Walter was consumed by her presence.

She was different from all the other black children he'd seen in Downtown. Her hair was not coarse like theirs. When their mother braided it, it hung in big thick plaits down Grace's beautiful brown back. Walter begged his mother to let him wash his sister's hair. It wasn't like regular Negro hair that would shrink as tight as sheep's wool when it got wet. Grace's hair would relax and hang, long and slippery, like wet strands of silk.

"Mama, where did Grace get that hair from? You and Daddy ain't got hair like that."

"She got it from God," Amalie said. "Same place you got yours."

Walter would spend all day with his sister, until Benny warned him that it looked funny for him to be playing with a girl so much.

"You ain't funny, is you, boy? I ain't gon' have no faggot for a son."

Walter knew what a faggot was. There were two in town. Deenie Henderson and his boyfriend, Tony. They'd been chased to the outskirts of Downtown years before, but Deenie ventured into town on occasion for groceries and other necessary business. He was always met with scorn. Walter had heard the word "faggot" chanted over and over as children and grown folks alike spurned the man.

Benny brought Walter into town one day to watch Deenie get beaten by three men outside the Lucky Star.

"See that?" his father said. "That's what happens to faggots. Is that what you want to happen to you?"

"No sir," the frightened boy whispered.

"You know why they treat faggots like that?"

"No sir."

" 'Cause they unnatural. That man lives with another man and they do unnatural things." Benny knelt down, face-to-face with his son. "Don't you never let me catch you doing nuthin' unnatural, or you gon' get just what Deenie's getting right now."

He pointed in the direction of the melee. Deenie thrashed in the dust as the men kicked and pummeled him from all sides.

Walter's eyes welled up with dread.

"What you cryin' for, boy? Cryin's for faggots. You just remember that, okay?"

Walter nodded, determined to avoid Deenie's fate.

He began to play rough-and-tumble games with all the other boys in town. His father was pleased.

"Now that's my li'l man," he said with approval.

When nobody was watching, Walter would take his little sister down to the creek and wash her hair. Then he would sit on the grassy bank next to her and make her lie on her back in the afternoon sun so the beams could dry her hair. He would spread it wide in a fantail shape and watch as each bead of water was absorbed by the sun. Little Grace would laugh as Walter blew on the hair to help it dry. Then they would run along the creek bank and wrestle as Grace's hair hung thick and long in the wind.

Walter cherished these moments. Grace was beautiful. And nobody else had hair like her. It made him feel special to be her big brother.

Little Grace adored her brother. He was smart and strong and fearless. She loved going on the creek bank with him and playing Bathin' the Angel, the name he gave to their private game. She was his angel, he said, and had the prettiest hair of everyone in heaven.

" 'Cept God," he said.

"How come my hair ain't pretty as God's?" Grace asked.

" 'Cause God is all-powerful and can make his hair prettier'n anybody's. Cain't nobody have nuthin' better than Him."

"But God made angels, and angels can fly like God," the little girl said. "That must make me close to being like God."

"Nope. That still don't make you God. That just make you a child of God."

"But Mama say we all God's children."

"Angels is special," he said. "God made them first."

Walter made her promise not to tell what they did down by the creek. And even though she was four, Grace kept their game a secret.

One day Grace became very ill, and Amalie had to keep her in bed for more than a week. The little girl was full of congestion and her throat was swollen. Every time she coughed, phlegm thick with blood came up from the bottom of her chest. When Grace began coughing up heavy clots of blood, Amalie sent for the doctor.

Walter was so frightened, he could no longer speak. He stopped eating. He feared God was taking his angel away.

"She's got pneumonia." Dr. Polk put his stethoscope back in his case as he stood. "Are you dressing her warm enough? Has she been out in the night air?"

"No sir," Amalie said. "She ain't out at night at all. She's just a child. And I always make sure to dress her extra warm."

Dr. Polk shook his head. "I don't get it. It's gotta be something. How often do you bathe her?"

"No more'n once a week," she said. "Rest of the time I just give her wipe-offs."

"How often do you wash her hair?"

"Once a month. Sometimes longer. It's too much hair for me to be foolin' with that often."

"Well," the doctor said, "maybe you need to cut down on washing her hair so much. Hair like that, you don't need to do nothing but wipe her head off every now and then with a warm rag."

Amalie began to cry as she looked down at her daughter bundled up in the bed.

"What I'm gon' do? She ain't gon' die, is she?"

"Now, now, Mrs. Martin. You just calm yourself down. She's obviously over the worst part of it. She just got a lot of congestion in her chest, and the blood is coming up 'cause her throat is raw. Put a washtub with some hot water, salve, and witch hazel in here. Place a towel across the top and let it fumigate the room. Make sure all the windows are closed so she can sweat."

"Won't she get too hot?" Amalie asked.

"No, just let her sweat. Rub some salve on her chest. That should open up her pores. After a couple of days, she should be a little better. But let her stay in bed for the rest of the week."

Amalie followed him out to the front room.

"You need to make sure you don't get her hair wet for at least two months. Her hair is too long to be washed so much. She might have a cold because her head took too long to dry."

"I'ma make sure I don't wash it for a long time, Dr. Polk."

She opened the door for him and walked with him out to the porch.

"Don't forget that salve now," he said.

"I won't. Doctor, my boy ain't eatin', either. I think he scared for his sister."

"Where is he?"

"Walter!" Amalie's tone was even but strong. Strong enough to reach her son as he huddled in Grace's room.

Walter had been hiding in the closet. He was crouched low among the tiny patent leather shoes and delicate ruffled frocks. When Amalie and Dr. Polk went outside, Walter stood next to Grace's bed, whispering, stroking the hair.

"Don't die, angel. Don't die."

Grace's eyes were shut tight in sleep. He could see her stomach rise and fall with each breath and hear the mucus pop inside her chest every time she inhaled. He laid his head against her hair.

"Walter, come here!"

He dried his eyes on his arm and ran into the living room.

Walter hung his head and walked out onto the porch to his mother and the doctor.

"Boy, why ain't you eating?" Dr. Polk asked, patting the wiry little boy on his head.

Walter looked up with tear-stained lashes.

"What you crying for?" his mother asked.

"I'm not crying," he lied, remembering his father's words. "My sister gon' die, Doctor?"

"No, boy, she ain't gonna die. She'll probably live longer than you do because she eats her meals every day. I heard you ain't ate since day before yesterday."

Walter grinned, his teeth shining white. His sister was going to live.

"You sure she gon' get better?"

"Walter," Amalie said, blushing. "He's the doctor. He knows what he's doing. 'Scuse him, Dr. Polk. He ain't got no sense."

Dr. Polk stooped down to Walter's eye level.

"Your mama said she's cooking some ham with biscuits and syrup for your sister for supper. And I hear she's a pretty good cook."

"My mama can cook real good," Walter said. He glanced up at her.

"Well, since you and your daddy are the men in this family, it's your duty to stay strong for the women," Dr. Polk said. "You need to eat, boy."

"That's right," Amalie said. "We don't need you to get sick, too."

"Promise your mama that you're gonna eat. She's got enough to worry about without you giving her trouble, too."

The doctor put his arm around the boy. Walter looked at him, then looked up at Amalie.

"I promise, Mama."

Dr. Polk stood and patted the boy on the head again.

"I'll be checking back with you, Mrs. Martin, to see how Grace is doing. Be sure to call me if anything changes. Otherwise, she should be up and at 'em by the end of next week."

"Okay, Dr. Polk. Thank you for everything."

Walter ran inside the house while Amalie watched the man crank his big red Chevrolet and drive away. Walter rushed into Grace's room and over to her. He stroked her hair as he whispered in her ear.

"You gon' be all right in no time. Next week we can play Bathin' the Angel again."

He kissed his sister on her warm brown forehead, still stroking the silky black hair. He slid into the bed beside her.

As he nestled his face against her cheek, Benny came and stood in the doorway. He had arrived as Dr. Polk was leaving and learned from his wife that Grace was going to be okay. He wanted to see her.

As he stood in the door frame, he wanted to know what his eight-year-old son was doing lying next to his sick sister, and why the boy was caressing her face like that.

More important, he wanted to know about Bathin' the Angel.

Two weeks later, Grace and Walter were once again racing down the bank of the creek.

"We still gon' play the game?" Grace asked.

"You still my angel, ain't you?"

"Yeah."

"And angels still gotta bathe, don't they?"

"Yeah."

"Then don't be asking crazy questions."

She grinned. Teeth too big for words.

Walter beat her to the water's edge, then held out his open arms to her. She ran into them and he kissed her on the forehead. One by one, he peeled away all of her clothing. The yellow dress with the blue apron came off first. Next came the yellow socks with the white lace, then the black patent-leather shoes. When she was left standing in her crisp white panties, Walter peeled them away from Grace's pecan-tan body.

The sun was shining warm and bright that afternoon, and Walter hugged his sister close and kissed her torso. He knelt close to the edge of the creek and opened his arms out over the water. She leaned back in Walter's arm in a practiced stance and he dipped her head into the cool water of the creek.

From the trees, Benny watched in horror as Walter held little Grace's head back into the creek until it was soaked. Then he leaned her forward, her hair dripping, and made her lie down on the moist grass on the bank. He combed her hair with his fingers, downward first, onto her body. Benny could see his daughter shivering as she laughed at her brother playing with her hair. Once all of her skin was wet, Walter pulled her hair back and combed it outward onto the grass in a fan. Then he went to the water and scooped a handful and ran back with it, drizzling it over Grace's head. Walter let the water fall onto Grace's hair and scalp, replacing the water that had been spread on her body.

Benny was seething as he watched his children playing this very sinful game. He had a tingling feeling in the pit of his stomach.

Walter stripped off all his clothes and laid down next to Grace's hair. He wrapped it around his neck and face and laid end to end with her. Walter turned around and blew on the hair. Grace giggled.

Benny's rage was too strong for him to remain still. He crept under the trees and stormed back up to the house. He snatched open the back door and burst into the kitchen, walking past Amalie.

"What's the matter?" She rose from the table and ran behind him into the living room. "What's the matter, honey?"

Benny swung around.

"I'm gon' kill that boy, that's what's the matter."

Amalie was confused. Grace was her baby, but Walter was her pride. She was very protective of him.

"I'm sure it ain't that bad," she said. "What did he do?"

"He's out there laying nekked in the grass with that baby, that's what he doing," Benny said, pointing in the direction of the creek. He paced, still unable to believe what he had seen.

"He what?"

Benny stopped pacing and glared at his wife. He nodded, a wild smile on his face. Amalie had seen the smile before. She'd seen it years before when he hit her for the very first time.

It was right after they got married. He punched her hard in the face with his balled-up fist for washing his underwear with the meadow-scented lavender soap powder she bought from Green Goods.

Benny came home and saw his boxers folded in white stacks on the bed next to her folded panties. He got a tingling feeling in his stomach, remembering how his brother, Hailey, used to wash and fold his own dainty, perfumed underthings. Amalie, happy to see her husband, smiled as she watched his face twist and contort into a series of half-smiles and frowns. Then Benny flew into a rage.

"I ain't no damn faggot," he screamed. "Don't be having me smelling like no fucking fags."

When he hit her, it was a point-blank blow that knocked her flat to the ground, blood gushing from her cheekbone in thick spurts. Benny left her laid out on the floor as he grabbed his underwear from the bed and went into the kitchen. She heard him snatch the washbucket from the wall and slam the screen door. Amalie struggled to get up.

She made her way to a mirror and examined the gash. Benny held his thoughts close. He wasn't a man too prone to share his feelings, but she had never imagined that he would be violent. She hadn't known him long when they married. He never spoke about his background and family. That was fine for Amalie. She figured all she knew was all she needed to know.

After she cleaned the blood from around her eye, she went into the kitchen in search of him. She could see Benny kneeling over the washtub in the cakey mud-dust, pounding his underwear against the washboard with a chunk of lye soap.

Years later, Amalie still had the faint, dark hint of a knuckleprint under her left eye from where the flesh had swollen and gone down, leaving a sunken, hollow depression. As Benny ranted now about Walter, she thought she could feel the dull and distant sting of that blow.

"That's your boy. I told you it's something funny 'bout him. He out there dipping that girl in the water, nekked, and he laying nekked next to her with her hair wrapped 'round him. That's how she damn near died two weeks ago. Doctor gon' tell you it's from washing her hair too much. Shit. I'm glad he don't know 'bout this."

Benny paced the room in his thick-soled work boots. Every few seconds he would stop to glare at his wife. Waiting, expecting, demanding, daring her to say something back.

Amalie was too dumbfounded to speak.

CHAPTER SIX

The beating Benny gave Walter was so severe, his hands began to bleed from striking the boy so much. Walter cowered on the floor and behind the bed while Benny chased him with the brown leather strap. Benny gripped the strap so hard, it tore into the meat of his palms with every blow he delivered. Walter stopped trying to outrun his father and slumped in a corner. Benny raised the strap and brought it down over and over against the boy's tender flesh. Walter's eyes were dry as they looked up at his father, which made Benny lay into him with deadlier blows.

Amalie could hear them from the kitchen. She sat at the table, her back stiff. Grace was standing between her legs, wrapped in a towel. Amalie could hear Benny's guttural grunts as the belt made *WopWopWopWop* sounds every time it came down.

"Mama, I ain't still wet."

"Hush, baby. Your hair is soaked. You gon' have a cold and be sick again. Y'all ain't had no business out there in that water like that."

"We was just playin'. Why he beatin' Walter?"

" 'Cause Walter knew how sick you was, and he had you out there playing in the water after the doctor told us not to get your hair wet."

Grace's eyes were pools of onyx. Tears fell onto her cheeks. She looked up at her mother's face, but Amalie's attention was elsewhere. She had her head raised as she rubbed Grace's body with the towel. She rubbed Grace so hard that the little girl began to squirm as the towel burned hot against her skin.

WopWopWopWop.

"Mama, I ain't sick now. I feel just fine."

"Hush, girl."

Amalie shook the little girl.

"Your brother's in there getting a beating now 'cause of you. If you'd'a told me 'bout this game, I coulda stopped him. It ain't right for no sisters and brothers to be running 'round nekked together like that."

"We was just playin'. "

Amalie's eyes were now fixed on her daughter. She rubbed her head with the towel, the long hair hanging free in damp, tangled locks.

WopWopWopWop.

Amalie looked at the hair as she listened to the sounds of the strap coming down on her beloved boy.

WopWopWopWop.

She fondled the hair, turning it over in her hands as she looked at each long and silky strand. It was beautiful. Her own hair was coarse and tight. This stuff in her hands was gossamer. Where did it come from, she wondered. No one in her family had hair like that.

WopWopWopWop.

Grace watched as her mother's gaze became lost in the luster of her hair. Amalie's hands stroked and tugged at the strands of hair that hung all around Grace's small body. Grace could hear circles of words shaping themselves and working their way up from the bottom of Amalie's feet to her mouth.

"This is the hair that gets my boy in trouble."

WopWopWopWop.

"He ain't bad," Amalie whispered. "This hair just makes him crazy."

WopWopWopWop.

Grace looked at her mother, puzzled by her tone, cradled by the stroking.

WopWopWopWop.

"We gots to get rid of it."

Amalie pushed Grace from between her legs. The towel dropped onto the floor and the girl stood naked, watching her mother's swift movements through the kitchen. She returned with a pair of scissors.

WopWopWopWop.

"We gots to get rid of this hair."

Amalie snatched the girl back between her legs and grabbed a thick lock of the hair. She sawed through it with the dull edges of the scissors as Grace fought against the motions. The girl made choppy, whiny sounds, but Amalie continued her crazed hacking at the thick rope of hair. It came free and fell in a thick ebony chunk around Grace's feet. She screamed and tried to pull away from Amalie's hands.

"Stop, Mama. This is my hair. This is my hair."

WopWopWopWop.

"This is the hair that's hurting my boy."

WopWopWopWop.

Amalie kept cutting, and hair fell in silky black masses upon the floor. Grace's scalp was visible for the first time in four years. The remaining hair on her head stood in a fuzzy jet fluff. The floor was a pool of inky down.

There was silence.

It was a silence so pronounced and thick, Amalie believed she could hear below her feet the sound of the wind stirring the hair into black whirlpools.

She looked up at the door. Benny's hands were bloody and his face was tired, but his eyes flickered with a brilliant flame. The flame skimmed the floor and Amalie could hear the sound of fire as it whispered through the inky masses of hair, crackling and popping as it scorched her feet.

Benny spoke in a slow, deliberate tone, breathing between every word.

"What . . . have . . . you . . . done . . . to . . . my . . . baby's . . . hair?"

Grace's face was a twisted mess, a knot of wrinkles, stained with tears as she stood still amid heaps of hair. Amalie studied Benny as if he had just walked into a dream she'd been having. She looked at him, past him, through him. His image was fuzzy, but she knew he was there, even as she mumbled garbled words in his direction. Grace could hear the words coming from the bottom of her mother's feet.

"That's the hair that hurt my boy," Amalie said. "I ain't gon' let my boy get hurt no more."

Benny's fiery stare rushed again through the inky swirls on the floor and rose up Amalie's legs, singeing the coarse hair that covered her thick calves, warming her thighs.

Grace, crying, stood rooted to the floor.

"You must be outta your fuckin' mind," Benny said. "That girl is bald-headed now."

He took a step toward Amalie, his bloody hands clenched and ready to swing. Amalie stood, pushed Grace from between her legs, and walked up to him, her legs still hot. Her eyes filled with an angry flash.

"I ain't gon' let that hair or you ever hurt my boy again," she said.

Benny swung at her, aiming for the sunken eye, but lost his footing when a sharp pain shot up through his chest. His eyes lost their brilliance as his flame was swallowed up by Amalie's own fire. The rest of her body remained motionless while her hand worked the scissors into the soft, fleshy folds in Benny's midsection. She could feel warm blood coursing over her hand as her husband wobbled, then sank to the floor. Grace went flying out of the kitchen, screaming, naked, bald, into the bedroom to her brother.

Amalie watched as Benny disappeared in an inky cloud of hair that rushed upward in little whorls, then settled on him and around him in a soft, silky nest.

She bent down and stroked his face. The fire was gone. It was replaced by the gentle wind of her voice.

"I ain't gon' let that hair, or you, ever hurt my boy."

PART IV

1932

HAILEY

*Men are what their mothers
made them.*

—Ralph Waldo Emerson

CHAPTER SEVEN

The ride in the car was cold and quiet as the black sedan wove its way up the hill to the cemetery. Grace cowered in the corner of the backseat. She had her face pressed against the window, blowing her breath on the glass and watching it mist up in the shape of a circle and dissolve.

Her hands were nestled in delicate black lace gloves. Her starched black frock with the white lace collar blended into her black-stockinged legs and patent-leather shoes. On her head was a black bonnet trimmed in gossamer white lace that tied underneath her neck. A hint of fuzz peeked out from the back of the bonnet—the sole vestige of the beautiful silky tresses that had hung there before. She traced the path of the dissolving mist with her nose until it vanished.

Amalie sat on the other side of the car looking down at her hands. They lay folded in her lap, holding the black mesh gloves her mother had given her years before. She stared ahead, enveloped by a profound sense of emptiness.

It whispered her name as she lay in bed the night of Benny's death. It was with her when the Downtown sheriff came to the house and questioned her about the murder of her husband. After an hour of interrogation, he dismissed it as a domestic incident.

"Nobody cares when niggers kill niggers," she heard him tell his deputy as the two of them walked out to the car. "It's when they start killing us that it gets outta hand."

She had notified Benny's family in Kentucky. It took her hours of sorting through Benny's personal things to find an address where she could contact his mother.

"Did you kill him?" the mother asked.

"Yes ma'am?" Amalie whispered into the phone.

The mother scoffed. "I'm not surprised. That boy was hateful anyhow."

Amalie knew that all she had now was her children. Most important, she had her son. She had murdered for him. That, more than anything, was something she had to find a way to reconcile within her heart and her mind. Walter had now become the center of her world. She watched him sleeping in the car beside her. She stroked his face with the back of her hand.

Walter stirred, then drifted off again, his head snapping forward. He dreamed he could still feel the strap coming down, the leather eating into his skin with its nappy roughness. He could smell its hidey scent. He could hear Benny's voice, filling his mind, filling his thoughts, filling his dreams with the wickedness of what he had done with his sister.

"Faggot. You a faggot. Only faggots play with they sister, 'cause they can't fuck no other girls. You ain't nuthin' but a faggot, and I'll kill you 'fore I let any son of mine be a fuckin' queer."

Walter didn't flinch anymore as the licks came down. Benny was so angry about seeing them at the creek. He couldn't have been upset about just that, Walter figured. What was so wrong with a brother loving his sister?

Benny's blows came crashing down on his arms, his legs, his back, his neck, his buttocks, his cheeks, the place between his legs where his lone testicle hung next to his penis.

"I knowed something was wrong wit' you from the day you was born. Ain't no man in my family never had one nut."

The welts rose in big, blistery humps. Benny beat him until the old blisters burst and new ones rose in their place. They ran in rivulets that stung him all over and later dried up in sticky flakes.

"Faggot . . . faggot . . . faggot . . . faggot."

The word turned over in Walter's head as he slept in the car. In his dream, he could hear it echoing, even as he watched little Grace run naked and crying to him with all the glorious hair cut away.

"Faggot."

Hearing the word hurt more than seeing Grace bald. More

than seeing his mama's crazed stupor as she mumbled disjointed phrases with clotted blood sticking to her hand. More than the stinging blisters. The "faggot" thing was something he would never forget.

CHAPTER EIGHT

Walter stood in the huddled throng of strangers around the grave site, clinging fast to his mother's hand. She was squeezing his palm tight. On the other side of Amalie, Grace kicked at the ground with her hard patent-leather shoes as the minister delivered Benny's last rites.

Walter's head was bent in reverence, but he was stealthy, scanning the faces, curious about these people with whom he knew he must have some sort of connection. Across from him was a large dark woman. Her face was massive, set in a permanent scowl. Her hair was a thick wool crown. She wore a tent of a black dress that draped over her dominating bustline and ballooned outward until it stopped just below the knees, revealing sturdy tree-trunk legs planted in a pair of solid black men's shoes. Walter studied the shoes. The feet were enormous. Everything about the woman was imposing.

He looked up at her face again. Her mouth was fixed in a tight line, her eyes upon the minister. Then her gaze fell upon him, the eyes glistening in a penetrating stare. He met her stare. She knitted her brow, deepening the scowl, and he averted his gaze from his grandmother's face.

When he fixed his eyes again, they were upon the curvaceous legs of the woman standing beside his grandmother. The skin was a supple pecan-tan. His eyes followed the shape of the calves up to the hem of the black dress, the delicate tapered waist and the slight bosom. The hands were folded in front in a dainty gesture, but they possessed a curious strength, the raised outline of large veins overlapping and crisscrossing just beneath the surface of the skin.

Walter's gaze continued upward, where the dark silky hair,

hair like Grace's, fell soft upon the broad, strong shoulders. He looked at the face. The plucked brows, dark mascara, and thin coat of lipstick could not soften the strong jawline. Walter stared unabashed. His mouth fell open. In his mother's clenched palm, his hand grew limp as he realized he was looking at a man.

His uncle Hailey watched him, a smile creeping across his lips. Walter gaped, eyes wide and unblinking. The man was a larger, masculine version of Grace. Hailey's smile widened as he studied the boy. He showed his teeth.

Teeth too big for words.

PART V

1966

LAY

Men of principle are always bold, but those who are bold are not always men of principle.

—CONFUCIUS

The Boten children were grown, but still living at home with their parents. Lay and Polo were now working with their father, and Ophelia did occasional laundry and sewing for families in the area.

Despite constant attention from the girls in town, Lay had no use for them other than for random acts of guiltless sex. His confidantes remained Ophelia and Sukie. Polo had been dating Coolie, a pretty, feisty girl who lived a mile down the road, for more than three years.

While Polo spent most of his nights out with Coolie, Ophelia and Lay would lie in the loft of the barn and talk throughout the night. Ophelia had just turned twenty-two, but was still very naïve about the world and the people in it. Lay felt a special obligation to see that she learned. Sukie was always at the core of their conversations.

"I'm scared of her," Ophelia said. "She ain't never liked me."

"Sukie's cool," he said. "She can do anything. She got dried chicken feet in her house. She say if she scratch somebody with 'em, they'll get sick and die."

"You think that's cool? Why she wanna scratch people with chicken feet, anyway?"

"Respect. You see don't too many people bother her. Look at Uncle Walter. He scared to death of Aunt Sukie."

Lay turned over on his side and blew straw into her face. She drew back, swinging her fist as though to hit him.

"Stop, boy. You so silly."

Lay brushed the straw out of her eyes. His fingers lingered over her skin, outlining the shape of her face.

"You look just like Mama," he said. "Me and Polo look like Big Daddy, but you got almost all her features, 'cept for your hair. Your hair ain't way down your back like hers. And it's kinda nappy, like Uncle Walter's."

Ophelia smiled at her brother as he brushed his fingers over her face.

"How come everybody think you so mean?" she said. "You always been so nice to me."

"They think I'm mean 'cause that's what I want 'em to think. Better to be feared than friendly."

"Hmph," she said. "I guess Aunt Sukie taught you that, too."

Lay stroked her chin.

"You ever wonder why you don't look like Big Daddy?" he asked.

"Nope. It's lots of people who don't look like both of they parents. You don't look like Mama, but you came out her belly, 'cause I saw it."

"You saw me come out her belly?"

"Yep."

"No you didn't," he said, still rubbing her face. "They wouldn't let you in the room with her. You was too little."

"So. They let me in there. And I saw it. Even before Big Daddy did."

"No you didn't," he challenged again.

"Uh-huh, 'cause Mama let me come close and see when they cut the cord. It was long and black and red and covered with nasty white stuff."

"You lying, Ophelia. You wasn't but eighteen months when I was born."

"So. I still remember."

"For real?" he asked with fascination.

"Yep. I saw it."

Lay rolled onto his stomach. He chewed on a piece of straw. "Aunt Sukie say it was something wrong with you when you was born."

Ophelia stared up at him. "What?"

"I'on know," he said. "She claim it was something bad. She said Mama committed some kinda sin before you was born and it messed you up."

"You believe her?"

Lay picked up a handful of straw and sifted it over her face.

"You seem normal to me. But I'on know. Sometimes you act goofy when you shut yourself up in that room and read them books all day."

She threw straw at him.

"I'm not goofy. Aunt Sukie's goofy. I told you she don't like me."

He threw straw back at her.

"Quit calling her goofy. Aunt Sukie is my friend. She shows me all kinda stuff. Mama don't take up no time with me like that. Sukie say Mama wouldn't never take up as much time wit me as she do. She say you Mama's favorite."

"Why is Aunt Sukie telling you all them stories 'bout Mama? What did Mama ever do to her?"

Lay sat up. He shrugged. "I'on know. But she say Mama part of the reason Uncle Walter so sorry. She say if it wasn't for Mama, she'd have a real husband and a family by now. She say Uncle Walter ain't got but one nut. That's one of the reasons why they can't have no kids."

"Don't tell me no more 'bout what Aunt Sukie say. You making me not like her for real."

"Fine," he said, "but I like her. She's my friend."

Ophelia leaned against his arm. "Ain't I your friend?" She looked up at him and batted her eyes for effect. He threw more straw at her.

"Yeah, I guess. You my friend. But you better not cross me. Or I'ma get my chicken foot Aunt Sukie gave me and scratch you and watch you die."

They tussled in the hay, with Lay landing in a pile on top of her. He ran his hands slow across her body, feeling through her blouse and under her skirts. It made her feel funny, nervous. Like something was wrong.

"Quit," he said, pushing her resisting hands out of the way. "You know this feels good."

"But you squeezing me too hard," she said with a whimper.

"I ain't squeezing you that hard. I'm just tryna show you what friends do. I thought you said I was your best friend."

"You are."

"I thought you said you loved me."

"I do. But I'm your sister."

"Then stop fighting me. I ain't gon' hurt you. You're old enough to do this now. It's time for you to learn."

Ophelia relaxed her hands and let his roam her body. She kept her eyes squeezed together while he pulled her panties down and unfastened her bra.

"Don't that feel good?"

"Nnh-hnh," she grunted, her eyes still shut.

His fingers probed too hard and she flinched, but he kept pushing and poking at her until he was inside, moving on top of her.

He whispered in her ear, telling her a story he'd heard about a brother and a sister loving each other, just like them. He told her that they weren't hurting anybody. He told her how good it made him feel. Ophelia loved her brother. She would have done anything to make him happy.

Grace couldn't sleep. Big Daddy had cracked the bedroom window, and the night air had given the room an uncomfortable chill. She rose from the bed and slipped into her robe and slippers. Big Daddy's snoring was undisturbed.

She walked out on the porch, to sit in the rocking chair. She pulled the thick chenille robe tight around her shoulders. Her brother's house was dark across the way, but Grace could see a flicker of light coming from the direction of the barn. It was almost three in the morning. She wondered if someone had left a lantern on.

She made her way across the yard. The barn door was open. As she went to go in, she could hear the sound of lowered voices. She stood just outside and listened.

"Wait, Lay," Ophelia whispered. "You going too fast."

"It's supposed to be fast," he said. "You gotta have friction. Else it don't feel good."

Grace pressed her hands to her chest, her eyes glistening. She stood at the door, trying to decide what to do.

After a few moments, she returned to the house and slipped back into bed alongside Big Daddy. Tears streamed down both sides of her face. She stared up into the dark of the ceiling until daylight, and Big Daddy's snoring, began to break.

Two months later, Ophelia learned she was pregnant. She panicked.

"I'on know what to do," she said. "What am I gon' tell Mama and Big Daddy?" She wrung her hands and tore at her hair.

"Calm down," Lay said. "Just tell 'em you gon' have a baby. People have babies all the time. That's how you got here."

They were in the loft of the barn.

"Who I'm gon' say the daddy is?"

"You ain't gotta say nuthin'. Mama ain't gon' ask you too many questions. You know how she is. Ain't too much she can say 'bout this, anyway."

"What you mean?" Ophelia asked.

Lay's face was twisted in a cryptic grin.

"Just trust me. From what I know, Mama ain't gon' start nuthin', and she'll make sure Big Daddy don't start nuthin', either."

He patted her belly. "You 'bout to have a baby. Be happy, it's a lot of people can't have none."

"But you my brother. What happened between us ain't normal."

"Says who?"

"It just ain't," she said.

Lay's expression darkened.

"Ophelia, did I ever hurt you?"

She shook her head.

"When we did it, I made you feel good, and you made me feel good back. That's normal, now, ain't it?"

"I guess," she said.

She looked down at her hands, still unsure. "S'pose the baby don't come out right? S'pose it's 'flicted or something?"

He put his arms on her shoulders and looked her in the eye. "Trust me, girl. That baby's gon' be just fine."

Because it was Lay, her brother and best friend, she told herself to believe him. That everything would be all right.

Deep in her heart, Ophelia knew that it wasn't.

CHAPTER TEN

No one knew what happened between Lay and his sister except for Grace, Sukie, and Walter. Sukie knew the boy spent a lot of time at night with Ophelia. She confronted him.

"You been with that gal, ain't you?" she asked.

Lay stood in front of her, kicking at the kitchen floor, nervous, afraid to lie.

"Tell me. You had sex with your own sister, didn't you, boy?"

Before he could answer, Sukie slapped him across the face. "They going to hell," she said, turning to Walter.

Walter sat at the dinner table, staring into his plate.

"You ain't got nuthin' to say to that?" Sukie asked her husband. " 'Course you don't. 'Cause you and your sister gon' be burning right 'long with them."

Grace knew what had happened between her children, but she also knew there was no way she could speak on it. Big Daddy never suspected what was going on around him. Neither did Polo.

When Grace heard that Caesar Bucksport's nephew was headed to Detroit, she saw an opportunity. She disappeared one afternoon on a phantom errand into town. She made her way to the Lucky Star Liquor Joint and asked Caesar a stream of questions about his nephew. When was he leaving, and was there room for anyone else to make the trip. She said it was time Lay struck out on his own in the real world, somewhere bigger than Downtown, Tennessee.

Caesar listened with interest. He had never seen Grace up close before. The Boten clan, except for Big Daddy and Lay, tended to keep to themselves. He admired the silky hair, wound tight in a ball at the back of her neck. A few errant wisps framed her face, giving her an angelic beauty and youthfulness that belied the hardships she'd seen in her thirty-nine years. Her figure was still impressive. Caesar nodded with appreciation, sucking on a cold peach Nehi as she spoke, his thoughts lurking in darker places.

"You think maybe Lay can catch a ride with him?" she asked.

Caesar swallowed the soda before he spoke.

"Don't see why not," he said, the smell of peach Nehi strong upon his breath. "Booty don't need to drive all the way up there by hisself nohow."

Grace nodded.

"So Big Daddy gon' let that boy go all the way up north, huh?"

Grace looked away.

Caesar studied her face. "He does know, don't he?"

Grace didn't respond.

"Now, Mrs. Boten, how you plan on sending that man's oldest boy off without him putting up so much as a protest about it?"

Grace looked at Caesar. "He'll do what's best for Lay. He knows there ain't nuthin' for him here."

Caesar sighed, turned up the bottle, and took a swig of soda.

"Well," he said, "there's room for Lay if he wanna go. But I ain't gettin' in the middle of no family spats."

"There won't be any," Grace said. "Me and Big Daddy done been together more than twenty-two years, and we ain't never fought yet."

She picked up her bag and prepared to leave. As she neared the door, she turned back to Caesar, who had been appraising her full, round buttocks as they moved with a gentle sway beneath the fabric of the dress. She saw the look.

"Thank you, Caesar. For what you are doing for my family," she said. "We won't forget it."

Grace Boten left the Lucky Star Liquor Joint and never set foot in it again.

Lay left for Detroit three days before the baby was born.

"We can't never talk about this to nobody," he said to Ophelia.

"But I thought you said wasn't nuthin' wrong with what we did."

They were sitting on the floor of the barn.

"I'm going away. I'm moving up to Michigan."

Ophelia began to cry. Lay sat beside his sister, steeling himself against her tears.

"Sukie says it's best. Can't nuthin' good come outta this."

"But what about me?" she asked. "What about the baby?"

Lay got up from the barn floor.

"I'll take care of y'all. I'ma get me a job and send y'all money. But we can't never talk about this again. When I leave here, this is the end of you and me."

"But you can't just cut me off," she wailed. "I'm your sister."

"Stop crying, Ophelia. You gon' make the baby come."

"You can't leave me, Lay. You can't do it. You just can't."

"I got to," he said, walking away. "Sukie say I got no choice."

Ophelia labored in the back of the house, writhing on the bed, violent contractions rifling through her body. She screamed and clutched her mother's arm. Grace stroked her daughter's forehead with a cool cloth. Through the shrieks and the snatching, she kept her eyes on Ophelia, recalling the anguish with which she had brought her into the world.

Ophelia named the baby Hamlet.

CHAPTER ELEVEN

Eight months later, Lay was settled in the new city. He had been back to Downtown twice to visit and was sending money home. He mailed it to Grace, who doled it out according to his instructions, to Polo and Big Daddy, giving the most to Ophelia for her and the baby. At first he was sending two hundred dollars a week. Two months later he was sending five hundred.

It was more money than the Botens had ever seen at one time.

"What kinda job that boy got?" Big Daddy asked.

"He started a business with some friends," Polo said.

"That's good." Big Daddy stretched and stood from the sofa. "I heard there's lots of opportunity for colored folks up north."

Lay was a heroin dealer.

In less than a year, through a few strokes of determination, positioning, and pure serendipity, he had become the most powerful pusher in downtown Detroit.

His initiation came within two weeks of his arrival in the city. The boy he rode up with, Booty, Caesar Bucksport's nephew, had friends who introduced him to the game. Lay was industrious, willing to do what he had to in order to learn the business.

His first job was as a runner. The man who employed him, a slick-haired, spats-wearing, chubby fellow named Crosstown Dickey, admired Lay's fearless attitude. Dickey ran sixty percent of the city's heroin trade. He paid Lay fifty dollars a day to shuttle drugs and money.

Lay relished the power of the role, often dishing out brutal beatings to users and would-be turf encroachers without even being instructed to do so. He knew how to hurt people so that they didn't wear their wounds. For those whose injuries were visible, Lay worked the art of the not-so-subtle threat. His first victim was a poor strung-out boy who owed Dickey twenty dollars. Lay stabbed him in front of two other addicts. He knew it would give him an instant reputation.

Dickey began to trust the intense young man with more coverage and responsibility. He liked this cocky kid from the sticks who protected his boss's territory as though it were his own.

Lay soon became Dickey's model for the ideal hustler: ambitious, aggressive, determined, and meticulous. He possessed a searing volatility that always threatened to break the surface, hovering in the undertone of conversation, the errant twitch of an eyelid, the semi-slack clench of a fist. That powder-keg trait was enough to make him the most feared member of Crosstown Dickey's crew. No one ever knew when Lay's lid was going to blow. Despite his hair-trigger temperament, he never once ended up in jail.

After six months with Dickey, rising in rank to number two man, Lay grew bold enough to want to strike out on his own.

"I think I can take over Cutty's business," he said, referring to Dickey's biggest rival in the city.

Dickey and Lay were having drinks at Bud's Monarch, a popular downtown club where fast women and money-flashing men came to mingle and swing to the hot new sounds of Berry Gordy's Motown hits and Jimi Hendrix's acid-laced rock and roll.

"You sure you ready for something that big?" Dickey asked, tossing back a shot of bourbon.

"What you think?"

Dickey puffed on a cigar, a fat Cuban with more than two inches of ash hanging from its tip. After three strong pulls, he exhaled the smoke into Lay's face. It was something he did to everyone. Lay loathed the smell.

"I think you got what it takes, if that's what you mean." Dickey took another puff; Lay clenched his jaw. "I just don't know if I'm ready to lose my best man yet."

Lay raised a snifter of brandy to his lips. He had learned to appreciate the cordial during his limited exposure to Dickey's world.

"You won't be losing me. It'll be like Cosa Nostra. We'll rule the streets. Be one big family."

Dickey ran his fingers around the rim of his shot glass, his jaws fat again with the stink of smoke. "One big family, huh?"

"Yeah. You raised me in this game. I can't just turn my back on you like that."

Dickey exhaled, enveloping Lay's head in a cloud. "Took me six years to get myself situated in this business," he said. "Young buck like you, you think you got it down in just six months?"

Lay sipped his brandy.

"That what you think?" Dickey repeated, his brow furrowed, leaning in toward Lay. "You think you so fucking bad, you can just bring your bumblefuck ass up here and take over half of Detroit?"

"I think I got a grasp of how things work. All you need is street smarts, a head for numbers, and some muscle and firepower to back it up. Respect."

Dickey laughed, a big guffaw ripe with the foul odor of the Cuban. He slapped the table with the flat of his big brown hand, knocking over his empty shot glass and causing the ashtray to fly up and land facedown with a thump, spilling ashes onto Lay's new silk shirt. Lay was still holding the brandy snifter. Some of the ashes landed in the drink.

"Muscle and firepower?" Dickey barked. "Kid, you're crazy. What about Bernie Coppola? I been fighting off that crazy wop for more than five years. His goons are always ready to close me out of the picture. They don't like no nigga running a show they can't get a piece of."

"Fuck Bernie Coppola. This ain't Chicago and New York. Niggas run Detroit."

"Oh, so now we fucking Bernie Coppola?" Dickey said, laughing. "For somebody who ain't never been nowhere but the sticks and here, you sole pop a lotta shit, black boy." He held up his thick fat finger, beckoning the waitress.

"Yessir?" All the waitresses were garbed in minidresses, outlandish butterfly eyelashes stacked with plenty of mascara, and shoulder-length wigs that flipped up at the bottom. This one seemed no more than seventeen.

"Look here, gal," Dickey said between puffs of his cigar, "get me another shot of bourbon. You want something, boy?"

Lay handed the waitress the brandy sifter. "I'm all right," he said.

"Yeah, I guess you is, ain't you?" Dickey said. "Fucking Bernie Coppola and all." He laughed again, and the waitress, on cue, laughed along with him.

"That's all, gal," he said, blowing the smoke in her face. "Clean these ashes up."

The girl leaned over the table, her rear inches from Dickey's face. Lay watched him as she cleared the table. Young girls were Dickey's weakness. He liked them "teenage tiny," he called it. It was the only flaw Lay noted in what seemed like an otherwise impervious veneer. That and his disgusting cigar habit.

Dickey slapped the girl on the behind.

"Go on," he said. "Get your tail outta here and fetch that drink. Sweet li'l ass gon' get me in trouble."

The girl giggled and rushed off.

Lay brushed the ashes from his shirt. Dickey watched him take great pains to clear them away.

"I don't know what to make of you, boy. I swear I don't."

"Between the two of us, we can run this city," Lay said.

Dickey took three long drags of the cigar, still eyeing the ambitious young man sitting across from him. He exhaled the smoke in Lay's face, laughing and shaking his head.

"Fuck Bernie Coppola. Boy, you something else. Next thing you gon' be saying is fuck Dickey, too."

After Dickey agreed to support him in the takeover of Cutty's turf, Lay made a tremendous show of his intent to combine forces with his mentor.

"I'ma give you a third of the profits for the first three years," he promised.

Dickey smiled. "I appreciate that. Makes me see you didn't take my help for granted."

"Not at all," Lay said.

Dickey puffed his cigar. "I'm not too sure 'bout them three

years, though. Way I see it, that turf technically belongs to me. I helped you get it. It's mine. I'm just letting you lease the space, per se."

Lay clenched his jaw. "So you want me to give you a third forever?"

Dickey puffed his cigar in response.

"I ain't got no problem with that," Lay said. "You done a lot for me. I can't never repay you for teaching me all the things you did."

Dickey exhaled a cloud of smoke.

"Exactly," he replied. "We just one big happy family. Ain't that what you said?"

Bernie Coppola's daughter Natasha was an exotic beauty. Although she was fifteen, the mulatto girl looked even younger, no more than twelve. Despite her youth, she exuded a bold sexuality and provocative charm that had been the source of many fights among the neighborhood boys competing for her attention. She had her father's fierce Italian attitude and wild mane of hair, and her mother's dark eyes and sensuous nature. Bernie had been keeping a mistress on the dark side of town for more than seventeen years. And while he made no public appearances with his forbidden family, he was a constant presence in their day-to-day lives. Natasha was fast, just as her mother had been when Bernie first met her. He kept a close watch on his daughter because of this. There was a strong probability that she would be the type to fall into a bad way.

"She's gonna cause me trouble, that one," he told his new friend Lay. "Maybe you can keep an eye on her for me when I'm not around."

Lay had introduced himself to Bernie after taking over Cutty's territory. He would help Bernie gain control of Cutty's old turf and Dickey's, he said, as long as Bernie would cut him in thirty-seventy—thirty for Lay, seventy for Bernie. Bernie was down. For once, he thought, here was a nigger with some sense. He felt more than confident about letting someone with brains enough to respect Italian authority watch out for his daughter as well.

Dickey had no idea the young thing riding him now, a birthday present from Lay, was that same provocative girl. Lay had been bringing her around with him for the past week and was not surprised to find her lured by the thrill of dangerous fun.

She sat perched atop Dickey's mountainous belly, her fingers playing in his gooey-slick hair.

"Work that thing, gal."

She bounced up and down on top of him, their bodies making smacking sounds as her lean body met the cushy folds of his. Dickey squeezed his eyes shut as the girl thrashed above him.

When the door opened, neither Dickey nor Natasha stopped what they were doing. Lay had come in and out of the bedroom several times. They had become oblivious to his many entrances.

"Natasha!"

The girl glanced toward the door and screamed. Bernie Coppola, a tall man, thin and wiry, clutched his thick mane of curls with both hands, his eyes wide with horror. Dickey raised up and hurled Natasha hard against the bedroom wall. He reached beneath his pillow and produced a gun. At the sight of his naked daughter being slammed into the wall, Bernie pulled a gun from his waistband. Both men fired several rounds in the other's direction.

At the sound of gunfire and screams, Lay, who had been lurking in the hall, raced into the room. Dickey lay slumped over the side of the bed in a bloody, gelatinous heap. Bernie was dead in the middle of the floor. Lay could hear whimpering coming from behind the bed.

He found Natasha, naked and frightened, cowering against the wall. She squinted up at him and, recognizing her friend, reached out her arms. When her eyes met his, she knew in an instant.

No one heard the gunshot Lay fired into her chest. He made

a phone call to the apartment where his gunmen were based. They were there within minutes.

"We gotta clean this mess up," Lay told them. "I guess Bernie was finally bold enough to make his move against Dickey."

"Damn," one of the men said. "This is fucked up." He surveyed the carnage, his hands on his hips. "I guess this means you're the big boss now."

The others muttered in agreement as they went about bundling the bodies for quiet disposal. Lay's lips were a tight thin line as he helped roll Dickey's bloody body tight in the sheet.

Hamlet was growing fast and strong, his body shaped like his father's, his hair delicate and soft like Grace's. He had Ophelia's questioning eyes.

Ophelia missed Lay, but there was no one she could share this with, and calls from her brother were rare. She placed all her focus on the baby, talking to him as though he understood her words. Hamlet sputtered and giggled as she played with him in her room, kissing his face, seeing her brother in his every movement. She sat with him on the porch in the afternoons, often catching glimpses of Sukie walking out to her mailbox to leave letters for the mailman.

"Wonder who she writin'," Ophelia said to the baby. "She so mean, don't nobody wanna hear from her."

Big Daddy never said a word about the baby. He thought she'd been with one of the locals. He'd even asked Caesar on the quiet if Booty was involved.

Caesar snorted. "You must be crazy. My nephew got more sense than that."

Ophelia spent most nights after the baby went to sleep in deep reflection. She sometimes lay awake in bed until dawn. Other times she wandered around the yard in the dark of night, always ending up in the barn where she and Lay had shared so many moments.

One night she was in the loft, hidden among the bales of hay and old musty furniture. She heard the door open and felt a blast of cold wind hit her face. As she looked down, she saw Polo and Coolie come in.

"Baby, won't nobody find us here. We can smoke this, get high, and you can give me what I need."

Ophelia hunched low against the scratchy hay.

Polo pulled a clear bag of green stuff from his pocket. He showed it to Coolie.

"What is that?" she asked.

"It's weed, baby. Some real good weed." He sniffed the bag, seeming to want her to think he knew the difference between good marijuana and bad.

"Lay sent me this from Detroit. He sell it up there. This and horse. Makin' big money, too."

"What's horse?"

Polo smacked his lips in impatience. "Damn, Coolie, you so country. Horse is dope."

"What kind?" she asked.

Polo's brows knitted. "Shit, I'on know. Just dope. Serious dope."

He reached into the bag and pulled out a wad pinched between his fingers.

"Lay say business so good for him up there, I can come, too, if I want."

Upstairs, Ophelia squirmed against the itchy straw.

"Can I go?" Coolie asked, rubbing her hand along Polo's thigh.

"I don't know, baby. You might weigh me down. Lay say he got plenty of women, round the clock, just jackin' his dick. You might get in the way." He looked sidelong at her, trying to hide his smile.

"Nigga, please. Fuck you and what Lay say. You can go to Detroit for all I care."

Coolie jumped up. Ophelia could see her face flushing red and crept to the edge of the loft, leaning over to get a better view. As Coolie tried to walk away, Polo grabbed her around the waist, one hand still balled up, holding the weed.

"C'mon, baby. You know you my heart. Anywhere I go, you gon' be right there."

Coolie pretended to be angry. She turned her head to the side, and Ophelia saw her break into a sly smile.

"You promise?" she asked, her tone still sullen.

"I promise. I swear 'fore God, baby, I ain't going nowhere without you."

He pulled her down and leaned her against a wide bale of hay, then he kissed her.

"Relax for a minute," Polo said, "while I do this."

He pulled a folded pack of rolling papers from his hip pocket, peeled one off, and spread it out on his lap. Still holding the wad of weed in the other hand, he dropped it from his fingertips in a straight line onto the paper. He turned the paper sideways and rolled it up, licking it fast all over like he had seen a boy in town once do. Coolie tried not to seem impressed, but her scope of experience was limited to the borders of Downtown. This was something new, something exciting, and Polo, his tongue flicking over the surface of the rolled cigarette, seemed to be a master of this brave new world.

"This gon' make you real hot, baby," he said. He waved the joint at her.

"How you know? You got somebody hot with it once befo'?" Coolie was sulking again.

"C'mon now, baby. Quit bullshittin'. I told you, ain't nobody but you." He lit the joint and took a long drag.

"Here, baby," he said, holding it to her lips. "This will make you real happy real quick."

Coolie hesitated, staring at the burning red ash at the tip of joint. The pungent odor wafted before her.

"Mama says I'll be a junkie if I do dope."

"Your mama's crazy," Polo said. "You know that already."

She pursed her lips, but she knew his words were true. Her mother was a petite woman with a strong hand and a fiery temperament, a trait she had passed on to her daughter in abundance. Coolie's father had abandoned his seven children and wife ten years before. In his absence, Coolie's mother was a dictator, a mean-spirited and intolerant woman who cursed and fussed at them at every turn. There was no latitude for anything other than work and chores for her children. All of the kids were forced to leave school by the age of twelve. Bringing money into the house was essential with so many mouths to feed. Coolie had little time for play. Her moments with Polo were intricate episodes of escape, calculated for when her mother was at work or asleep. During the day, Coolie, who had just turned eighteen, worked part-time at the beauty salon in town, washing and straightening hair.

"Suppose I smoke this and get hooked on dope?" she asked.

"This ain't no dope, baby. It's reefer. Ain't like I want you to shoot up or nuthin'."

A piece of ash fell onto his foot.

"Ouch. Damn. The shit's burning out."

He pulled it back to his lips and drew on it long and hard. He held the smoke in his mouth, sucking it in with tiny gasps. Then he swallowed it and blew it through his nose.

"Where you learnt how to do that?" she asked.

"Don't you worry 'bout that, baby. You want some or not? I'm 'bout ready to get down to some real nasty business."

He ran his hands across her full breasts, breasts that made him fall for her long before he ever discovered the rest of her soft, full body. He held the joint back up to her mouth.

Coolie took a slow puff of the joint, trying not to burn herself with the fresh piece of ash hanging from the tip. She coughed and spat, choking on the smoke that was coming from her mouth, nose, and what seemed like every opening in her head.

"Boy, you tryna kill me," she sputtered, glaring at Polo through watery eyes. Polo smacked her on the back, fearful that she might be choking for real.

"Girl, ain't nuthin' wrong with you," he said. "You just tryna smoke it too fast."

"Stop hitting my back like that," she said, still coughing.

Polo's smacks became a soothing rub as he tried to calm her. Coolie leaned back and the coughing subsided. The joint Polo was holding had burned out.

"Let me relight it," he said. "It's just a roach now." He used the term as though he said it all the time. "It's too little for you to smoke." He lit the nub again. "I'll give you a shotgun," he said as he brought the weed to his lips.

"What's that?" Coolie asked, afraid of choking again. Polo rubbed her back to reassure her.

"I'll smoke the roach, baby, then I'll blow some smoke in your mouth and you suck it in. It's almost like kissin'."

Coolie relaxed. "Okay, but do it slow."

From above, Ophelia watched, transfixed.

Polo took a long toke of the roach, which was now so small that Coolie could not even see it between his fingers. All she could see was the bright red glimmer of ash as he inhaled. He sucked the smoke, his cheeks sinking in. He leaned over to Coolie, gesturing with his hand for her to part her lips. Polo blew in all of the smoke, then sucked a little back into his mouth.

Coolie pressed her lips together tight, holding in the smoke.

"Just let it stay in your mouth," Polo said, exhaling. "When I tell you to, swallow it."

Coolie held the smoke in her mouth, smiling as she realized that she was not choking. Polo groped her breasts, his hands rough and aggressive. Coolie squirmed, still holding in the smoke.

"Now swallow," he said.

Coolie gulped the smoke, smiling again as some of it came out of her nose on its own.

"That was good," she said. "Let's do it again."

Upstairs, Ophelia could smell the sharp aroma of the weed as it rose to the top of the barn. She imagined that she, too, could feel a high coming on.

Polo reached into the bag and pulled out another clump of

marijuana. He laid another piece of paper on his lap, spread the weed out on it, and rolled and licked it. He lit it and brought it up to his lips, ready to take the first pull. Coolie stopped his hand.

"Give me another shotgun, baby."

Polo smiled at this.

"Oh, you like that, huh, baby?"

"Yeah. Give me another one just like before."

"Your mama was right. You is a junkie."

She ignored him. Her lips were parted, ready for the smoke. Polo took an extra-long pull of the joint, then held the smoke in his mouth. Coolie squirmed, leaning into his lap. He leaned toward her, into her open mouth, blew in all the smoke, and sucked some back before she could close her lips.

This time Coolie needed no coaching. She leaned away from Polo, closed her eyes, and swished the smoke around in her mouth. Polo stood, holding the joint in his mouth, and stepped out of his jeans. Ophelia could see from above that he was naked. His penis jutted out from a thicket of hair, denser and bushier than Lay's. She knew she should feel shame in watching Polo, but he reminded her so much of Lay that she could not turn away. She could feel the moisture welling up just south of her navel, and she began to wriggle amid the straw. Polo sat on the hay, still watching Coolie twirling the smoke around in her mouth with her eyes closed. He puffed on the joint some more.

"Swallow it," he said, talking around the smoke in his mouth.

Coolie swallowed, then opened her mouth wide to exhale, licking her lips. She bent her head down into Polo's lap and took his penis into her mouth. Polo leaned back with a deep moan, still smoking the joint.

Ophelia could see Coolie's head navigating Polo's crotch. She felt her own hand move downward as she kept her eyes fixed on the activity below. The smell of the smoke and the excitement of voyeurism left her reeling, and her hand moved with the same speed and intensity of Coolie's head. Soon she was no longer watching what was happening below but was caught up in her own erotic whirlwind.

Polo's moans deepened and quickened. Ophelia stifled her own sounds by pressing her face into the hay.

Coolie and Polo began to writhe in a series of sexual calisthenics.

In the loft, Ophelia drifted off to sleep.

PART VI

1944

WALTER

*He that is childless
has no light in his eyes.*

—PERSIAN PROVERB

CHAPTER TWELVE

By the time Walter was twenty, the memory of Benny had carved a crippling niche into his character. He was a study in contrasts: whorish and timid, mannish and frail. The realization of his heritage with the discovery of Uncle Hailey rendered him alarmed and determined. Alarmed because he believed homosexuality was his destiny–Benny's pronouncement and the lone testicle assured him of that. Determined, therefore, to fight against his destiny.

He battled overwhelming shyness to talk to women. To be near them. To flirt with them. To dance with them. To seduce them. He cultivated a rakish reputation and had plundered Downtown and eight surrounding counties of all semblance of women before he was even sixteen. He sexed church matrons, neighbors, sisters of friends, blushing backwoods virgins, and seasoned juke-joint tramps. They loved him with desperation, whined for him, turned terrorist in anguished hope for his requited love. Walter was the king of the stick-and-move. He was the envy of every man in Downtown.

Walter loved none of these women. He saved all his emotion for Grace, whom he loved with a regard that transcended the physical. It was a sublime, beatific, ethereal thing.

After Benny's death, Amalie became singular in her existence. She lived for Walter. She consulted him on every decision she made. Meals were planned around his whims of appetite. Her mood was dictated by the color of his. She had killed for her son, and everything that happened after the scissors collided with Benny's flesh revolved around the magnitude of the deed.

Amalie lived in the shadows of Walter's world, despite her desire to be at its core. She often waited for days for his return from the sexual safaris that dominated his time. She would sit in the hand-carved rocking chair in the living room, humming hymns and reading the Bible by the light of a single lamp.

She filled her vacant time with the Word. After Benny's death, Amalie's conscience had driven her deep into religion, desperate for consolation for what she had done. She didn't regret the act. She would do it again, given the opportunity. Instead she sought justification for her actions. Justification for everything she did. She became a master of Scripture, superior at distorting the words to fit her needs.

When Walter was away, even if it was for days, Amalie didn't sleep. She stayed awake in case he came in late and was hungry for a hot meal. She wanted everything perfect upon his return. When he did stumble in, drunk and unwashed, she was always welcoming.

Walter was the love of her life. To a woman who had committed the ultimate act of choice, he was the living measure of the vast chasm between maternity and marriage.

Walter was indifferent, verging on spiteful, to his mother. He thought her ability to reason was suspect. How could she, he'd ask, be stupid enough to marry a man she knew nothing about? How could she, in turn, then kill her own husband?

"The woman answered and said, 'I have no husband.' Jesus said unto her, 'Thou hast well said, I have no husband.' John 4:17" was her favorite response to the question about Benny.

"What is that supposed to mean?" Walter asked one day.

"It's God's will. Jesus said it was well that he's gone."

"And when was Jesus last here? I must have missed that."

It was the one time Amalie ever struck her son. The surface of his brown cheek flushed a faint red at the blow. Amalie grabbed his shoulders and pulled him tight to her breast.

"Wherefore I say unto you, all manner of sin and blasphemy shall be forgiven unto men: but blasphemy against the Holy Ghost shall not be forgiven unto men. Matthew 12:31."

"You're crazy," he said, pushing her away.

He left the house for ten days. When he returned, she kept her Scripture quoting to herself.

• • •

Amalie gave no thought to Grace other than to despise her, even though her spirit nagged her with a deep native sense of guilt. Amalie blamed her daughter for inciting Benny's death and Walter's depravity. She blamed her most for consuming all of Walter's love.

The two women coexisted as strangers in the house. Amalie's hymn singing in Grace's presence was her scorn. The girl stayed out of her mother's way, hurt by the rejection.

Walter returned once just before dusk, reeking of sex and Seagram's, ignoring his mother as he searched for his sister.

He raced through the house. Amalie sat at the kitchen table, docile and obeisant as she watched him, waiting for any sign of his attention.

"Where is she?" he demanded.

"You want something to eat?"

Walter sucked his teeth and stormed out of the screen door.

He found his sister in the woods, down by the edge of the creek, sitting on the ground. Her crossed legs were pulled up to her chest, and her arms were wrapped around them. The gentle waves of water sloshed against her feet. Her chin rested on her knees.

From the corner of her eye, she could see him. A smile began at the corners of her lips and spread to the middle of her mouth.

Walter flopped down on the bank beside her, leaning back on the grass. His palm lay on a pebble. He picked it up and skimmed it across the surface of the creek.

"I smell you," she said without looking at him. "Why didn't you wash before you came home?"

Walter smelled his armpits, making an exaggerated effort of it. He sniffed each pit three or four times, then dropped his arms.

"I don't smell nuthin'," he said.

"You smell like you've been doing it."

"I have."

"Well, you could at least wash up afterwards."

Walter lay flat on the moist grass.

"Naw," he said. "Can't do that."

Grace looked at him. "Why not?"

Walter rubbed his chin. He stared off into the woods beyond the creek.

"Why not?" Grace repeated.

"Because. If you start washing up at their house, they start thinking they own you. They start buying you your own set of towels, laying them out, running your bathwater. Next thing you know, they buying you clothes and cooking you dinner."

"They make you dinner anyhow," she said.

"Yeah, but they do that just to show me they can cook. They trying to win me over with they culinary skills."

"Culinary? What that mean?"

"It means cooking."

She laughed. "Then just say cooking. Stop acting like you got so much experience. You ain't nuthin' but a silly country boy."

He rubbed his chin again. "Yeah. Anyway, if I washed up over at they house, they'd think I was settlin' in. And I ain't 'bout to settle in with none of them sluts."

Grace considered her brother. His dark, chiseled features were striking. She could see why women clamored for him so. She reached over and touched his face. Walter's eyes grew moist. He looked away.

"Walter, if they sluts, why you lay with them?"

Silence hung between them.

"Because," he said, "I'm a man. And that's what a man's supposed to do."

Grace leaned back on the grass. She reached out and took her brother's hand, bringing it to her lips. She kissed the fingers. The hand smelled of sex.

Walter looked over at his sister. His eyes were wet.

"You're a good man, Walter. Everybody knows that. You don't have to prove nuthin' to nobody."

Walter turned away again.

"You've been the best example of a man I've ever known. No matter what Daddy said."

Walter's breath caught in his throat. He wondered at what his sister knew of his torment.

"No matter what Daddy said," she repeated. She deposited a flurry of kisses in the palm of his tainted hand. "You ain't never been no faggot. So you don't have to keep laying with all those women to prove it."

Grace could not see Walter's face as he bit his lip and tears fell across his nose onto the grass.

The two lay on the bank in silence, Grace kissing his hand, Walter crying silent tears of relief because his beloved sister understood his anguish and motivation.

"Wash my hair, Walter."

It was more a plea than a demand. Walter turned to look at her. Her eyes softened when she saw his tear-streaked face. She sat up on the bank and freed her hair from the legions of pins that held it back. The hair fell around her shoulders and torso in heavy abundance. Grace stood and stepped out of the cotton dress. She removed her bra and panties.

Walter stared at his sister, whose body he had not seen naked since the day of his father's death some twelve years before. She leaned back onto the bank, waiting for him. She was more beautiful than any of the women he'd been with. She was the standard to which none of them could ever rise.

Walter stood, stepped out of his clothes in haste and waded into the creek. He bent down and scooped the cool water in his hands, ran back and dropped it onto her hair. His manhood rose before him, and she reached for it, pulling him down onto her. Walter fell into her arms, his tears fresh, his sobs audible. Grace embraced him, rocking him as he cried against her breast.

"Don't cry, Walter," she said. "No matter what Daddy made you think 'bout yourself, I know the truth."

He sobbed harder.

"I love you, Grace."

"I know you love me. You're the only one who loves me and takes care of me. And for that you'll always be as much a man as any man can ever be."

Grace kissed his neck and rubbed his back. He leaned above her, tears falling onto her face as he kissed her forehead, her eyes, her cheeks, and then her mouth.

In the shadows of the woods, Amalie watched her grown children naked on the bank. Christian outrage and shame churned inside of her as she witnessed Walter clutching the hair in his hands, moving on top of Grace. She began to cry, cursing and spitting upon the ground. She thought of Benny.

Amalie had loved two men in her life, her husband and her son. One had betrayed her with violence. And now the other one, the one she had lived for the last twelve years, was writhing on top of his sister in sin.

As dusk fell around her, Amalie trudged back through the woods, her voice a twisted whisper of the Word.

"Thine eyes shall behold strange women, and thine heart shall utter perverse things."

While the dusk turned to darkness, Amalie prayed and sang, bending Scripture to her will as she moved with purpose about the house.

"This is my justice. My punishment from God. Numbers 35:31. *Moreover ye shall take no satisfaction for the life of a murderer, which is guilty of death.* "Nuthin' ain't been right. Nuthin' can't be right. I gots to fix it at the root."

Amalie wiped her hands on her skirt and picked up the rusted can.

"So ye shall not pollute the land wherein ye are: for blood it defileth the land: and the land cannot be cleansed of the blood that is shed therein, but by the blood of him that shed it. Numbers 35:33."

She hummed in affirmation as she doused the furniture with kerosene. She made her way from the kitchen to the bedroom, pouring a thin trail of fluid behind her.

She went back into the living room, struck a match, and

threw it upon the sofa. Making her way down the hall, she prayed as she drenched herself with kerosene.

The fire raged from the front of the house toward the back. Amalie was in her bed, her voice a blend of the Word, supplication, and song.

"Save my children, O Father I pray, that they not suffer for what I've done."

She hummed as the roar of the fire sent a swoosh of smoke down the hallway.

"Forgive me for killing my husband."

As she breathed the words, the smoke invaded her lungs and rent her body in a spasm of coughs.

"Forgive me for hating Grace," she gasped, "forgive me for loving my son more than I have loved You."

The fire licked the walls of the hall, framing the bedroom doorway, rushing across the wooden floor.

"Forgive my children for their sins. Take me so that they may be saved."

The flames made their way around the bedroom, creeping upon the bedcovers. Once the fluffy chenille of the spread was lit, the fire rushed to the kerosene on Amalie's clothing. She struggled to pray, her body wild with coughs, her vision blurred by the stinging puffs of gray filling the room.

"And if thy right eye offend thee, pluck it out, and cast it from thee: for it is profitable for thee that one of thy members should perish, and not that thy whole body should be cast into hell."

Amalie thrashed on the bed.

"Matthew 5:29."

The fire swept across her, first scarring, then charring her body to the bone.

Walter and Grace were oblivious to the brilliance in the distance as they lay entwined, sleeping on the bank of the creek.

CHAPTER THIRTEEN

Grace took a job as a housekeeper after her mother's death. Her employers, Canada and Piedmont Deveaux, were a successful young couple in their mid-twenties with a large ranch just out-side of Downtown. Canada was a tall, elegant woman, almost six feet, with fair features and a dancer's body. She was a Vassar graduate who'd been raised in New England. She met Piedmont the summer before her senior year while vacationing with friends at Martha's Vineyard. They were married a year later, and he brought her to Downtown, the place of his birth, to as-sume the helm of the agricultural stronghold and livestock trade his family had established there years before.

Piedmont was as tall as his wife, and as dark as she was fair, with broad shoulders and clear blue eyes. His reputation for fairness preceded him. His grandparents had been among the first settlers of Downtown, and the Deveaux name had been re-spected for years by whites and blacks alike.

By the time Grace's belly had grown big, the Deveauxs were too attached to her sweet temperament and hearty cooking to be that concerned about why she was an unwed mother. Canada felt a special affection for the soft-spoken sixteen-year-old. She had no children of her own and delighted in caring for the girl. She prepared a place for Grace just off the library, not far from where she and her husband slept. Together, the two women decorated the room, adorning it with all the comforts a baby might need.

While Canada wondered about the father of the child, she respected Grace's privacy. The girl kept the Deveaux house in perfect order, and in return, Canada exerted great effort to pro-tect her from judgment and unnecessary questioning.

Walter came once a week, on Sundays, to pick Grace up and take her out for the day. It was during these moments that Canada witnessed the most significant change in the girl. She was radiant.

"Walter's rebuilding the house," she told Canada.

"Which house is that?" Canada asked. She knew very little about Grace's life and even less about the residents of Down-town. Although it was a small place where everyone seemed to know everyone else, she didn't leave the ranch often. In most instances, she relied on Piedmont to keep her informed about the town's goings-on.

"The house where our mama died," Grace said. "It burnt up in a fire a few months ago."

"Oh goodness, child. Amalie Martin? Was that your mama?"

"Yes ma'am."

"Piedmont told me about that. His parents knew your mother. I'm so sorry."

Later that evening, as the Deveauxs prepared for bed, Canada questioned her husband further.

"Honey, did you know that Grace's mother was that woman who died in the fire a little while back?"

Piedmont was sitting at his desk signing paperwork, a pair of glasses perched on the edge of his nose. He glanced in his wife's direction, squinting at the bright light that came from the lamp beside her.

"Yes, I knew."

"Why didn't you say something?" she asked.

"Because it's not important."

"It's important to me."

Piedmont put down his pen and took off his glasses. He got up from the desk and came over to the bed. He sat on the edge of the mattress.

"It makes no difference, pumpkin," he said. "She has no family other than her brother. She needs us, we need her. Those facts still remain. Knowing who her mother was doesn't change any of that."

Canada stroked her husband's dark hair.

"You're so logical sometimes. Is that what Harvard does to people?"

He leaned down and kissed her.

"I just focus on the facts," he said. "Now slide over."

He slipped under the covers as she turned out the light. He spooned his body behind hers, kissed her neck, and settled in for sleep. Canada remained awake deep into the night, thinking about Grace.

How sad, she thought. The girl had no mother, and she had no father for her baby. Canada was grateful that Grace had a brother. At least his regard for his sister, though unspoken, was apparent.

The two women would sit in the library in the evenings, after Grace had put away the dinner dishes and Piedmont Deveaux had retired to the sitting room to drink bourbon and read the paper. Canada had a degree in English literature and a particular fondness for the works of Shakespeare. She initiated the routine of reading to Grace when they convened each night, first the sonnets, then the plays. Grace would listen as she knitted, darned, and sewed, captivated by the cadence of words.

"Iambic pentameter," Canada said.

"What's that?" Grace asked, intrigued by the mysterious phrase.

"It's the number of beats he uses, and a special way of inflection."

"What's inflection?"

Canada smiled, realizing how rudimentary she would have to be in her approach.

"It's how you use your voice when you say something. The way Shakespeare wants you to say his words gives them a certain rhythm. Almost like music."

"That must be why I like it so much," said Grace.

She could not understand the language at first. Canada, anticipating this, took painstaking care to explain the meanings of words and phrases. This effort belabored the readings, often stretching out a play for weeks, as Canada attempted to impart the significance of each word, each emotion, each moment of conflict and interaction. By the time Canada had read *King Lear, Macbeth,* and *Othello,* she no longer had to explain meanings. Grace understood the style and diction and gave the appropriate responses to the action taking place.

Canada loved these moments with Grace. In this unwed black girl with little family, no home, and incomplete schooling, she had found a most unexpected, fastidious student. She came to realize that she was learning more from Grace than the reverse, something that defied the logic her blue-blooded upbringing had instilled in her.

By the time Grace was seven months pregnant, they were reading *Hamlet*. Grace took a personal interest in the story, often asking Canada to go over certain passages two, sometimes three, times. Because of her fascination, *Hamlet* took longer to get through than any of the other plays.

After Canada read the last scene, before she could even close the book, Grace was pleading with her to read it again.

"Why?" Canada asked. "*Hamlet* is a good story, but it's not one of my favorites. I think I'm one of the few people who has no compassion for the Melancholy Dane."

"I don't know, Mrs. Deveaux," Grace said. "It's something 'bout that story. I kinda feel sorry for him. He wasn't a bad person. He just didn't know what to do 'bout the situation. Ain't you never felt like that?"

"No. I can't say that I have."

Grace put down her knitting so that she could gesture with her hands.

"I mean, look at him. Having somebody, a ghost at that, asking you to kill for them when you ain't never had to kill before? And that poor Ophelia. All she wanted was for somebody to love her. She ended up losing everybody she cared about. Wasn't nuthin' left for her to do but go crazy."

The two women were quiet, the sadness in Grace's voice lingering between them.

"I guess I never looked at it that way," Canada said. "I always thought Hamlet was just a sorry excuse for a son."

"Oh no," Grace said. "It's got to be more than that. Otherwise Mr. Shakespeare would have never wrote that story, don't you think? I mean, he must have had a message, and I don't think it was 'bout a pitiful man."

Grace lay in bed many nights, thinking about the play.

King Claudius and Queen Gertrude, to her, were Benny and Amalie. She saw parallels that did not match but were close.

Benny was not the stepfather who had killed her real father. But he did try to kill her brother as he beat him. And while Amalie hadn't cheated on Benny by marrying his brother, she did adore her son to the exclusion of everything else.

In the middle of it all, Grace loved Hamlet the most. With every word his character spoke, she was reminded of her brother and his personal torment.

She had a feeling in her spirit about the story. Somehow the vengeance, murder, and marital betrayal touched her in a way that she couldn't explain.

"So what do you think Shakespeare's message was in this story?" Canada asked a few nights later. Grace had been pressing her to read the story a third time, and she was doing everything in her will to avoid it.

Grace paused, her hands folded in her lap.

"You know, I think he was trying to say that all we really want is love. And even in the middle of all that craziness and death, everybody was fighting to get their little piece of it. I mean, look at Claudius. He killed his brother 'cause he was jealous. He wanted to be king so the people would love him like they did his brother."

Canada listened to her words.

"And then Gertrude. I don't think it was so much that she just jumped into the arms of Claudius 'cause she didn't care 'bout her dead husband. She was lonely and needed somebody to care about her. I can't imagine no woman wanting to be by herself after she done had a husband all that time."

"Makes sense," Canada said.

"And all Ophelia wanted was for Hamlet to love her, but he was so set on killing Claudius, he didn't even pay her no 'tention. Then he killed her daddy by mistake. It was just a mess all the way 'round."

"Yes. It was indeed a mess for everyone. I told you, it's not one of my favorites."

"Just 'cause it's a mess don't mean it ain't good," Grace said. "This story is more than what it looks like. It's a love story. It's just a love story gone wrong."

"A love story?" Canada said with a laugh. "I don't think so."

"A story ain't gotta have no happy ending to be a love story. Just 'cause nobody got love the way they wanted, it don't mean the love wasn't there."

Canada sat in her comfortable armchair, holding the closed book in her lap. She looked at the sixteen-year-old girl, her belly filled with a fatherless baby, and realized she envied her. She envied her profound simplicity, her tenderness, and her ability to see something she herself would never see on her own.

Canada couldn't stop thinking about Grace's words. The girl's sense of deduction was so acute, there had to be something more for her in life than what her immediate future seemed to hold.

"Have you ever thought about going to college?" she asked Grace the next morning at breakfast. Piedmont looked up from the paper at his wife and smiled.

Grace waved her hand as she placed a hot plate of biscuits on the table.

"That's crazy. I ain't even finish regular school. It takes smarts and money to go to college, and to be honest, Mrs. Deveaux, I ain't got too much of neither. Else I wouldn't be walking 'round here looking like I do now."

Canada shook her head, her heart hurting for the girl.

"I went to college," she said, "and you have far more smarts than I do."

Piedmont shook out the pages of his paper so he could read them better.

"You're just being nice," said Grace, standing at the stove. "Tell her how crazy she sounds, Mr. Deveaux. I ain't got no business going to nobody's school."

"She's just being honest," he said. "You're a pretty smart girl, as girls go. I thought I had the only smart one on the planet. And then you show up. You two have got me surrounded."

Grace laughed.

"Well, as far as money is concerned," Canada said, "Piedmont and I would be more than happy to pay to send you."

Piedmont put down the paper, stood, and kissed his wife on the cheek.

"You're leaving?" she asked. "You're not going to eat?"

"I've got to go into town. You two smarty-pants just don't rewrite the laws of gravity while I'm gone."

Grace placed a dish of eggs and breakfast meat on the table. Piedmont grabbed a strip of bacon and walked out the door.

"You're really ought to think about it, Grace. It's not like Piedmont and I have any children of our own to send to school," Canada said.

"How you know, Mrs. Deveaux? You might decide you want children in a couple of years."

"I don't think so."

"You never know. You're young. You can't be much older than me. Having children is a blessing. The Lord might bless you with kids when you least looking for it."

Grace glanced at her employer. Canada's mouth was a thin, tight line.

"I guess you don't like kids, huh?" Grace asked, slipping into one of the chairs. Canada didn't answer. "I'm sorry. I didn't know. You been so helpful to me with my baby coming, I just assumed–"

"I can't have children."

Grace's hand flew up to her mouth.

"Oh, Lord, ma'am, I'm so sorry. I didn't mean no harm."

"No harm taken," Canada said.

The women sat in silence. Canada picked at a biscuit in the middle of her plate.

"I still think you should consider what I said. Piedmont and I could get you into an excellent school."

"I got a baby coming. I can't go to no school with a baby. Plus, it ain't right for no white folks to be paying for a colored gal to go to college. Folks would never stop talking 'bout it. It's lots of white folks out there for you to send instead."

"What people say is the least of my worries," Canada replied. "And you could always go to college after you have your baby. I think there's a treasure trove in that head of yours waiting to be opened, and it would be a shame if that never happened."

Grace blushed. "I'm going to say thank you and ask that we stop talking 'bout this," she said. "You reading me all those books every night is education enough for me."

"Okay," Canada said, "but I want you to remember one thing: as long as Piedmont and I are alive, the offer stands. Maybe one day you'll change your mind."

"Thank you, ma'am."

"You're welcome. And Grace, I want you to do me one more favor, but this one you can't refuse or else I'll have to let you go."

"What's that, Mrs. Deveaux?"

"Call me Canada. Can you at least do that?"

Grace smiled. "Yes ma'am. Yes, Canada. I think I can do that."

"Good. Now pass me the syrup. My biscuit's getting cold."

CHAPTER FOURTEEN

Grace was in her eighth month of pregnancy when she met Big Daddy Boten.

One Monday morning she walked into the sitting room to bring Piedmont his coffee and found him talking with a black man who was far too big for the small armchair he was sitting in. She returned to the kitchen for another cup. When she came back in the room, she took a closer look.

The man wore crisp jean overalls and a white T-shirt underneath. His arms were massive and muscular. Grace found herself studying these arms as she poured the coffee. He gave her a pleasant smile. His face was very attractive and friendly.

"Grace, this is Leonard Boten," Piedmont said. "He's going to be my primary cattle handler."

The man nodded as he smiled. Grace nodded back.

"Grace is our housekeeper," Piedmont continued. "She makes the best pork roast and blackberry cobbler this side of heaven."

"Mr. Deveaux, I may as well tell you. Ain't nobody called me Leonard since I was knee-high to a ant. I'd feel much more comfortable if y'all just call me Big Daddy. I don't think no explanation is necessary why folks call me that."

Piedmont laughed. "Okay. Big Daddy it is. You think you can remember that, Grace?"

"I don't think I'll have a problem," she said.

"Good," Piedmont said. "Grace, why don't you take Big Daddy to the guest house. That's where he'll be staying."

Grace nodded.

Piedmont stood and extended his hand to Big Daddy. Big Daddy stood, too, towering so high his shadow fell across Piedmont's face.

"Glad to have you aboard." Piedmont shook his hand with vigor. "Grace can help you with anything you need. And you should feel free to see me if you have anything you don't quite understand."

"Thank you, sir. I shole appreciate you taking me on here."

"Call me Piedmont."

Big Daddy grinned.

"Yessir. Yessir, Mr. Piedmont."

"So how long have you worked for the Deveauxs?"

"A little over eight months."

Big Daddy watched Grace sidelong as they walked through the yard to the guest house. He thought she looked about eight months pregnant. She was a very pretty girl. He didn't see a ring on her finger.

"Does your husband work for the Deveauxs, too?" he asked.

Grace looked down.

"I'm not married."

Big Daddy tried again, treading with care.

"Your boyfriend?"

"No sir, I don't have a boyfriend." Grace's voice was a whisper.

They continued to walk without saying anything more.

When they reached the guest house, Grace opened the door and showed him inside. There was a big four-poster bed and a lamp, a dresser, a highboy, and a chifforobe. There was a small bathroom and a kitchen area. Grace pulled the curtains back. Big Daddy looked around in astonishment.

"This is where I'm gonna be staying?"

"Yessir."

Big Daddy walked around the room, touching the fine cherry-wood furniture, running his massive hands along the posts of the bed.

"They're gonna let me stay in this nice house all by myself?"

Grace looked at Big Daddy. He was a very handsome man. Big. Strong. Bigger than anything she'd ever seen with arms, legs, and a face to go with it. He looked to be twenty-two, twenty-three years old.

"The Deveauxs ain't like regular white people. They treat us colored folks like we just like them."

"I see," he said, still not believing his good fortune.

"Every night Mrs. Deveaux—Canada—reads books to me. Plays by Shakespeare," she said with pride. From the expression on Big Daddy's face, Shakespeare could have been the man next door.

"That's right nice," he said.

"Shole is," Grace replied. "She wants to send me to college, but I told her that was crazy talk."

"Why is that crazy talk? We can do anything white folks can do, sometimes better."

Grace looked out the window toward the field of cows standing around munching hay.

"I got a baby to be thinking 'bout. Canada gave me lots of stuff for him. And she didn't even know me fo' I came here."

"How do you know it's a him?" Big Daddy asked.

" 'Cause I can feel it. I just know." Her voice was distant.

Big Daddy sat on the bed, watching her. Grace walked away from the window to the door.

"I'll put fresh linens on the bed. Dinner is always at noon.

Supper's always at six. I serve breakfast at four for the farmhands. The Deveauxs don't eat until later. If you can't make it to a meal on time, let me know, and I'll keep it hot for you."

Big Daddy watched her in silence.

She turned to leave, pulling the door behind her.

"Grace."

She opened the door.

"Thank you. I appreciate all your help. You've made me feel very welcome here." His smile was warm and broad.

Grace looked at the floor, fidgeting with the doorknob.

"It's okay, sir. I know how it feels to be a stranger in a new house. I'll help you any way I can."

CHAPTER FIFTEEN

By Grace's ninth month, she and Big Daddy were living in the guest house together. The Deveauxs were just as pleased about the union. They had watched Big Daddy court Grace with an awkward shyness, lifting things for her, reaching for objects that were too high, undertaking the smallest of tasks to assist the girl, whose energy levels diminished with her pregnancy. They whispered together at meals and as they passed each other in the halls. Grace began to laugh again. Canada had seen her laugh this way only when she was with her brother, Walter.

They were married two weeks before the baby's birth. Canada was Grace's matron of honor. Big Daddy wanted the baby to have a last name, and more than that, he wanted Grace. Grace wanted him just as much. She still loved Walter from the deepest place in her heart, but Big Daddy's love was so consuming, she knew it would be more than enough for her and her baby to rest in. His big strong arms made her feel secure and protected. It was best she marry Big Daddy. There was no other option. She would never be able to acknowledge what had happened between her and Walter. She would never be able to tell the world about their baby.

Walter was jealous of Big Daddy, but the man's personality

was so large and welcoming, it was impossible to hate him. During the day, Walter worked on a cattle farm ten miles outside of town. After supper and on weekends, he and Big Daddy rebuilt the house that had burnt down.

"I'm gon' do my best to buy that plot of land next to this," Big Daddy said.

"What for?" Walter asked.

"Well, me and my family gon' need a house. We can't stay with them folks forever." Big Daddy pounded a nail into a ceiling beam. "Once we finish rebuilding this house, I wants us to start working on one for me and your sister."

Walter's insides knotted up at the words. He could hold on to Grace with invisible hands, but he knew, no matter how tight he held on, she was already slipping into a grasp that was more binding, more acceptable, than his.

Big Daddy never once questioned Walter about the father of Grace's baby.

"I love her so much," he said. "It's like God just dropped an angel into my arms by mistake. I'd take her if she had ten babies. Long as I have her, I don't care what else comes 'long with her."

Walter cringed inside.

"I want us to have our house ready by the time the baby's 'bout three months. Think we can do it?"

"I reckon," Walter said.

The last thing he wanted to discuss was Grace making a home with someone else. Big Daddy stopped hammering to glance at him. Walter's expression was as stony as the pile of bricks around his feet.

"So that's all right with you?"

"I reckon."

"Well, hell, man, we gon' need more than a reckon. It's gon' take some long weekends and a lotta late nights and such to pull it off."

"I reckon so."

Big Daddy scanned Walter's face, then sighed and shook his head.

"You's a strange bird sometimes, you know that?"

Walter gave a wan smile. "I reckon so."

"Grace says she knows it's a boy, but I kinda hope it's a girl," Big Daddy said one night as he and Walter sanded pieces of wood.

"Why do you want a girl?"

"Man, Grace is the prettiest thing I done ever seen on God's green earth. You know how special it makes me feel to know somebody like her could love somebody like me? The greatest thing God could do is send another one just like her to share with the world. 'Cause I'm not sharing Grace. Lawd hammercy, no. She's all mine."

The beefy sound of joyous laughter came rising from the middle of his gut.

The sizzle of acid backwash and bile clashed in the pit of Walter's stomach.

The baby came two days later. Big Daddy was a wild man, his hysterical bellows breaking the still of the quiet night as he ran from the guest house, pounding on the Deveauxs' front door. Canada, already dressed in her robe and slippers, followed him. Big Daddy was so frightened and fidgety, she feared something had gone wrong with the baby.

Canada could hear Grace's cries as she neared the house. Inside, she found her wrestling with the bedcovers, clutching her stomach. Canada rushed to the bed and held her hand. She turned to Big Daddy.

"Get me some hot water and towels."

Big Daddy stood in front of her, rooted in terror.

"Quick!"

He ran around the guest house, fearful that not following her instruction would result in Grace's death. He heated water and gathered towels and rushed them to Canada.

"Dip a washcloth in some cool water and bring it to me," she whispered. "Bring the sewing shears, too."

He rushed away again. When he returned, he handed her the

cloth and shears, then hovered over her, fidgeting with panic, like a hen whose eggs had just been stolen from beneath her.

Grace screamed and clutched Canada's arm so tight that a blue handprint appeared against the woman's delicate skin. Canada wiped Grace's face with the cool cloth and whispered to her in a soft, comforting tone.

"It's okay, Grace. The baby will be here soon."

With every stroke of the cloth, Canada's elbow hit Big Daddy's thigh. He was standing so close to her that his shadow darkened the bed. She turned to him with a scowl.

"You're either going to have to leave," she said, "or give me some room to do this. She needs air. Could you back up a little?"

He shrank away from her, and slumped down in a chair in a corner of the room. Tears were streaming down his face. In desperation, he began to pray.

"Please, God, don't take her. Please don't take her. I don't know what I'd do if you let her die."

Canada was working between Grace's legs now, squatting beside the bed, helping her push as the baby moved down the birth canal.

"One more time," she whispered. "One more push and he'll be here. I can already see the head. My goodness, this baby has a head full of hair just like yours."

Grace groaned, squeezing against Canada's hands, forcing the baby farther out of her body. The shoulders came through, and Canada grabbed hold of the baby and pulled.

"One more, Grace. One more and we're all done. I promise."

Big Daddy was shaking with such violence, the wooden legs of the chair began to rattle.

Grace pushed again and Canada pulled the baby free. She cleared the mouth and slapped the buttocks until the baby cried, a gusty passionate squall that made Grace forget her pain and think of Walter. Canada cleaned the baby, cut the cord, wrapped it in one of the towels, and laid it against Grace's bosom.

"Grace, honey, I know you said you were hoping for a boy."

Big Daddy froze in the chair.

"But this is about as healthy and pretty a girl as I ever did see. It'd make anybody forget about having a silly old boy. Sure would. Just look at her." Canada stroked the baby's head.

Grace smiled, her eyes wet.

"What are you going to call her?" Canada asked, her own eyes filled with tears. "A beautiful little baby like this has to have a special name."

"Ophelia," Grace whispered, cradling the child.

From across the room, Big Daddy's trembling grew even more distressed.

"Now that's a special name," Canada said. "But don't you want something happier? Something more befitting such a pretty little girl?"

Grace coughed, shaking her head.

"No. The name is perfect. And this Ophelia won't have to worry. She will be loved. She will be loved very much."

Canada wiped away her tears as she studied the tiny baby in the arms of its mother. "Come here, Big Daddy," she said. "Come see your brand-new baby girl."

Big Daddy rushed over to the bed and knelt down beside it. He kissed Grace and the baby on their foreheads. His body was still shaking. He caught sight of the blood-soaked bed. He turned his head away.

"Are you okay, Grace?" His voice was husky and thick. "Do you feel sick or anything?"

Grace smiled up at him.

"Right now," she whispered, "I'm the happiest I ever been in my life."

Canada backed away and slipped out of the house, leaving the new family alone to share in their moment of joy.

She found out very early in her life that she couldn't bear children. But Canada loved babies, and while at Vassar, she often volunteered in the maternity ward at the nearby hospital. This was not the first baby she'd helped to deliver. She was just as sure that it wouldn't be the last.

"Just because I can't have one doesn't mean that I can't help," she said to the darkness.

As she walked back to her house, she recalled the face of the baby as she had cleared away the blood and held it in her arms before handing it to Grace.

She stopped in the middle of the dusty backyard, the chill of the night washing over her. She thrust her face into her hands and burst into tears.

CHAPTER SIXTEEN

When Big Daddy, Grace, and baby Ophelia moved into their new home, the Deveauxs gave them all the furniture from the guest house.

"We can't take this," Grace said. "There's no way we could ever pay for it all."

"It's a gift, Grace," Canada replied. "You're not supposed to pay for gifts."

"But you already done too much. Buying that land for us was more than we could wish for."

The Deveauxs remained firm. "It's all yours," Piedmont said. "We want you to have it."

Big Daddy reached for Piedmont's hand, gripping it tight. He knew his employers well enough to know that when they insisted on something, there was no turning them down.

"Well, we thank you, Piedmont," he said. "We shole thank you for all you done."

As Big Daddy, Walter, Piedmont, and a few of the farmhands loaded up the furniture, Canada called Grace into the library. Grace held Ophelia in her arms. The baby thrashed against her, a burst of gurgles and grins.

"That girl's a real busybody, isn't she?" Canada asked.

Grace smiled at her baby.

"Yes, indeed. She's gonna be something else when she starts walking. I'm gon' have a time keeping up with her."

Canada walked over to the secretary and opened a drawer.

She pulled out a box wrapped in white tissue paper, tied with a large gold bow. She held it out to Grace.

"What is this, Canada?" Grace asked. "I can't keep taking stuff from you. I feel like I don't deserve what you've given me already."

"You deserve everything and more, Grace," Canada said. "You and Big Daddy have given me and Piedmont so much joy while you've lived here with us. We want to give some of it back. I don't think you realize the impact you've had. The times you and I spent in this library have meant a great deal to me."

Her hand was still outstretched as she walked toward Grace, holding the box.

"Take it, please. For me," she said.

Grace shifted the baby in her arms and took the gift. She stared at the paper, fingering the soft tissue. Ophelia slapped at the object in her mother's hand.

"It's so pretty. I don't want to open it and mess up the paper. It looks so nice."

"That's why I brought you in here. I wanted us to open it together."

Canada reached for the baby, taking her so Grace could open the package. She tried with great effort not to tear the paper. When she pulled the tissue back, she found a beautiful leather-bound copy of *Hamlet* inside.

"Oh my goodness." Her hand flew up to her mouth. "Canada."

Canada smiled, bouncing the baby in her arms.

"I think you appreciate that story more than Shakespeare himself. I felt like you had to have it. Don't ask me why. It just feels that way."

Grace's shoulders shook as she clutched the book to her bosom.

"You been so good to me." She embraced the woman in a tight hug. Ophelia gurgled, snatching at Grace's hair.

"You're my friend," Canada said. "I have to tell you, Grace, when I first hired you, I was just looking for somebody to cook and keep my house clean. It doesn't even feel right having you do that anymore. Almost makes me feel ashamed of myself. God truly works in mysterious ways."

"Yes, He does. But don't you feel no shame about hiring me. Cooking and cleaning is the kind of work I choose to do." Grace shifted the baby on her hip. "I think God had something else going on with me and you. Maybe we can't see it yet, but it's there. He brought us together, and it's been nothing but a blessing from the day we met."

Both women's eyes were filled with tears. Baby Ophelia snatched at her mother's hair until it fell free from the pins.

"Nyyaahh," she screamed in triumph once the hair was loose.

Canada and Grace both looked at the baby in wonder and laughed.

Walter helped the Botens settle into their new home. He and Big Daddy had already painted the house, inside and out, by the time they brought in the furniture. Walter worked the land with Big Daddy, helping to plant and cultivate a small crop of vegetables and tend to the five pigs, three cows, one bull, and eight chickens that Piedmont had given them. Every evening, Walter went across the way to his empty dwelling. He never stayed over for supper. In the middle of the night, he slipped out to see one of the many women with whom he slept. Grace could hear him leaving and was awake to see him return.

Walter said nothing to or about baby Ophelia to anyone. When the baby played in the house within sight of him, Walter ignored her. It pained him too much to see his child yet not be able to acknowledge her.

He made the decision to shut her out of his mind and out of his heart.

Ophelia bore a strong, innocent adoration for him. There were many times when she crawled over to him as he worked in the house, clung to his legs, and smiled up at him with a toothless grin. Walter would stand still, staring down at her, refusing to move or respond. Grace always arrived in time to witness these moments. She would run over to pick up the baby, whose cries would turn to hysterics as she clung steadfast to Walter's legs. Walter would remain rigid as Grace pried the baby away. Grace made no eye contact with Walter whenever this happened, nor he with her, as she rushed the shrieking baby from the room.

Walter always left right after one of these episodes. Sometimes he would not reappear for days.

One day when Walter was tightening a doorknob, Ophelia crawled up behind him and sat on the floor. She had been sitting quietly for several minutes before he turned around and saw her. She looked up at him with her beautiful toothless grin.

"Dada," she squealed.

Walter opened the door and left.

It was six months before they heard anything about him again.

"Caesar Bucksport said that Walter got some gal over in the next town pregnant," Big Daddy said at supper one night.

Ophelia sat in a high chair, flinging crumbled cornbread to the floor. Grace looked up from her plate. "What?"

Big Daddy shrugged as he took a bite of chicken. "You know how your brother is."

"Well, who's the girl?"

"I'on know. Caesar said he saw her with Walter and she big as a house, like she 'bout to pop any day now."

Grace put down her fork and pushed away from the table.

"What's the matter, baby?"

"Nuthin'."

"Yes it is. You worried 'bout your brother, ain't you?"

Grace stood at the kitchen sink, staring out of the window into the pitch of the night toward her brother's house. It had been dark for months.

"No. I was just wondering why he didn't tell nobody, that's all."

Big Daddy kept eating.

"Well, that's just Walter," he said between bites of chicken. "He so closed-mouthed. He'on talk 'bout too much of nuthin' no way."

Grace returned to the table and started clearing the dishes. She stooped to gather errant crumbs from around Grace's high chair. She took the dishes to the sink and washed them in silence. Then she wiped Ophelia's face and lifted her from the chair. Big Daddy was still eating.

"You finished?" he asked.

"I'ma go lay down. The baby wore me out today."

Big Daddy nodded.

"You feel all right, don't you?" he asked.

"I feel fine. Just a little bit tired, that's all."

Grace made her way down the hall, holding Ophelia in her arms. As she entered the shadowy darkness, far from the light of the kitchen, tears began to stream down her cheeks.

Walter waited in the back of the room as the midwife helped the girl deliver the baby. Pammy's cries frightened him, but he sat in silence, awaiting the arrival of his very own child. One he could claim. The midwife screamed at the girl to push, and Pammy strained, sweated, and groaned until, moments later, after ten hours of labor, she squeezed the baby into the world.

"It's dead. It was a boy." The midwife's face was expressionless.

At the sound of her voice, Benny's words rang in Walter's head.

Faggot. I knowed something was wrong wit' you from the day you was born.

Walter turned away from the woman, abandoning the room and Pammy's hysterical cries. Pammy never saw him again.

Walter left Tennessee that same day.

Two months later, he returned with a wife.

PART VII

1966–1968

COOLIE AND POLO

We are not the same persons this year
as last; nor are those we love. It is a
happy chance if we, changing,
continue to love a changed person.

–W. SOMERSET MAUGHAM

CHAPTER SEVENTEEN

After the second fire destroyed the Boten house and the baby, Ophelia lapsed into a depression so deep, no one could bring her out of it. Big Daddy lifted her from the mucky ground and the shadows of the dark trees and brought her into Walter and Sukie's house. They put her in one of the back bedrooms, where she lay for three days. Her sooty face was tear-streaked. She refused to let anyone touch her. Her eyes bore a faraway look that would remain with her for the rest of her life.

Walter and Sukie lived in a spacious four-bedroom home. All the rooms were decorated with great detail. Most were unused. The Martins had hoped their house would someday be filled with many children, the happy sounds of life and laughter reaching out to them at every turn. Sukie wanted to be the nucleus of affection for her husband and her brood, something that had never held true within her own family.

There had never been much life in the house, from the moment the two inhabited it as husband and wife. There never would be. Whatever spark had first drawn Sukie and Walter together was now a tentacle of obligation that she was unwilling to release. He feared her. That fear, and the threat of repercussion should he ever try to leave, was what kept them together.

The marriage was a sham. Walter surrendered to it in body, but his mind was never a willing participant.

"My baby ain't gon' be right no mo' after this, I can just feel it," Grace said to her husband the night of the fire, just after he had put Ophelia to bed.

Walter sat across the table from his sister. Her hair was a tangled mess around her face, hanging heavy down her back and over her breasts. He wanted to hold her, but Big Daddy's arms encircled her in a tight hug.

Sukie washed dishes. Her back, stiff and straight, was facing them. As Grace sobbed into Big Daddy's chest, Sukie turned sideways and watched Walter from the corner of her eye.

"Y'all can stay here till we get your house built again," Walter said. "Ain't no need to go nowhere, since we got all them empty rooms upstairs."

Sukie's back was steel.

"We can't do that," Big Daddy said. "These quarters is too tight for so many people."

Grace pulled her face from her husband's chest. "Thank you, Walter. We'll stay. We ain't got nowhere else we can go."

"What about the Deveauxs?" Big Daddy said.

"The Deveauxs ain't family," Walter replied.

A dish slipped from Sukie's hands and made a crashing sound in the sink.

"I just hope my baby don't have no breakdown from this," Grace said. "Losing a child is the hardest thing a woman can ever go through."

A piercing pain shot up from Walter's stomach to his throat.

"This is the second time that house done burned down," Sukie said, looking around at them. "The earth is tryna tell you something. And it ain't saying pull up roots and move in here."

She dried her hands and left the room.

"I'm going to Detroit to stay with Lay," Polo announced to his parents the next day.

Big Daddy heaved a sigh and shook his head.

"You talked to him about it already?" Grace asked.

"Yes ma'am."

She pulled him into her chest and kissed his forehead.

Polo glanced over her shoulder, into his father's face.

"Big Daddy, you ain't got nuthin' to say?"

"Ain't nuthin' I say gon' make a difference," he grunted.

Grace rocked her son in her arms.

"Much as we don't want you to go, you got to make it on

your own," she whispered. "Ain't nuthin' for you 'round here but a hard row to hoe."

Polo held on to his mother, lingering in her embrace.

"I love you, Mama."

"I love you, too, baby boy."

Polo waited for his father's words.

"My whole family done fell apart," Big Daddy said.

He left the house and went into the fields.

Polo refused to stay in the Martin house. He went home with Coolie, who slipped him into her room through the bedroom window.

"If my mama finds you in here, boy . . ."

Polo slid beneath the covers alongside her.

"I'ma be quiet. I know how she is."

Coolie pressed her body against his, wrapping her legs around him.

"Just make sure you're outta here before sunup," she whispered.

He pulled her close until there was nothing between them but the nuance of flesh. "Don't worry, I'll be out."

She stroked his head. "Where you gonna go?"

"I'll make a way."

"You ain't gon' go to your uncle's house?"

Polo's body grew rigid. "No."

Coolie stroked his shoulders and began to massage his back. "Why not? They got plenty of room over there."

He shrugged her hands away.

"No. Aunt Sukie watched us tryna put out that fire and save the baby, and she stood right in the door of her own house just lookin', like it wasn't nuthin'."

Coolie squeezed him tight, pulling him into her body. She could sense the rage building within him and realized it was best to try to cut it off. Polo was hot-tempered, a short man with a short fuse. She knew that once he got his thinking caught up a certain way, there was no getting him to change his mind. And it wasn't right that he should feel that way about his uncle and aunt. Right now, their house was the lone option that he had until his family could rebuild theirs.

"Relax, baby," she said. "It's gon' be all right. Just relax. Calm down."

"No, Coolie. Something ain't right 'bout all this. Something 'bout her and that fire just don't seem right."

"Baby, you gon' have to stay there. Least 'till y'all can get your house back up."

"I don't have to stay nowhere." His voice dropped so low, Coolie had to strain to hear it. "I'm going up north with Lay. I told you he said I can come up there with him any time I want to."

Coolie's arms released him and she turned onto her back.

"I'm leaving tomorrow," Polo said.

She lay in the darkness, her mouth pursed, her eyes stinging, staring up at the ceiling. What did his decision mean for her? He'd said before that he would take her with him wherever he went. There was no way she wanted to remain in Downtown. Without Polo as a safe haven, she knew she would crumble, or strike out against her mother's dominion.

He pulled her close to him again.

"You gon' go with me, right?" he asked.

Coolie threw her arms around him.

"You ain't never getting rid of me," she whispered. "So don't even try."

CHAPTER EIGHTEEN

Three months later, Polo and Coolie were living with his brother in a three-bedroom apartment in Detroit.

It was ideal for Coolie. Most days, she and Polo were together at home. Lay was almost always there with them. The three spent their time drinking, smoking marijuana, cooking or eating take-out, playing spades, and watching television. They didn't meet any of Lay's associates or friends for the first few weeks, and Lay didn't appear to have any kind of job to speak of. But there was always money. Coolie marveled at how, no matter how much they spent, it repopulated itself again and again. Once a day, in the evening, Lay would leave and return with more.

"I thought you said your brother sold dope," Coolie said.

"He do."

"How come we don't never see it, then?"

They had been watching television while Lay went out for one of his evening runs.

"I guess he'll show us when he's ready."

Lay left town once a month. Coolie and Polo never knew where it was he went. He would go on a Friday morning and return the following Sunday. They never questioned him. His departure meant they had the apartment to themselves. It made them feel like newlyweds.

The phone rang often, always for Lay. He preferred that they not answer it. "You know it ain't for you. Y'all ain't met nobody since you been here."

"Suppose it's Mama?" Polo asked.

"Mama don't call. She like to write."

Coolie answered it one day out of boredom when Polo and Lay had gone for takeout.

"Hello?"

She could hear someone on the other end, listening, breathing. A quick dial tone followed.

On another occasion Polo answered the phone after it rang seventeen times and Lay refused to pick it up.

The three of them were watching television. Polo and Lay had been drinking.

"You ain't gon' get that?" Coolie asked after four rings.

"I'm tired. I'on feel like talking to nobody," Lay said.

The ringing continued.

"Damn, man, why don't you answer that shit?" Polo said. "I'm tryna watch this movie."

Lay ignored him and stared at the television screen.

Polo got up from the couch and walked to the phone.

"Hello?"

"Lay?" a soft voice whispered.

"Naw. This is Polo. Who this?"

The phone went dead.

Polo pursed his lips and walked back over to the couch. He kicked Lay's foot as he sat down.

"Man, who that be calling you all the time like that and hanging up?"

Lay shrugged.

"Could be anybody. Nobody told you to answer it."

Polo leaned back against the cushions.

"Kick my fucking foot again," Lay said, "and I'll cut your throat."

Polo glanced over at his brother. "Man, please. Quit playing."

Lay's face was rigid as he sipped his brandy and watched the rest of the movie.

Polo had run down to the store for more beer and brandy. When Coolie walked out of the bathroom, she heard Lay whispering into the phone.

"I told you to stop ringing my phone like that. I'm not the only one living here anymore. Damn. I'll call you if you just give me half a second to catch my breath."

Coolie listened from the hallway.

"I'm sorry," he said, his tone changing. "I didn't mean to cuss." He paused. "Yeah, I know." Another pause. "No, I haven't forgot. I know what you did for me. I owe you everything. I do. I know that." He was quiet for a long moment. "Yeah, Susu, I know. I'm tryna work that out now. Just give me another month or so, and I'll work it out so you can come."

Coolie never heard him terminate the call. She walked out and saw him placing the phone on the hook.

"Who was you talkin' to?" she asked.

"Nobody."

"Stop lying," Coolie probed. "Who that? One of your girl-friends?"

"Something like that."

The phone rang again.

"I'll get it," Coolie said, racing to pick it up.

"Just leave it alone." His voice was steel.

She stopped and looked at him, her hand in midair.

"I'm sorry," he said, his voice softer. "I'm sick of that woman calling here. No matter what I do, I just can't get her to leave me alone."

"Okay." She shrugged and walked away from the phone.

"Good," he said, smiling. "When Polo gets back, let's play us some spades."

The first few months after Coolie and Polo arrived, the three of them spent a great deal of time in the apartment, not even bothering to dress. Most days Lay and Polo were in boxers and Coolie wandered around in a slip. Some days they never even went outside. They didn't have to. Lay had now let them in on things, and they ran the business from within the confines of the apartment.

Polo and Coolie learned that Lay was the biggest heroin dealer in the city of Detroit.

People would come by the apartment from early morning until deep in the night, purchasing nickel and dime bags of the stuff. Some of the harder-partying folks went for more. Lay made a point to know all of them by name.

"Keep your users close," he told Polo. "Make sure you get to know 'em well. Who they kids are, where they mama live. That way they won't mess around and tell the wrong person about what you doing. They too scared to make a stupid move like that when you know too much about 'em."

The people in the immediate neighborhood had seen Lay kill before, and they knew his reputation from his days with Crosstown Dickey. Many months before Polo and Coolie arrived, he'd murdered someone right in front of the building where he lived, shot a man in the throat for trying to cheat him out of more heroin than he had paid for. As the man lay dying on the sidewalk, Lay urinated in the bloody gaping hole in his neck.

"That's what happens when you fuck with me," he said to the crowd that had gathered. "Anybody want some, I'm in apartment 504."

When the police arrived, no one admitted to seeing what had happened. Lay stood in the midst of the crowd, watching as the cops harangued and questioned bystanders for a clue about who'd committed such an outrageous act. No one conceded. Lay owned the mean streets of the Detroit hustle. He knew there wasn't a soul bold enough to challenge his role.

"How come you live in this small apartment if we making so much money?"

Coolie was sitting on the sofa beside Lay watching television. Polo was in the bedroom asleep.

"This apartment is fine," Lay said. "The last thing we wanna do is draw attention to how much money we got. The police'll be on us like ticks."

"Oh," she replied. "Is that why we don't have no car?"

"I got a car."

Coolie shoved him. "No you don't."

Lay looked at her hand on his arm. She followed his eyes. They met hers and were icy cold. Nervous, she drew her hand away.

"Sorry," he said, softening. "I just don't like people pushing on me."

Coolie closed her mouth and turned her attention back to the television.

"I only use the car to go outta town or for special reasons," Lay said. "I try not to flash too much stuff. It causes more trouble than it's worth."

Coolie didn't respond.

"You mad at me, Coolie?" he asked. "I ain't mean to snap at you."

"I'm okay. I'm just tired. I think I'll go lay down with Polo for a while."

• • •

Lay was smart enough not to fool with heroin himself. He had seen too many people with addictions to horse do foolish things.

His vice was marijuana.

"Weed, wine, and women," he sang to his brother. "That's all a nigga need."

Lay had many women. Women who tricked for him. But he realized that Polo was still too naïve to accept that his big brother was a pimp as well as a dope dealer. He figured he'd school Polo about that side of the business later. Once he was in deep enough not to consider getting out.

Polo was impressed by the money and all the freedom that came with it. When Lay's gunmen became more visible, he was even more enthralled. They had not been there when Polo and Coolie first moved in. A month later, six of them patrolled the halls just outside the apartment.

"Who that?" Coolie asked.

"Them? Oh, those are just my boys."

"What you need them for?" she said, watching the burly thugs sidelong as they returned to the apartment with takeout.

"Detroit is dangerous. Can't do what we do and not have nobody looking out for us."

"Yeah, baby," Polo said. "Don't be stupid. We gotta protect what's ours."

Coolie frowned at Polo. "I'm not stupid."

"Naw," he said. "You just country, is all."

Lay hadn't brought the gunmen around at first by design. He wanted to wait until Polo and Coolie were comfortable within their new lifestyle. A lifestyle where there was always money and where, when they walked down the street, people showed such deference, it was heady, intoxicating.

"Good afternoon, Mr. Boten," a lanky brown-skinned woman said as she brushed past Polo.

"Who she talking to, you?" Coolie asked. "How she know you?"

"I'on know."

Coolie gripped his arm tighter as they walked down the block.

Lay watched them enjoy the spoils and begin to ease into this new world and adapt it as their own. The two had even started picking up some of the lingo they heard spoken in the clubs and on the streets.

"Plant me now?" Coolie would ask Polo whenever he was about to leave the apartment without her, which wasn't often.

"Dig you later," Polo would shoot back.

Lay smiled as he watched them, his plans for the two of them taking on a beautiful shape.

One night Lay took them out to the club Bud's Monarch. Neither Polo nor Coolie had ever seen anything like it. There were platforms and stage areas where women danced, alone in go-go boots and short dresses, or with swift-footed, flashy men who moved as smooth as James Brown. Coolie was in a daze. This was nothing like the Lucky Star Liquor Joint. Bud's Monarch was something light-years away.

She sat at their table in a reverie, listening to the loud music and taking in the bright lights and all the glamorous women with their perfect hair, wigs, and makeup, smoking, drinking, dancing in moves so provocative that she almost felt ashamed to watch them.

Her attire was painfully inappropriate. She wore a tea-length cotton frock, an A-line calico dress that was as drab as a gray Detroit day. She knew nothing about makeup. On this level of sophistication, her fresh face was a flaw.

She watched Polo ogle the smorgasbord of sensuous women and their risqué garb. Tight chemises clung to the curvy backsides, miniskirts rode high on thighs. Coolie couldn't even begin to compete with what she witnessed in the club that night.

Lay sat back, sipping brandy and watching her terror, watching his brother fall easy prey to the lure of the fast world around him. It would not be long for Polo, he knew. Soon enough, he would be able to let him know about the stable of whores. Coolie would require more attention. As he watched her, he could see the fascination. She wanted to be like the women around her.

The next day he gave her a knot of money for shopping. She snatched it from his hand and counted it.

"This is three thousand dollars," she said. "You gon' let me use all this for new clothes?"

"That's up to you."

Polo sat at the dining table eating breakfast. He put his fork down.

"That's too much money for her to be spending," he said, frowning. "What she need new clothes for? We don't go that many places."

Coolie stormed over to the sofa and sat down.

"That money's yours," Lay said to her, ignoring his brother. "And guess what? I'm gon' use the car today. Just so we can drive around and get you all the stuff you need."

Coolie squealed, clapping her hands together.

"I don't see why we need to go with her to get no clothes," said Polo, getting up from the table.

"Well, we do," Lay said. "I got an eye for ladies' fashions." He smiled at her. "Don't worry, Miss Cool. We gon' fix you up good. You gon' make the rest of these women walking 'round here look like shit."

Coolie grinned.

Lay pulled his brother aside as he tried to pass.

"Look, man," he said, "you got this fine-ass girl. You need to be trying to show her off to the world."

"I'm not going," Polo said. "I'm not trying to see her dressed like them girls at the club."

"All right then," said Lay. "Let's go, Miss Cool."

Coolie had heard his words to Polo. Pumped full of confidence, she walked out of the apartment, making an exaggerated display of swaying her hips.

Polo watched his girlfriend go.

For the first time in his life, he began to wonder how well he really knew his brother.

Polo began to notice even more of a change.

Lay and Coolie had become coconspirators while Polo watched the two of them from a distance. Every day, the three worked together in the apartment, handling the business, rationing the product, and counting the money, with Coolie playing more of an active role in the dealing of heroin. She packaged the bags, monitored the stock, and made direct contact with Lay's gunmen.

In the beginning, she would watch television while Lay and Polo did the bulk of the work. Now Lay encouraged her aggressive participation. Polo had no say in the matter at all. She no longer listened to him the way she used to.

Weed was becoming even more popular, and they started dealing it heavy when the demand began to rise. Lay placed Polo in charge of that end of the business. He distributed the marijuana to the runners and collected the funds at day's end. This business became more and more profitable over a short period of time, with as many clients as the heroin side of the trade.

Lay let Polo control the weed and claim all the profits for himself. Polo saw this as an opportunity to woo Coolie back from Lay's influence. He took pride in having his own enterprise and soon became daring enough to leave the apartment to collect from the runners on the street, instead of waiting for them to bring the revenue to him. He figured this allowed for less possibility of theft.

"Plant me now?" he said as he stood in the doorway to leave, prompting her for the phrase she used to give up on her own.

"Yeah, yeah, yeah," Coolie replied. "Dig you later."

Before long, he was spending most of the day on the street, leaving Coolie and Lay to run the heroin business alone.

Which was what Lay had been working toward all along.

"Let me show you something," Lay said to Coolie one afternoon, not long after Polo had gone to make his rounds.

Coolie had been putting the nickel and dime bags of heroin together, using a scale to measure exact amounts before she spooned the substance into the tiny plastic pouches. She wore a thin slip, her usual attire in the confines of the apartment.

"Show me what?" she asked, taking a drag of the cigarette that lay burning beside her in an ashtray.

She had come a great distance from her innocent puff of reefer in the barn with Polo. She had been smoking cigarettes for two months and had graduated to a two-pack-a-day habit. It was more style than addiction. Her technique was still very sophomoric. She puffed the smoke through her nose almost as fast as she inhaled it.

"I got a new use for the stuff in those bags," he said.

Coolie stopped measuring the heroin and looked up at him. He was standing behind her.

"What's that?"

She had begun to enjoy learning to run the operation, and Lay had convinced her that she was now an active partner in the heroin enterprise. She watched him as he smiled, his expression cryptic.

He leaned closer, peering over her shoulder at the product on the scale. He touched the powder, letting it sift through his fingers like dust. His chest grazed her naked shoulder, sending a nervous charge throughout her body. Lay seemed oblivious to her shudder. His voice was a whisper when he spoke again.

"Do you understand the power of this stuff?"

He let the white dust drift through his fingers.

"Hell yeah," she said. "The same people come through here three and five times a day trying to buy some of this power. Making us a whole lotta money and buying me a whole lotta dresses. And I thank them very much." She took another drag of the cigarette.

"No, Cool, you don't hear me. Do you really understand the power of the horse?"

His head was now alongside hers. She studied his face as he marveled at the drug sifting through his hand. His profile was strong and structured. It possessed a feral quality that fascinated her, not soft and unsure, like Polo's. Coolie could see a calm savagery in Lay's face, and she was pleased to know he was her friend, her confidant, her mentor.

He stared ahead. His eyes glazed as she watched him now.

"I don't think you understand the power, Cool. And before you can rule it, you gotta understand."

Her pulse had quickened. She felt the adrenaline push through her as Lay leaned close, the bare skin of his chest against her back.

"What are you talking 'bout, Lay?" Her breath was quick. "We already rule the horse. We have the money to prove it."

He shook his head.

"We don't rule the horse, baby. We're just selling tickets for rides. You and I, we're a couple of nickel-and-dime-selling hookers for the pony."

His voice was hypnotic.

"The horse is wild and free. It's an untamed maverick. But we gotta rope it in, baby. To rule it, and rule it right, we gotta catch it. When we do that, man, won't nobody be able to touch us. Ever."

Coolie listened, charged by the sensation of flesh against flesh and the mystery of his words.

"We gotta rope it in," he repeated. "When we do, we won't be scared of nuthin'. 'Cause we'll have been to the edge and back. Once you go to the edge and look into the depths of the pit, let me tell you, Cool, nuthin' won't scare you no mo'."

"So how are we supposed to go to this edge and rope in the horse?"

"I've been to the edge, Cool," he whispered close to her ear. "I've looked in the pit. I rode the horse, and he didn't throw me off."

He played with her hair.

"But you're my partner. Polo's not in the business with us anymore. Not really. He's got his weed. It's just me and you. And I want us to be equals. Same approach. Same experience. Same everything, fifty-fifty. But Cool, there's only one way to get you there."

She looked down at the table, the cigarette between her fingers burning close to the flesh.

He turned to look at her, his eyes intense. He grabbed her chin and lifted her face until she was caught in his gaze. "You gotta do it, Cool."

She stared back at him, trembling. He nodded as he spoke, stroking her face.

"You gotta ride the horse."

Coolie's habit was heavy inside of a month.

Polo didn't know what was happening, because she took her hits in the bathroom. He was away during the day, and at nights they were always at Bud's Monarch. Coolie drank and smoked heavily, and her dresses became more and more seductive. She was changing. In a way that he'd never expected before.

He watched Lay watch Coolie. She was beautiful. Not like the calico princess he'd known before. Almost overnight, his country innocent had become a sophisticated urban queen.

"Baby, maybe you need to stop drinking so much," Polo said one night at Bud's Monarch as he watched her down her fifth cognac. "That stuff takes its toll on your face and your body after a while."

Coolie stopped drinking long enough to roll her eyes at him. She took a long pull from her cigarette, blowing the smoke in his face.

"Listen to you trying to tell me what to do. What you saying, I look hard now or something? I don't see nobody else complaining."

Lay sat at the table in silence, taking in the exchange. Polo glanced at him after Coolie's remark. Lay's eyes were on the dance floor.

Coolie took another gulp of her drink. The waitress arrived with a new one and set it on the table. When Coolie reached for it, Polo knocked it away, sending liquor flying onto the couple sitting at the table beside them. Coolie jumped up.

"Now look what you did," she screamed. "You don't own me, motherfucker."

She picked up her near-empty glass of cognac, tossed the liquor into his face, then aimed for his head. He ducked, raising his hands. The glass shattered into pieces somewhere just behind him. Coolie snatched her purse from the table and stormed off toward the bathroom.

"What's happening to her?" Polo asked. "It's almost like I don't know her anymore." He reached for a napkin to wipe his face.

"Miss Cool is growing up," said Lay. "She's learning to adjust to the big city. I think she's doing all right. You need to cut her some slack."

"No, Lay, she's not doing all right. She drinks way too much. Like a man. And she smokes all them damn cigarettes. And those dresses fit her like the skin on a onion."

Lay twirled his brandy snifter. "You don't have a problem admiring other women wearing them same onionskin dresses," he said. "You oughta be proud your girl can compete."

"You started all this. She was fine till you took her shopping that day. Now she got her ass on her shoulders. She's a totally different person. And she so damn moody these days. I'm telling you, man, she's like a stranger to me."

Lay shook his head. "You're just plain stupid," he said. "You should be sportin' Miss Cool like a prize. She's fine, and she's got street smarts. She's running the business like a champ. Hell, every man in here has his fucking eye on her."

"Is that right?" Polo asked. "Funny, I only know of one."

Lay smirked and took a sip of his brandy.

Coolie returned to the table, her face euphoric. She leaned over and kissed Polo on the mouth, plunging her tongue through his unsuspecting lips. She pulled back a little, her face hovering close to his as she licked her lips. She burst into laughter as she fell into her chair.

"I'm sorry, baby. I didn't mean to throw that glass at you. I just get so mad sometimes."

She rubbed Polo on the arm, then motioned for the waitress. She tapped her feet in time to the music, "Going to a Go-Go," by Smokey Robinson and the Miracles. She sang the words and swayed her body as the waitress made her way across the crowd over to their table.

Lay watched Polo from the corner of his eye.

Coolie writhed in her seat. She seemed high, but her behavior was so erratic, Polo wasn't quite sure. Just as the waitress arrived at the table, Coolie jumped up, snatching him by the arm.

"C'mon, let's dance. I'm 'bout to go crazy, I wanna move so bad."

Polo remained in his seat.

"C'mon," she said, "before the song go off." She jerked him from the chair and onto the dance floor, bumping against the waitress's tray in her haste.

"Why did she call me way over here so she could walk off in my face?" the waitress asked Lay. "I don't know who that skinny bitch thinks she is. I'll whoop her ass, pushing me like that."

Lay crooked his finger for her to come closer.

"What?"

"C'mere," he whispered.

The girl leaned in toward him.

"You know who I am?"

"You're Lay Boten, the dealer."

Lay smiled. "No, I'm not."

The girl put her hand on her hip, her voice loud. "You are Lay Boten. I know who's who in this place. And people talk."

He beckoned her closer. She leaned in.

"Let me tell you something," he said, "and I'll only tell you once: I am not Lay Boten. I'm Mr. Boten. You got that? And as long as you see me and speak to me or about me, I better not ever hear you address me without a 'Mr.' before my name, or a 'Sir' after it, or you'll come up missing, and when they find you, your own mama won't know you from deviled ham."

His expression was pleasant. His eyes were ice.

The girl nodded in fear.

"And don't ever talk negative to me about any woman you see me associated with." He pointed toward Coolie. "I don't

care what you think, if that girl's ever within a mile of your stupid ass and I know about it, you better break your neck to get to
her. Wipe her ass, lick her fucking feet if she wants you to."

The girl kept nodding.

"If I hear you did or said otherwise . . ." He paused. "Understood?"

The girl stood rooted in front of him.

"Understood?"

"Yessir."

Lay smiled and leaned back.

"Good," he said. "Now get the fuck outta here and bring
back two brandies. And I better see nuthin' but teeth when you
return. Go on."

The girl scurried away, tripping on the feet of a woman sitting at the table across from Lay. The waitress fell onto the floor,
her tray flying off a few feet away. The woman across from Lay
jumped up from her chair to help, glancing back to see if Lay
was going to join her in aiding the fallen girl.

He didn't.

The woman frowned at him and offered a hand to the waitress, who refused it, managing to stumble forward and rush off
to the bar. The woman sat down, glaring at Lay.

He gazed past her to Polo on the dance floor. He was standing still.

Coolie flailed around him in a trance.

CHAPTER NINETEEN

"Hurry up and shoot it," Coolie shrieked, holding the rubber
tube around her arm. Lay injected the heroin into her vein,
watching her body's instantaneous response as the chemical
coursed through her bloodstream.

She slumped limp on the edge of the bed, breathing much
easier than she had been just seconds before.

"Are you all right now?"

Coolie took deep breaths. She looked up at him, her face

twisting into a scowl. "How come you never do this? It's always just me. You said you rode the horse."

"But I conquered him," he said. "All it took for me was one hit and I walked away. I expected the same thing to happen with you."

She sat next to him, her breathing slowing.

"I thought you were stronger than that," he said with disgust. "I guess I was wrong."

"Is Coolie strung out?" Polo asked.

It had been three months, and Coolie's unpredictable highs and lows were too recurrent for him to ignore.

"What do you mean?" Lay never took his eyes from the television.

Coolie was asleep in the bedroom. The two brothers had been watching football, and Polo was leaving for his afternoon collections, even though it was Sunday. Sunday was his busiest day. Everybody wanted to get high the day before going back to work. He stood in front of his brother with his leather coat in his arms.

"You know what I mean, man," Polo said. "You deal heroin. You know what someone looks like when they strung out."

Lay sipped a snifter of brandy and glanced at his brother. He shrugged. "I don't know. She don't seem no different to me." He returned his attention to the game.

" 'Course, she packages the stuff," he added. "Anything is possible."

"How would she learn how to shoot it, if not from you?"

"Have you ever seen me shoot heroin?"

Polo sat down on the edge of the sofa, his head in his hands.

"That's what I thought," said Lay. "She didn't get no fucking tips from me. You spend so much time in the damn streets chasing money, you letting your lady go to shit."

He twirled his brandy glass.

"I can't watch the bitch all day. I ain't no baby-sitter, little brother."

He leaned forward, watching the screen.

"Awwwwwwww, shit. They 'bout to score a touchdown."

Polo's head was still in his hands. Lay looked down at his brother.

"Did you check her arms for track marks?" he asked. "That's the main giveaway."

"I don't never see her arms. She claim she always cold, so she always wrapped up in sweaters and robes."

"Umph," said Lay. "Well, don't you see her nekked when y'all—"

Polo lifted his head. "She don't never hardly wanna do it no more."

Lay shook his head as he got up from the couch. He went into the kitchen for more brandy.

"So maybe the girl just got low blood," he said. "And she sound like she frigid. Don't be so paranoid, baby boy. Everybody in Detroit ain't a damn junkie."

He refilled his snifter and came back into the living room. He sat down on the couch, slapping his brother on the knee.

"Maybe she just a low-blooded, frigid, moody bitch. Shit. Let it go. I'm tryna watch the game."

He turned his attention to the television, getting up to raise the volume, then sitting down again.

Polo watched him, the intensity of his anger making the surface of his skin prickle. He walked in front of the screen and turned it off.

A grim smile formed on Lay's lips. "Now, now, little brother. What's on your mind that's heavy enough to tempt you to piss me off?"

"I think it's time me and Coolie got out of here and got a place of our own."

Lay smiled, rubbing his chin.

"So now little Polonius has outgrown his brother. Ain't that some shit? So who's supposed to run the weed business and do Miss Cool's share of the heroin operation?"

Polo's eyes met Lay's.

"Way I see it," Polo said, "I do all the legwork, money management, everything for the weed business, so I'm taking it with me."

He seemed unsure but determined. Lay was amused at his naked audacity.

"Do tell."

"That's right," Polo replied. He felt bolder now, having divulged his intentions. "And Coolie won't be working in your heroin operation anymore. If she does any work with heroin, it'll be for me, where I can monitor her. Like you shoulda been doin' from the start."

Polo waited for a reaction.

Lay leaned forward on the couch.

"Oh . . . now I get it. Dum-di-di-dum-dum me. My little brother is gonna be the competition."

He smacked his knee.

"Looks like I been had," he said. "Here I am, bringing you two bumps up from the country to teach you 'bout life, and you learn the business right up under my nose so you can move me out. Ain't that a bitch?"

"Nobody's tryna move you out," said Polo. "It's just that I gotta look out for me and my lady. That's what I was tryna to do, hustlin' out there on the streets. I thought you was looking out for her for me, since y'all was always together. Looks like you been up here turning her out instead."

"Be careful of the words you use, baby boy. A little accusation can go a long way."

Polo turned the television back on and walked toward the door. "Don't matter now, anyway. Me and Coolie gon' be outta here by the end of the month. I'ma take my baby as far away from you as she can get. You ain't been nuthin' but bad news for us."

He walked out, slamming the door behind him.

Lay leaned back on the sofa. "Don't speak so soon, little Polonius," he said in a low voice. "I still owe you the satisfaction of turning your lady out."

He twirled his snifter of brandy, breathing in the aroma.

"He thinks I been trouble for him and Miss Cool," he said to the television screen. "Baby brother, you ain't seen trouble till you see what kinda trouble I got."

"This is your brother's girl, ain't it?" the man asked. He was one of the regular johns who frequented Lay's stable of prostitutes.

"Don't worry 'bout that. You been asking when I was getting some fresh meat on the circuit. Here it is."

Coolie was in the bed, facedown beneath the covers. She seemed to be sleeping. Her soft curls framed her face. Lay had given her a heavy dose of heroin when she awoke earlier, and she nodded back off into a hazy, euphoric sleep. He had positioned her in the bed, then made the phone call to the john.

"Looks like she's knocked out," the man said.

"That's part of her game. She likes to be taken from behind. She may put up a little resistance, but she always gives in. It's how she works. She'll be awake soon enough."

"You sure?"

Lay frowned and pushed the man toward the door. "You know what? Fuck this. Here I am, tryna take care of you, and you giving me the fucking fifth degree."

"All right, all right, all right," the man said, stopping him. "So what's this going to cost me?"

Lay sighed, shaking his head. "Damn, bruh. You just determined to take me through changes."

"No I'm not. I just wanna make sure I got enough cash."

Lay patted him on the back. "Listen, you're one of my better clients. This one's a gimme. How 'bout that?"

The john's eyebrows raised. "You shittin' me, right?"

"I wouldn't do that to you," Lay said. "It's all yours, on the house. Have at it."

And with that, he left the eager john and his gift horse in the bedroom, closing the door behind him.

The john stripped and slid into the bed on top of Coolie.

He couldn't believe his great fortune. This was the prettiest one yet, even though she was a bit on the underfed side.

The apartment was empty when Polo returned.

There was no sign of Lay, and the television was off. He checked the kitchen. It was empty. He headed for the bedroom. The door was shut.

He figured Coolie was sleeping.

He went back into the kitchen and took a beer from the refrigerator. He opened it and drank as he walked over to the sofa and sat down. He turned on the television. *The Wonderful World of Disney* was on. Polo stared at the screen, not registering the images and the sound.

He wondered if Coolie was okay.

Polo set the beer on the table and went to the bedroom. He cracked the door, pushing it open.

The smell of sex invaded his nostrils as the air from the room escaped through the door.

His chest tightened when his eyes focused on the bed.

Coolie was on her knees, giving a man a blow job.

"Polo, don't leave me," she cried. "Please."

Naked, Coolie chased Polo through the apartment, following him as he carried the two suitcases he'd packed in haste into the living room.

The john had fled after Polo hit him in the jaw.

"I'ma leave you right here with Lay. Y'all can do your dirty work together," Polo said. "You think I'm crazy enough to take you with me? You probly done fucked half of Detroit since you been here."

Coolie collapsed on the floor, crying into her hands.

"No I haven't. I ain't been with nobody but you."

He stepped over her, one of the suitcases hitting her in the head as he passed.

She grabbed at his legs.

"Polo. Polo. Polo."

Her voice made a warbling sound at the back of her throat as she pleaded with him through her tears.

He dropped the suitcase and grabbed her by the shoulders.

"Quit calling my name, you filthy bitch. Ain't no need for you to cry 'bout it now. You shoulda thought about that before."

"Don't leave me, Polo. I love you. I love you."

"Oh? You love me?" He glared down at her with savage eyes.

"Yes," she sobbed. "Yes, yes, I love you."

"Then show me," he said.

"What?"

"Show me, dammit, you love me so motherfuckin' much."

Coolie sat confused as Polo stood in front of her.

"Go on," he said. "Show me."

She reached for his zipper. Repulsed, Polo pushed her away.

"So all you know how to do now is suck dicks, huh?"

"No, baby, I can do–"

"I know you can," he screamed, cutting her off. "I'ma show you what I want, you nasty slut. And since you love me so much, I know you gon' be happy to give it to me."

He reached down, grabbed her by the shoulder, and turned her onto her stomach.

"Raise up on your knees, bitch."

Coolie fell forward, sticking her backside high into the air.

Sex had become almost nonexistent between them since Coolie's addiction had taken over. Polo had been indulging a vivid fantasy life as an alternative. Coolie was always the star of his erotic focus. In his dreams, she submitted to things he could never ask for. Things he saw in the quarter movies at the Bijou. He was never once unfaithful. She was all he wanted.

As she knelt in front of him, all of Polo's fantasies burned at the surface of his mind. He grabbed her by the hair and snatched her body back toward his.

"Give it to me," Coolie said with a whimper, desperate to calm him so that he would stay. She wriggled her backside.

Polo unzipped his pants and dropped his boxer shorts without ceremony, his member erect and angry. He grabbed her up-turned buttocks, parted the cheeks with his hands, and thrust his penis into her.

Coolie screamed, her body slumping to the floor away from him.

"Where you going?" he grunted. "I thought you loved me so?"

He reached down and pulled her up, bringing her buttocks close to him. He reentered her as savagely as before, ignoring her cries of pain.

"Aiiiii, Polo, please. It hurts. Please. Please. Please. It hurts so bad."

He kept thrusting, his penis covered with blood and tattered skin from Coolie's torn rectum.

He pumped and pumped against her, feeling his fury bubble up inside him. He pulled out of her and let his seed splatter across her backside.

"Now," he said, shoving her away from him, "I guess that's how you like it."

Coolie fell to the floor, hysterical. When she realized Polo still intended to leave, she grabbed him by the leg and held on.

He shook her loose, kicking her back onto the carpet.

Polo made his way to the door, opened it, and headed down the hall. Lay's gunmen lined the corridor.

Coolie struggled up and attempted to go after him. She stumbled naked, unabashed, past the men, tears and snot streaming down her face. Pain tore through her with every footfall.

"Polo, don't leave me, please. It won't happen no mo', I promise."

The men watched her, none of them offering to help.

"Stay here with Lay, you junkie bitch," Polo said. "Y'all deserve each other."

He took the stairs two at a time, running with the heavy suitcases.

Coolie lay naked in the corridor, trembling, bleeding. Waiting for him to come running up the stairs and take back the horror of what had just happened.

"Polo? Polo?"

She pushed up from the floor. Her entire body shook.

"Polo?"

The men watched her with bored distraction.

Coolie stood in the hallway for a long, impossible moment.

"Plant me now?" she asked the air in a strangled voice, the faint hope hanging in her heart that Polo would answer.

The crashing sound of the blood rushing to her head as her knees buckled under was the only response she was to receive.

Lay returned to find a naked Coolie curled tight in the middle of the living room floor. One of the gunmen had brought her in and left her there. Across her bottom was a smear of dried blood.

She had looked up, her eyes hopeful and teary, when he opened the front door. She struggled to her knees, managing to stand and stumble toward him. She babbled in a mixture of unintelligible groans.

"Calm down, Miss Cool, calm down," Lay said. "What's going on here?"

She clung to him, her words a mash of sounds. Lay gripped her shoulders and pushed her onto the sofa. She gasped in pain as the cloth made contact with her bottom.

"What's wrong, why can't you sit down right?" Lay asked.

"Polo . . . Polo . . . Polo."

She began to cry again.

"All right now. Just lay down here on the couch. I'ma go get you some clothes."

He went into the bathroom, grabbed a washcloth, and ran some cool water over it. He opened the medicine cabinet and took down a bottle of hydrogen peroxide, a jar of salve, and some cotton balls. He took her robe from the back of the door and brought it with him to the living room.

"Turn over."

"No, Lay, no. What are you gonna do?"

"I'm not gonna hurt you, girl," he said. "I'm just gonna clean you up."

Coolie turned over, her body tense and untrusting. Lay dabbed at her skin with a cool, moist cotton ball. She could feel the hydrogen peroxide bubbling around the cuts. Lay carefully cleaned off the dissolving blood with another moist cotton ball. Then he wiped her with the cool cloth. When he finished, he smeared salve around the area to soothe the pain.

"Can you stand?"

Coolie struggled to sit up on the couch.

"That's good enough," he said, offering her the robe. "Put this on."

Coolie slid her arms into the wrap and closed it tight around her body.

Lay knelt beside her. "You feeling a little bit better?"

She sobbed as she nodded.

"Good. Now, tell me what happened."

"Polo left me. He took all his clothes and left me."

"Left you for what? Did y'all have a fight while I was gone?"

Coolie shook her head, her tears renewed.

"Well? Come on, tell me. What happened to make him leave? Where the hell did he go?"

Coolie dropped her head into her hands and sobbed with breaths so deep that her entire body shook.

"Cool," Lay said, the tone of his voice one of harsh concern. "Tell me what happened right now. I can't take too much of this crying. Not from you. So come on with it."

Coolie hugged herself tight and began to rock. She wiped her arm across her nose.

"P-P-Po-Polo."

Lay waited.

"H-h-he caught m-m-me with another man."

"What?"

"H-he c-caught me—"

"I heard what you said. You bullshittin' me, though, right? I know you ain't stupid enough to be cheatin' on my brother with another man."

Coolie shook her head.

"I-I-I ain't been s-s-seeing nobody."

Lay stood and began pacing the room.

"I'm sorry, Cool, I don't understand this. If you ain't been seeing another man, then how the hell did Polo catch you with one?"

"I don't know. He c-c-came home, and he f-f-found us in the bed together. I don't know how it h-h-happened, but I was . . . I was . . ."

Lay stopped pacing. "You was what?"

"I think I was sucking his . . ."

Lay was now standing in front of her. He stared down at her with disgust.

"I think that I was sucking his . . ."

Lay slapped her. Hard.

"Hush," he shouted. "Just shut the fuck up now." He put his hands over his ears. "I don't want to hear no mo' of this shit. I can't believe you brought another motherfucker into my place and fucked him right underneath me and my brother's nose."

He stormed off toward the bathroom and slammed the door. He locked the door, closed the lid on the toilet, and sat. Waiting.

Coolie stumbled after him, pain ripping through her. She banged on the door. She was frantic.

"Lay, don't you turn on me, too. Please. You're all I got. I ain't got nobody no mo'. I can't go back home to my mama. I ain't go nowhere else to go."

"You got to get outta here, Cool. You done turned into a junkie freak, picking people up off the street, bringing them into my house. You must be outta your fucking mind."

Lay was screaming at her through the door.

"Oh, God," she cried, sinking to the floor. "What am I gonna do? I gotta feed my habit, and I ain't got no way to do it without you."

Lay didn't respond.

"Please. I'll do anything. Please. Just don't put me out."

She lay on the floor, listening for some kind of sign from him, then pleaded, "I'll do anything. Anything."

After a few seconds, the door opened.

Lay stood over her.

"Anything?" he asked, his voice gruff.

She looked up at him. "Anything."

He snatched her by the arm.

"Get your ass up, then. I just might have a way for you to feed your monkey and keep a roof over your head, too."

He dragged her toward the living room.

Coolie turned her first trick the next day.

Her first customer was Caesar Bucksport's nephew, Booty. The boy Lay rode up to Detroit with.

He paid three hundred dollars for her. Lay had no idea he could pull that much for Coolie.

"I 'member that gal when she was in Downtown," Booty said. "I thought your brother was the luckiest man on earth. She was fine then, but she ain't look nowhere near as good as she look now. I'd pay a grand if I had it."

Lay let Coolie do Booty in the apartment. In her and Polo's old room.

Coolie took a heavy hit of heroin. By the time Booty arrived, she was ready for anything.

She sat on the edge of the bed in her bra and panties.

Booty stood in the doorway, licking his lips.

"Girl, you look like a piece of candy sitting over there."

Coolie was a shell. She parroted the lines she had rehearsed.

"Straight screw is fifty. Round-the-world, seventy-five. I'll suck your dick for ten. What's your pleasure?"

Booty grinned at her. One of his front teeth was missing.

"Girl, I paid three hundred dollars for you. I wants it all."

Coolie stared at him, unblinking.

"You know why they call me Booty, don'tcha?" he asked, a vulgar sneer across his face.

Coolie shook her head.

" 'Cause I gots to have it." He laughed. "Booty gots to have that booty. Don't look at me like that, I know you know what I'm talkin' 'bout. The dookie trail. I'm a dirt-road daddy."

Coolie froze, the memory of Polo's violent act the day before still vivid.

"I know you like it, too," Booty kept on, his image growing more repulsive and grotesque as she studied him. "Lay told me you did. Matter of fact, he said you love it. So we should both be happy. I get me some front- and back-door action. And you get to do your favorite and get paid for it too."

Coolie could hear, but her focus was off. There were now three Booties swirling before her in a kaleidoscopic haze. They took off and flew around the room, a series of popped balloons that whizzed, zinged, and zoomed past her head like fairies, making her duck and cower to get away.

"What you doin'?" Booty asked, watching the girl as she bobbed and weaved.

She leaned back on the bed to get away from the flying Booties.

"Nothin'," she said. "You ready?"

"Shiiitt," he replied, laughing. "How you gon' ask me that? You must not see this pole stickin' up in my pants."

Booty shut the door behind him, unzipped his fly, and stepped out of his jeans. He came toward her on the bed.

Coolie reached over and turned off the light. To shut out the flying Booties. To hide the tears streaming down her face.

CHAPTER TWENTY

Grace sat across from Canada in the library where they used to spend their evenings reading together.

"So how is the family?" Canada asked. She was still very elegant. Errant wisps of gray framed her face.

"That's why I'm here. You've always been a friend to us, and I figured I could come to you."

Canada leaned forward.

"Of course you can, Grace. You can come to me for anything. Piedmont and I consider you family."

"I know. But it's been a few years since I worked for you."

"That doesn't mean we're not family. Here, drink some tea." Canada poured her a cup from the serving set on the table. "Whatever the problem is, I'm sure we can help."

Grace took a few sips of the tea.

"So tell me what's wrong," Canada said.

"It's Ophelia. She done shrunk up into herself ever since her baby died in that fire. She don't do nuthin' but stay locked up in her room. We can't hardly even get her to eat."

Canada leaned toward her. "Oh, Grace. That's awful."

"Yes it is," Grace said. "Big Daddy and me, we so scared. We try to get through to her, but it ain't no use. We hear her talking to the baby, but Canada, there ain't no baby."

She wrung her hands.

"The few times we do get her to come out to eat, we see her cock her head at the table, like she hear the baby. Sometimes she just jump up and go running off, talking 'bout she hear the baby crying."

Canada shook her head.

"We don't know what to do. She used to be so bright and lively. Ain't a ounce of happiness left in her now." Grace's voice caught. She cleared her throat and drank some more tea.

"But ain't too much we can do 'cause she's grown now. Ophelia's twenty-four. And we worried she gon' spend the rest of her life in a shell, 'less we can help her somehow."

"So what can we do?" Canada asked. "Just say the word. I helped bring her into the world. I'll do anything I can for her."

"Well, ain't too much none of us can do to help her no mo'. She used to be close to her brother Lay, but him and Polo live up in Detroit now."

Grace finished the last of the tea. She looked around the library.

" 'Member back when I was sixteen and pregnant, when you used to read to me every night in this room?"

"How could I ever forget it? Those were some of the happiest moments in my life."

Grace set the teacup on the table. " 'Member you used to tell me how smart I was, and that I should go to college?"

"You were smarter than me," Canada said with a laugh.

Grace smiled.

"Well, Canada, my baby's smart like that. And I'm afraid that if we don't find a way to make her realize there's more inside of her than the part that's done died, she's gon' die herself."

She hesitated.

" 'Member you told me that if I ever decided I want to go to college, you'd send me?"

"Of course I do. I told you that as long as Piedmont and I are alive, the offer stands. I meant it."

Grace's eyes met Canada's.

"Well, it's too late for me to go. But I want to send my daughter. Ain't no way she gon' know her possibilities without somebody teaching her. I figured you and Piedmont could help her get into a college somewhere."

"Hmm," Canada said. "Tell me, Grace, how did she do in high school?"

"Well, that's what's gon' make it a little hard for her. She never did finish. Ophelia was just kinda off and on like that about school. Polo is the only one who finished. Me and Big Daddy didn't make her go."

"I see," Canada replied.

"But she loved to read. You know that. She been reading ever since she was a tiny little thing."

Grace fidgeted with her hands. "It's gon' be hard for her to get into college 'cause of that, ain't it?"

"It'll be nearly impossible," said Canada. "Ophelia's going to have to graduate high school first, or at least get a GED."

"A GED?" Grace asked.

"Yes. It stands for General Educational Development. Colleges accept them. It means she met the requirements equal to graduating from high school."

"Can y'all get her one of those?"

"Well," Canada replied, "we can't exactly give it to her."

"Oh," Grace said, discouraged.

"Don't give up so easily. It's not the toughest thing in the world to get. You say she's got smarts and I believe you. But she still needs to study before she can take the test."

"Would you help her? Like you helped me years ago?"

"I'd be honored. I'll gladly take on any role I can play to help her along."

"Thank you, Canada."

"Don't even think about it," the woman said. "It's been lonely around here for years. I'm bored. Piedmont's always talking about new-generation cows. I don't know what a new-generation cow is."

Both women laughed.

"Yes. A little busywork will do me some good. It'll be something for me to throw myself into again."

"So what do I need to do?" Grace asked.

"Well, honey, I'll take care of the paperwork. You just make sure Ophelia shows up here at nine A.M. sharp Monday through Friday. I'll tutor her until three, then you can have her back for the rest of the afternoon."

Grace embraced her. "Thank you for doing this."

"Well, once we get past the GED, which I'm sure we can do if we put in the work, we'll pinpoint a college to send her to. Do you have any idea where you want her to go? Somewhere here in-state, maybe?"

"No," Grace said. "I think she should get away from here. Ain't nuthin' but bad memories for her. I was thinking maybe we could send her somewhere not too far from her brothers. That way, they can at least go see 'bout her every now and then."

Canada thought for a moment.

"I believe Piedmont has an uncle who's a dean at Michigan State."

"Is that a long ways from Detroit?"

"No. Actually, it's close enough for her brothers to visit often."

"That's what we want," said Grace.

"We'll see what we can do to get her in. Let's get this girl a GED first." She poured more tea in Grace's cup. "Now sit back down and visit with me. And don't you worry yourself anymore. Ophelia's going to be just fine. We'll make sure of that."

PART VIII

1967–1968

OPHELIA

*Education doesn't change life much.
It just lifts trouble to a higher plane
of regard.*

—ROBERT FROST

CHAPTER TWENTY-ONE

Ophelia showed up at the Deveaux house at nine o'clock the next Monday morning.

When Canada opened the door, she was greeted by the dismal face of the woman-child standing on her doorstep. Ophelia was clutching a box of pencils and a tablet.

"My mama said you wanted me to be here this morning," she said. Her voice was almost as lifeless as her appearance.

Canada embraced her.

"My goodness, child. Look how you have grown. I don't get to see you nearly as much as I used to. Come on in." She guided her into the foyer. "Piedmont. Come see Ophelia."

Piedmont was smoking a pipe when he walked out of the sitting room. Ophelia was embarrassed as she stood before her parents' friends.

"Well, don't you look just fine," he said. "Come on in here, girl. You ready for some schooling?"

He started to guide her down the hall toward the library, while Canada closed the front door. Ophelia turned back, listening to the creaking of the wood.

"You hear that?" she whispered.

Canada clasped her hand.

"No, honey, I didn't. Have you eaten breakfast?"

Ophelia lingered, her eyes cutting to the side.

"I said, did you have breakfast?"

The girl turned to her. "Yes ma'am."

"Good," Canada said. "That means we can get started right away."

She led her to the library.

"This is going to be our tutoring area. I used to read to your mother in this very same room. When she was pregnant with you."

She smiled at Ophelia. The girl's expression was empty.

"Sweetie, please relax," Canada said, putting her arm around her. "Think of this as your second home. Your mother will tell you, this was not just a place of employment for her. She's always been family to us, and so have you and your brothers."

"Yes ma'am."

"Now, I know we've never spent any real time together, but I've watched you children grow up. I helped deliver you, you know, so it's almost like you're my daughter, too."

Ophelia grabbed the woman by the arm.

"You helped deliver me?" she said.

"I sure did. I was right there."

Ophelia smiled.

"I'd like to hear 'bout that sometime," she said. "I had a baby, too, you know."

"Well, I'd be happy to tell you about it," Canada replied. "But first things first. Let's hit these books. This is going to be fun. I remember you being into books since you were little, always running around with one tucked under your arm. I gave your mama that copy of Hans Christian Andersen that you used to love reading so."

"Really?"

"I sure did."

Ophelia followed Canada to a table filled with children's books, a chart of the alphabet, and pictures of animals. She was surprised to see such elementary material.

"We're starting from scratch, honey," Canada said, noticing her expression. "I don't know how much you know. The best way to gauge is to start from the very beginning."

By the end of the week, Ophelia was talking. Canada paid particular attention to moments when the girl's attention drifted. She focused on keeping her busy. In time, Ophelia began to respond. She seemed curious about her studies and even more curious about Canada's life.

"Is this where you were born?"

"No ma'am," the woman said. "I'm originally from New England."

"New England," Ophelia repeated in a dreamy voice. "That sounds like it's nice."

"It is. It's very pretty there. Perhaps one day you can go."

Ophelia gave Canada a bashful glance. "But I ain't never left Downtown before," she said.

Canada leaned close to her ear.

"Well, honey, maybe it's about time you did."

"What's this?" Ophelia asked, chewing a salmon canapé at lunch. In her hand she held a piece of bread topped with a green straw and what appeared to be a leaf.

"That's a watercress sandwich," Canada said.

"It looks like grass."

"You know," the woman said with a laugh, "to be honest, it kind of tastes like grass, too."

She picked up the sandwich and turned it over in her hand.

"Piedmont and I have been eating these things for so long, we convinced ourselves we like them. When you get down to it, I guess it really is just grass."

"Tomorrow we're having chicken for lunch," Piedmont said, walking into the kitchen.

They laughed. Ophelia gave a shy smile.

"Come on," Canada said. "Let's head back to the library. We've got work to do."

Ophelia spent a year with Piedmont and Canada.

She showed up at nine A.M. five days a week. She often stayed well after four. Her diction was still informal. That was the area upon which Canada concentrated most. But Ophelia read well with good comprehension, and had a decent understanding of math, thanks to Piedmont's help.

The day arrived for her to take the GED exam.

"Are you scared?" Grace asked Ophelia the night before.

"No ma'am. I coulda took it a long time ago. I just wanted to make sure I was as good as I could be."

"What time you got to be at the place?"

"Eight o'clock. Piedmont and Canada are gon' pick me up."

"That's nice of them," Grace said. "Those are some good people, you know. And I don't mean just good white people. In God's eyes, no matter what color they is, the Deveauxs is just flat-out good people."

"Mmm-hmm," Ophelia said. "They shole is, Mama. They shole is."

Grace smacked her on the leg.

"I know I ain't send you over there for no year for you to still be talking as bad as I do."

Ophelia smiled.

"I know, Mama, I'm trying. Sometimes I just can't help it. It's like slippin' on old shoes."

The two of them laughed, and Ophelia fell into her mother's embrace.

She came running from the mailbox with the letter.

"I passed it, Mama. Big Daddy. I got it. I got my GED."

She waved the letter at Grace, who ran down from Walter and Sukie's porch. Big Daddy stood on the steps nearby, his mouth a wide grin.

"I got it," Ophelia exclaimed, out of breath as she ran. "I can go to college now. Mama, I can go."

Big Daddy's smile tightened.

Sukie stood in the doorway and watched Ophelia, her eyes narrowed.

The wind whisked past them, rustling the letter in Ophelia's hand. She cocked her head. As she looked up, her eyes met Sukie's.

"Did you hear that?" Ophelia whispered to no one in particular.

"No, baby," Grace said, realizing that her daughter was still haunted. Even after a year. "It's just the wind. They say it's gonna rain today. Now, come on. Tell me about that GED."

Ophelia's eyes remained fixed on Sukie. Sukie's eerie eyes, always dark and commanding, now seemed troubled.

At that moment, Ophelia knew that Sukie heard. She had been hearing baby Hamlet's cries being carried on the wind.

Sukie turned away and disappeared into the house. Grace rushed to her daughter and threw her arms around her.

"I'm so proud of you, baby," she said. Ophelia smiled, the image of Sukie's face still troubling her.

When Sukie went into the house, Walter was sitting in the living room. As the door opened behind his wife, he caught a glimpse of his sister and his child in an embrace.

As the door closed, he listened, uninvited, to his daughter's celebration.

"Canada and Piedmont are gonna send her to college somewhere near Detroit," Grace announced at supper.

The Botens were still living in Walter and Sukie's house, so the two families ate all their meals together. Walter and Big Daddy worked every day to rebuild the house destroyed by the fire. It had taken most of the year because of bad weather and Big Daddy's work schedule. Now the house was almost finished.

Big Daddy didn't look up in response to Grace's statement, but he nodded his approval. Sukie dined in silence.

Walter glanced around the table, confused. "Piedmont and Canada are sending who where?" There was an edge to his voice.

Grace was startled by Walter's tone. So was Sukie. Her fork dropped against her plate with a clang.

"They gon' get Ophelia into a college," Grace said. "It's a school up north called Michigan State."

Big Daddy remained silent. He was hurt by Grace's idea of sending Ophelia off to school, but he had resigned himself to it. He had raised her for twenty-four years as though she were his own. The thought of her leaving them tore at his heart.

"How they gon' send a grown woman off somewhere if she don't wanna go?" Walter said.

"She do wanna go. She been working for this for a year. You seen her with them books she been studying."

Walter's face contorted.

"This is a good thing," Grace said. "Ophelia wants to go. She'll be closer to her brothers."

"How come nobody told me 'bout this?" Walter said, pushing his chair from the table and standing. The chair fell back onto the floor.

Big Daddy looked up at the sound of the chair crashing against the wood floor. He surveyed all the faces in the room.

Grace cut her eyes at Sukie. "Walter," she said, "we're telling you now."

Walter stormed out of the house, down the porch steps, and into his car.

Big Daddy kept eating, taking everything in.

Sukie glared at Grace from across the table. Her eyes flashed with anger and her lips began to twitch.

"Y'all going to hell," she said. "Both of you. Evil sinners. That's why they took her baby, and that's why we can't have no chillun now."

Grace clutched her breast, her eyes falling upon her husband.

"Sukie, that's not true," she said. "That's not why—"

Before she could finish, Sukie stood and reached across the table and slapped her face. The force sent Grace flying back onto the floor. Big Daddy leaped from his chair.

"Don't talk to me 'bout Walter," Sukie screamed. "I know everything there is to know 'bout him. I told you a long time ago to stay out my way. I'm gon' put a stop to all this foolishness befo' long. Just watch."

She stormed out of the kitchen and up the stairs.

Big Daddy picked his wife up from the floor.

"What was that all about?" he shouted, his nostrils flaring with rage. "Did she hurt you, baby?" He looked toward the living room. "I'll tear her apart, you just give me the word. I don't care if she is your brother's wife."

"Leave it alone," she said. "Just leave it alone."

As Big Daddy stood before his wife, he saw Sukie's handprint on Grace's cheek rise in a swollen burst of red against the pecan-tan skin. He wrapped his arms around her.

"What foolishness was she talking 'bout?" he said. "I wanna know. Somebody better tell me." He rocked back and forth as they stood holding each other. "And why is Walter so mad about Ophelia going off to school?"

"Just leave it alone, Big Daddy. Please. Leave it alone."

She leaned into his chest, terrified at the prospect of discovery. By Big Daddy. And worst of all, Ophelia.

Big Daddy rocked her in his arms, his chin resting on the soft crown of her hair.

Above her head, his brows were knitted.

He wanted to know why Walter cared so much about Ophelia's welfare. He was determined to find out.

Outside, Walter tried to crank the car, but the engine wouldn't turn over. He quit after several attempts, slamming his hand against the dash. He leaned his head upon the steering wheel and began to cry.

Ophelia was upstairs in her room. She lay in bed, daydreaming. She had been too excited to come down for supper. There were so many things on her mind about going away. Part of her was afraid of being in a new place, unsure of what the change would bring. Canada said there were thousands of students at Michigan State. The thought of so many people at once made Ophelia nervous. She wondered if she would suffocate from the throng. She had never been around more than twenty folks at a time in her whole life.

She was ready to leave. Ophelia prayed that the change of environment would bring her peace of mind as well. Though she didn't talk about it much anymore, she never stopped being haunted by the sound of her baby's voice. The incident with Sukie wasn't the first time she'd heard Hamlet's cry. Earlier that evening, as she walked along the creek, she could hear his gurgles in the rippling of the waters.

She heard a car door slam. She rose from the bed and went

to the window. Ophelia watched as Walter sat inside his car. He seemed overcome with emotion, filled with a sadness she somehow seemed to understand.

She felt connected to him, connected to his pain. She had known the sorrow she saw rifling through him now. She knew her uncle Walter, like her, was alone, even though there were always people around. He sat in the car. She could see his body shaking.

As she watched him drop his head to the wheel, Ophelia began to cry.

Six months later, she was well into her first semester of freshman study. She had feared that being thrust into a new environment with so many people would be stifling, but instead she felt liberated.

She was able to blend with ease into the thousands of students on the campus, even though she was older than most. They were busy protesting the war in Vietnam, burning bras and draft cards, touting the power of peace, and losing themselves in dramatic displays of free love, chemical experimentation, and loud music.

Piedmont pulled a few strings, and she managed the unheard-of freshman privilege of a single dorm room.

It was as if she was still alone.

Ophelia immersed herself in study, spending late nights in the library and reading in her room until early hours of the morning. With her newfound focus, the haunting cries began to fade. Not all at once. The sounds still visited her dreams in the deep of the night.

All of her classes, except for Expository Writing and English 101, were held in large lecture halls.

Her writing class was held in a small room with only fifteen students. It was there that Ophelia began to flourish.

And catch the attention of her professor.

• • •

Polo came to visit near the end of the semester.

"Why didn't Lay come with you?" she asked. "And where's Coolie?"

She and Polo were having lunch in one of the campus cafeterias. He was in town on business and could stay but a couple of hours. He promised to return in a few weeks.

"I haven't talked to Lay in over eight months," he said.

"You mean you don't live with him anymore?"

"No."

Ophelia put down her fork.

"Then how have you been getting my letters?"

"The address you have is a P.O. box. It's mine, not Lay's. He don't give out his address."

She shook her head. Her brow was furrowed.

"I don't understand this. Lay was the one who asked you to come to Detroit. I thought he was looking after you. Where's Coolie? Is she here in town?"

"I guess she's still with Lay," he said. "I left the two of them in that apartment and moved my stuff out."

He turned his head away.

Ophelia reached across and put her hand on top of his. He drew his hand back and put it in his lap. His voice was thick when he spoke.

"I caught her in the bed with some stray nigger. She was so strung out, I couldn't take it no mo'."

"Strung out?" she said.

"Yeah, strung out. A junkie. A dope fiend."

"No, Polo." She put her head in her hands and took a few breaths. She looked up at him. "And you think Lay knew something about this? Is that why you left?"

Polo's eyes met hers.

"You're wrong," she said, shaking her head. "Lay's not like that. He wouldn't never let nuthin' happen to Coolie. You must have misunderstood."

"Ophelia, you're crazy. Lay's a dog. A low-down dog who don't care 'bout nuthin' and nobody but himself."

"That's not true. He always cared about me."

Polo studied his sister's face. He realized how oblivious she was to the true spirit of their brother.

"If he cared 'bout you so much, how come he ain't been up here to see you yet?"

"He's got business to tend to," she said. "But watch, he'll be up here. I just bet that he will."

"Do you know what his business is?" he asked.

"He's got his own distributorship."

Polo laughed.

"Yeah, that's right." He sucked his teeth. "C'mon, Ophelia, don't be stupid. Did he ever tell you what he distributes?"

"No."

"Did you ever stop for five minutes to think about what it could be?"

Ophelia searched his face. "Yeah, sure, I've wondered 'bout it."

"He's a heroin dealer. Your brother deals heroin and weed. He helps people kill themselves and ruin they families." Polo's expression was stern. "And he had me doing it for a while. And I won't lie. I enjoyed it. I made a lot of money. Enough money to not have to do it no more."

"It's not true," Ophelia said. "You're making this up. You've always been jealous of Lay. You were always trying to be just like him."

"Oh really?" he said with a smirk. "And why would I wanna be like somebody whose baby dies and he don't even seem to give a fuck?"

Her face contorted as he said the words. The tears were poised, about to fall.

"How could you be so cruel to me?" she whispered.

Polo closed his eyes and lowered his head.

"Yeah. I'm sorry. You're right," he said. "I used to try to be like him."

Ophelia pressed her lips tight as she wiped away her tears. "I know you did."

"But I'm not like that anymore," Polo said. "Once I found out what Lay was really about, I couldn't get away from him fast enough."

He leaned closer toward her, reaching out for her hand.

"You wanna know how evil he is? One time one of his boys, these so-called security motherfuckers Lay has working for him, was looking off, and somebody tried to rob us. Me and Lay were standing on the street. When the robber saw backup coming, he ran off." Polo shook his head at the memory. "Lay was so mad at his boy for looking off, he had the other ones pin him down while Lay stuck him in the eye with a knife. Told him next time, he'd have an excuse for not seeing someone coming. Then he stuck him in the gut for good measure. Left him bleeding right there on the street. Folks just walked on by, like they saw this shit every day."

The tears found their way down the sides of Ophelia's face.

Polo closed his hands around hers.

"Look at me," he said. She turned her face away. "Ophelia, look at me."

Her eyes found his.

"Lay ain't gon' come up here. He don't give a shit about you. He don't give a shit about nobody. So don't even think about him no mo'."

She wrested her hands from his grasp.

"No," she said. "I know him. He loves me. He always has."

"Lay don't love nobody but Lay," Polo replied. "And maybe Sukie. She was the only one who understood him. He's evil, just like her." He picked up his glass of tea and took a sip. "Do you know he brought that bag of voodoo bones to the apartment a couple of times to visit?"

"He brought Sukie to Detroit?" she asked, a sick feeling in her stomach.

"Shole did," Polo said.

"You saw her? She saw you?"

"No," he said. "I never saw her at all. But that smell of hers was all over the house."

He looked at his watch.

"Look, sis, I gotta go. I got a few people I have to go see."

"What for? What do you do now, since you claim you're so much better than Lay and don't sell dope no more?"

Polo wiped his face with both hands and sighed.

"I didn't come here to turn you against Lay, okay? Believe me, I idolized him. I was hurt more than I could ever tell you. My brother was my heart." He patted his right hand against his chest. "I didn't turn against Lay. He turned against me. Sooner or later, he turns against everybody."

"I don't want to talk about this anymore."

"Ophelia, c'mon. Face facts. It damn near killed me to see him for what he was. But you know what? Sometimes the truth is there, right smack in front of you. All you gotta do is be brave enough to look."

Polo's expression was intense.

"So what are you here for?" she asked.

"I told you, I saved up a lot of money. I applied for school. They haven't accepted me yet, but I ain't out for the count."

Ophelia's face brightened.

"You applied for school here?"

"Yep. Right here. So I could be close to you."

She smiled.

"I'd be so happy if we were up here together," she said. "What were your grades like when you graduated?"

Polo laughed. "You know, I used to be so proud that I was the first one in the family to graduate from high school. But that shit came back to bite me. I barely squeaked through school. I spent too much time messing around. Hanging with Coolie."

He cleared his throat and drank some more tea.

"My grades were garbage. Low Cs. Shit, they was almost damn Ds. But they got this new thing now, something called affirmative action, and because of that, I might have a shot at gettin' in. I talked to a minority counselor on the phone. She told me to come in if I could so we could go over the requirements."

Polo smiled, nodding.

"So ain't that somethin'? I might get to go to college with you, even though my grades don't stack up to shit."

"Well, that's good," Ophelia said, "but it's not gonna keep you in. It's just gonna help to get you through the door. You've gotta do the work once you make it inside."

"I know that," he said. "I ain't scared of a little hard work. Especially when I got my sister close by."

They smiled at each other across the table, the haze of anger over Lay fading into the background.

"I wrote Mama and Big Daddy and told 'em about it. They got they hopes up so high, I gotta get in, one way or another."

He checked his watch again.

"All right, I gotta run." They both got up from the table. "Oh yeah," he said. "I almost forgot. Mama said Uncle Walter left Sukie. Not too long after you left. Ain't nobody seen him since."

"What?"

"Yep. Brother broke outta there. More power to him for gettin' away from that bitch."

Ophelia walked along beside him in silence as they left the cafeteria.

"I'm gonna get an apartment off campus," he said. "Close enough so I can walk to school. I was wondering if you wanted to be my roommate. I got enough money, so you don't have to worry 'bout paying none of the bills. Just maybe cook us a dinner or two every now and then."

"I'd like that," she said. "But you sure you wanna eat my cooking?"

"Aw damn, that's right, you don't cook. Always been too busy with your nose in a book." He smiled at her. "Ever since we was kids."

"I guess so. But I can try."

"Then you got yourself a roommate," he said. They stopped in front of the building. "Gimme a hug," he said. "I'm already runnin' late."

Ophelia stepped inside her brother's open arms. He held her close and kissed her on the forehead.

"Be easy," he said.

"I will. I got an appointment with my writing teacher. He said he wanna talk to me about my work. Maybe it ain't good enough."

Polo tweaked her left cheek.

"Don't worry 'bout it, sis," he said. "It's prob'ly the best in the class."

Javier Trueba was a young man, twenty-eight, of South American descent. His accent was thick but uncluttered, his features lean and aristocratic. He was almost a foot taller than Ophelia, his skin a burnished hue, the color of resin. He moved with a grace and fluidity that she had never seen before in a man. He glided from behind the desk with winged feet, his footfalls imperceptible. His hair was a tuft of jet-black curls that softened his eyes and sharpened the edge of his jaw. Javier's English was fluent, but his emphasis on words was magical, almost musical, in tone. Ophelia found it amusing that her writing professor taught others how to master a subject that wasn't even his native tongue.

"Where are you from?" the professor asked.

"Tennessee," she said as she sat across from him.

Professor Trueba sat behind a time-worn desk. He leaned toward her.

"Where in Tennessee? As I recall, it's a very large state."

His gaze was fixed upon her as he spoke.

This unnerved Ophelia. Until now, her exposure to people had been limited to her family and a few random people in Downtown. Even though she had managed to assimilate into the crowds at the college, she was still unaccustomed to strangers.

"You wouldn't know it if I told you," she said, playing with her hands. "It's a real small place."

"So tell me anyway."

She looked up.

"Downtown."

"That's the name of the town?"

"Uh-huh."

He laughed. "You're right. I have no knowledge of that place. Is that where you were born and reared?"

"Uh-huh," she said. "Downtown's not a place where people move to. People tryna get out more than anything else."

"I see."

He began to rifle through the stack of papers in front of him. Ophelia took the opportunity to study his face. His jawline was strong. The color of his skin reminded her of dried popcorn kernels. He stopped sorting through the papers when he located the one he sought. His eyes made rapid movements across the page. He looked up, ensnaring her in the web of his gaze. He smiled again, his keen eyes a gold-flecked hazel.

Her cheeks flushed.

"I called you here today to discuss the assignments I've given you this term."

"Okay."

"I've been sitting here reading them over. In fact, I've been reading them for the past few nights. I thought we needed to talk about what you've written."

"I know," she said. "My writing prob'ly ain't as good as everybody else. I read well, but I ain't got the best . . ." She hesitated, searching for the word she had heard Canada use. "Diction. My diction could be better. It's not like I don't know. It's mostly just me being lazy, I suppose."

"Okay."

"But I'm willing," she said. "I wanna learn anything I can get my hands on."

He waited.

"Are you done?" he asked.

"Uh-huh."

"Good. Because I didn't bring you in here to criticize your writing. In fact, I called you in for just the opposite."

"What?"

"I gave you ten assignments this semester. Each of them, every single one, has managed to touch me in some way."

"What do you mean?" she asked. She leaned toward him.

"Well," he said, sorting through the papers again, "the first week, your assignment was to write about a place. Your description of what must have been Downtown was so vivid, I could actually see it in my head. I could see the dust on the streets. I saw the four hills that made up the town. I saw the Green Goods Grocery. And the man with the peach Nehi."

"Caesar Bucksport," Ophelia said.

"Incredible. That name suits your description of him well."

She searched for a response but couldn't find one. She didn't know what to say to him. This man had just handed her an identity. Ophelia felt as if the world's focus had shifted, and she was now in the forefront, risen out of a background she had blurred into so well for most of her life.

Professor Trueba kept going through the papers, then pulled out another.

"And then there was the one where you had to write about a strong emotion you recently felt. You wrote about the loss of a child." His voice softened. "I assume the child was yours."

"Yes," she said. "My baby, Hamlet. He burned up in a fire at our house." She breathed in and out. "I feel it every day. The pain is like a walnut at the back of my throat. Every time I swallow, it's just sitting right there."

Professor Trueba was quiet, watching the woman across from him.

Ophelia wanted to say more. She glanced at him. She was accustomed to measuring her words. His silence gave her permission to let them pour.

"Sometimes," she said, her voice a whisper, "I still hear his cries. I hear him laughing. Sometimes, when the wind changes direction, I feel him reach out to me."

Professor Trueba listened, his hand on his chin.

"Ophelia, do you know the history behind your name?"

"Yes," she said, the question bringing with it an unexpected flicker of light in her eyes. "My mama liked Shakespeare. Her favorite story was *Hamlet*. She used to read it to me when I was little. The lady who sent me to school here used to read it to my mama when she was pregnant with me."

Just as soon as it had flickered, the light within Ophelia's eyes grew dim. Her face took on a faraway look.

"I liked that name," she said. "Hamlet. That's why I named my baby the same thing."

"That's interesting," Professor Trueba said. "Through your writing, I could see him. I could feel your love for him, and so very much of your pain."

"There was lot of pain," she said. "It's the only real feeling I've known since he died."

Professor Trueba went through the papers one more time. He pulled one from the middle of the stack.

"This one about your family was particularly interesting. You said you wish you were closer to your aunt and uncle. Was your relationship with them distant when you were growing up?"

Ophelia's gaze rested on his face.

"Hmmm . . . yeah, I guess so. My aunt Sukie has always been strange. She never liked my mama or me. And my mama's brother, Uncle Walter, never talked to me. But I always felt for him, you know? Like he wanted to get to know me but just didn't know how. He seems like he's in so much pain, but he don't never tell nobody 'bout it. I know how it is to feel pain and not know how to tell nobody 'bout it."

Professor Trueba scribbled a note on the paper.

"Ophelia," he said, "let me make something clear. I didn't bring you into my office to play therapist and try to get into your psyche."

She listened to his soothing accent.

"I brought you here for another reason. You obviously have a lot to say, and you need a way to say it. Through your writing, your voice is very clear and expressive. It's strong. It has the ability to move the reader. That is a rare gift, and I feel you should explore it. Have you chosen a major yet?"

"No." She leaned closer, lured by his voice. "But I know I like books, and I like writing things down on paper. It's like screaming. I can empty myself, and when I fill up again, as long as there's paper, I have a way to let it all out."

"I think you should think about English as a major. Your grammar and vocabulary need some fine-tuning, but there's a power in your words that you should explore."

Ophelia was smiling.

"You really think I'm that good?" she asked.

"I think you're very good," he said. "Do you have any evening classes?"

"No."

"Okay," he said, searching through a notebook on his desk. "How about if I tutor you on Tuesdays and Thursdays from six to eight in the English lab?"

"Oh, Professor, that would great."

He stood, reaching across the desk with his palm outstretched.

"I enjoyed talking with you, Ophelia."

"Me too, Professor," she said, extending her hand.

"Please, call me Javier. I don't think I'm that much older than you. You can address me by my first name."

"Hobby-air?"

"No. Javier. Like Hobby, only with a V. Hovvy-air."

She released his hand and walked toward the door. She glanced back at him.

"Okay, Hovvy-air. I'll see you on Tuesday."

He smiled. "I'll be looking forward to it."

PART IX

1967–1968

TRANSITIONS

There is a certain relief in change,
even though it be from bad to worse.

—WASHINGTON IRVING

It was rainy and cold the night Walter checked into the Chero-kee Motel on the outskirts of Lansing, Michigan.

"How far away is Michigan State?" he asked the plump white woman behind the counter.

She wore a tattered poncho stained with coffee and mustard. Her face was pocked and her hair greasy. The remains of a sandwich sat on the counter. An unthreatened cockroach feasted upon its outer edges.

"No more'n ten miles up the road," she said. "You stayin' just for the night?"

She assumed he was one of the hundreds of parents who came at the end of each semester to watch their children gradu-ate or pick them up for the holiday vacation.

"What's your weekly rate?"

The woman was surprised. No one ever stayed for more than a few nights. She wasn't even sure the hotel had a weekly rate. She picked up the sandwich and took a large bite.

"Billy," she yelled, her mouth full. The cockroach sat on the counter, waiting for his turn at the sandwich.

From the back, Billy appeared. Despite the cold, he wore a torn tie-dyed T-shirt and slack jeans, his gut bulging above the waistline.

"What, Esther?" he said, annoyed.

"What's our weekly rate?" she asked.

Billy eyed Walter. He looked safe enough, Billy thought. But he wondered why this older black man wanted to stay in a tran-sient motel for a week. Without a woman.

"I don't know, Esther. Hell, thirty dollars oughta be enough."

He scratched his backside and went back to where he had appeared from.

"Thirty dollars," Esther repeated.

Walter peeled off two one-hundred-dollar bills and a ten. Esther's eyes bulged.

"That oughta get me 'bout seven weeks, right?" Walter asked.

He held the bills toward her. Esther set the sandwich back on the counter and snatched the money from his hand.

"Sure oughta," she said, not caring why the man needed a motel room for seven weeks. "You're in room 16."

A few inches away, the cockroach resumed his meal.

CHAPTER TWENTY-THREE

Walter sat at the breakfast table alone. The boys were already gone, out into the city where they had jobs as day laborers. The shadowy guests who came and went at the Chateau le Lux were either sleeping or away. Madame Lucien was in the parlor.

The plump Creole cook placed a dish before him: a plate of bacon, spicy sausages, and fresh beignets. She exited the kitchen without a word, leaving him alone to eat.

Walter bit into one of the beignets, daydreaming as he chewed the pillowy bread. Its buttery sweetness dissolved in his mouth. He devoured it and reached for another.

"Marie makes the best beignets in the Quarter."

He looked up. Sukie slid into the chair across from him, her robe falling open. The abundant red hair fell around her shoulders, dwarfing her face. Her eyes penetrated his.

Unsure of himself, Walter said nothing. Sukie grabbed a beignet and consumed it in two bites, then grabbed another.

"What you gon' do today?" she asked, her mouth full. "You got a job somewhere?"

He shook his head.

"So how you gon' pay my mama to stay here? You must be rich or somethin'."

He smiled, his body tingling at the memory of the prior night's events.

"I got a little change. Not that much. Just enough to hold me till I find me a piece of a job somewhere."

"So you ain't got nuthin' to do today?"

She licked sugar from her fingers.

"No," he said.

"Good," she replied. "I got somethin' I wanna show you."

Walter's breath caught. Sukie's foot danced up his thigh, her toes working their way into the center of his lap.

She took him to her room in the house.

"This is where my daddy and my sister died. It's my room now," she said.

Walter stood in the doorway and glanced around the room. The lights were dim. A fan turned slow in the window. Strange markings were on the walls and floor, and candles were everywhere. The air was thick with the smell of cinnamon. A fire crackled in a massive stone hearth. A fireplace poker sat upright beside the bed.

"How do you like it?" she asked, falling back onto the mattress.

"You're not scared to stay in here?" he asked.

"Scared of what?"

"Ghosts."

"What ghosts? There's only spirits," she said. "I'm not afraid of spirits. My nana comes and talks to me. She protects me."

Walter remained in the doorway of the room.

"What about the spirits of your daddy and sister?"

"They don't bother me. They dead. Ain't nuthin' to fear from the dead."

She lay sprawled on the bed, her feet kicking behind her.

"Come in, Walter," she said, her finger crooked, beckoning him. "And shut the door behind you."

Walter stepped inside the room but stayed near the door.

"You're still afraid of me?" she asked. "Even after last night?"

"I'm not afraid of you," he said, looking around. "We can't

lay up in here now. It's broad daylight outside. Where's your mother?"

Sukie waved her hand.

"Don't you worry 'bout Madame Lucien. She won't bother us. She won't bother us a'tall." She patted the bed. "Come here."

He walked over to the bed.

"Sit down."

He did.

"How long are you gonna keep this up?" he asked.

"What?"

"Taking me from room to room and telling me to shut the door and come here."

"Till I get what I want."

Walter felt his body growing warm.

"And what is it you want?" he said.

She reached up and pulled him onto her.

"You," she whispered into his ear. "When you walked through the doors of the Chateau le Lux, I knew why you were here. I asked Nana about it last night. She said that you're for me. You came to this house to take me as your wife."

"Get out of my daughter's bedroom. Get out of my house."

Walter awakened, naked, entwined around the girl. Madame Lucien stood above him. Her eyes were narrowed and blazing. She clutched the claw around her neck. His eyes opened and his focus adjusted, his mind not yet aware of what was happening around him.

Madame Lucien spat into his face. He let go of the girl and sprang from the bed.

"Get out of this room now," Madame Lucien demanded.

Walter grabbed his clothes, his heart racing.

"Get out," she screamed. "Get out of this house now."

"Mother," said the girl, "you get out. Leave me and my man alone."

Madame Lucien spun around toward her daughter.

"You're evil, child. I should have put you out of my house long ago."

She clutched the claw tighter.

"You can't put me out," Sukie said, her nakedness a knowing affront to her mother. "This is my domain. You may run the Chateau le Lux, but this room belongs to me."

Walter stuffed himself into his clothes. He was bent over, having just secured the laces of one boot. He held the other boot in his hand.

Madame Lucien came at him again. Behind her, Sukie shifted on the bed, slipping over to the side.

"Get out of my house," the old woman screamed, beating Walter on the back with her hands.

The blows surprised him. He jerked upright, the boot in his hand. The heel of the shoe caught Madame Lucien in the face.

She let out an anguished wail and, still clutching the claw, fell flat, straight back on the floor. Her head hit the hard wood with a solid thwack.

Just behind her, Sukie was standing naked.

Walter dropped to his knees and picked her up. Madame Lucien's body was limp.

"Oh God," he cried, looking up at Sukie. "She's bleeding. Oh God."

Sukie came over to him.

"Put her down before you get blood all over yourself."

Walter laid the bloody body of Madame Lucien on the floor.

A pool of blood formed at the back of her head. She didn't move. Walter felt her wrist for a pulse. There wasn't one.

"I just hit her in the face with my shoe," he said. "It was an accident. It wasn't hard enough to hurt her."

"She's a gnarled-up, bitter woman," Sukie said. "It wouldn't take much to kill her."

At the word "kill," Walter began to sob.

"I killed her. Oh God, I killed her. I'ma go to jail for this."

"Just calm down."

Sukie walked over to the open door of her bedroom and pushed it shut, turning the lock.

"Pull that sheet off the bed," she said.

Walter kept sobbing.

"Stop crying like a baby and pull the sheet off the bed. We gotta take care of this now. Unless you wanna go to jail."

Walter glanced up at the girl through his tears. He pulled the sheet away from the bed.

"Now wrap her body inside of it," Sukie said.

"What?"

"Just do it. If the police find out you killed my mother, even by mistake, you'll rot in jail, if they don't kill you first."

Walter rolled Madame Lucien over, facedown, on top of the sheet. Blood spurted from the hole in her skull, staining the sheet a vibrant red.

"I accidentally hit her in the face," he said. "Why she got this big gash in the back of her head?"

"She must have fell hard when she hit the floor," Sukie said.

Walter stared at the wound.

"Hurry up."

He draped the edge of the sheet over the dead woman's body.

"Wait," Sukie said. She came over, reached inside the sheet, and pulled. Her hand emerged with the dried chicken foot curled around the twig.

"She wore this as protection from me," Sukie said with a laugh. "Look like it didn't do her much good."

Walter stared as she held the claw up to his face. Her eerie eyes met his. She laughed again and walked over to the fireplace, tossing the claw into the open flame. There was a brilliant explosion. A yellow cloud of sulfur-scented smoke filled the room.

Sukie opened a box on the mantel and reached inside. She sprinkled a handful of brown dust in the air.

"Cinnamon," she said. "Nana says it's my power. I take my color from it. Cinnamon is my strength."

Walter knelt beside the dead woman's body and finished rolling it up in the sheet.

Sukie clapped her hands free of the spice, then walked over to the bed. She pulled the rest of the bottom sheet free, then pushed the mattress. It didn't budge.

"*Come here,*" *she said.* "*I need your help.*"

Walter went to her without question.

"*We need to get this mattress off the bed. Then we need to turn it over.*"

Sukie walked to her dresser, opened a drawer, and pulled out a dagger. She handed him the knife.

"*Cut open the bottom of the mattress. Cut a hole big enough to fit her inside.*"

Walter didn't want to go to jail. He cut away at the fabric of the mattress with the sharp edge of the knife. She stood next to him, close to his ear, whispering as he tore away at the cloth.

"*She was so crazy 'bout Celine,*" *she said.* "*Celine was always better than me.*"

She twisted her voice into a singsong pitch, meant to imitate her mother.

" '*Ain't she pretty with her long red hair?*' '*Don't she have pretty green eyes?*' '*Ain't she smart?*' '*Don't she look nice in her new Sunday dress?*' "

Walter kept cutting at the mattress, afraid to look at her.

"*I got red hair. I got pretty eyes. But nobody ever talked about how pretty I look.*"

Walter sawed away.

"*I got Celine's old Sunday dresses. Ha.*" *She stood next to him without any clothes on, her hair tumbling over her shoulders, tickling his ear.* "*Guess I got the last laugh, too.*"

When he had cut an opening, Sukie moved him aside and began pulling out the stuffing. Cotton flew in big tufts around the room. She opened a hole large enough for Madame Lucien.

"*Now let's put her in.*"

Walter didn't move.

"*Grab her legs,*" *Sukie said.* "*Do it. Do you wanna go to jail?*"

Walter picked up the bottom of the sheet, holding Madame Lucien's feet. He and Sukie dragged the body over to the mattress. Without his help, Sukie pushed her mother's limp body into the hole. She jumped on top of the bloody corpse, cram-

ming it in to make sure it would fit. After she had arranged her
mother inside the space, she began repacking the cotton around
her.

Walter sat on the floor in a daze.

Sukie took a large needle and some thread from a drawer.
She perched her small frame on top of the mattress and sewed
the fabric back in place with long stitches.

"Help me put it on the bed."

"You can't leave this here," he said. "The blood will soak
through it. The room's gonna stink."

"You got a choice. You can do it my way, or you can end up
in jail."

Walter was helpless. He lifted the mattress and positioned it
back in place, with the stitches facing down.

He leaned against the mantel while Sukie scurried around
the room, tossing errant cotton puffs from the mattress and
other debris into the fire. She wiped the dagger and the needle
and returned them to the drawer. She emptied a pillowcase and
used it to wipe up the remaining blood on the floor. She threw it
into the flames.

"What about your brothers?" Walter asked in a weak voice
as he watched her at work.

"It'll take them some time to miss her. Sometimes they don't
come home for days."

"This won't work. I have to tell the police," he said. "It was
an accident."

Sukie turned to him.

"Don't be ridiculous. This is New Orleans. You're a nigger.
They'll hang your black ass so fast, folks'll think you was a
painting."

His mind was racing.

Sukie's tone softened as she came over to him. She put her
arms around his neck and pulled him in to her naked breast.
He could smell the cinnamon. Her hair fell heavy upon his
shoulder.

"It's all right," she said, stroking his back. "We'll go away *from here. Nobody will ever have to know that you killed my mother."*

Tears fell from Walter's eyes and dripped onto the bloodied tip of the poker lying next to his foot on the floor. He didn't remember seeing the poker before and wondered why there was fresh blood on the tip. He stared at the metal stick until his focus was so clouded that everything else became a dark red blur.

CHAPTER TWENTY-FOUR

Polo and Ophelia moved into their apartment a week before Christmas. Ophelia cooked a small turkey with all the trimmings. They decided not to go home to Downtown. It was important for them to spend the time together in their new home.

It was Ophelia's first attempt at cooking a holiday dinner. The bird wasn't quite done in the center, but they ate it anyway.

Polo gave her a leather-bound diary and a Cross pen. She gave him an embroidered Michigan State sweatshirt and a canvas bookbag.

That year, 1968, Christmas Eve fell on a Tuesday. Javier Trueba continued to tutor Ophelia, even though the semester ended the second week of December.

"What are you doing for tomorrow?" Ophelia asked him.

"Nada," he said. He had taught her a handful of Spanish words, something he did for fun during breaks in her studies. "I've been spending the holidays alone ever since I came to this country. I usually don't have the time or the money to fly home. So I stay here and get a head start on the next semester."

"Where's home?" she asked.

"Argentina," he said. "Buenos Aires."

"Oh," she replied. Ophelia didn't know Buenos Aires from *buenos días.* She thought it sounded like it had something to do with the weather.

• • •

On Christmas afternoon, as she and Polo feasted on half-done turkey, dried clumps of stuffing, and very candied yams, she thought of Javier.

"I'd like to invite my professor over," she said.

He shrugged, his mouth full of water. He was trying to free the thick clod of candied yams clinging to the roof of his mouth without offending his sister.

"You don't mind if he comes over?" she said. "He's really nice. And he's all alone for the holidays."

Polo's expression indicated indifference. He used his finger to loosen the goo.

Ophelia got up from the table and went to the phone. She dialed the number. She'd long before committed it to memory.

"*Hola?*"

"*Feliz Navidad,* Javier."

"*Feliz Navidad,* Ophelita. This is a surprise."

She loved when he called her Ophelita. He said it meant "Little Ophelia." It made her feel exotic.

"What are you doing?" she asked.

"I was reading Goethe. *The Sufferings of Young Werther.*"

"It sounds so sad for such a happy day."

"Well, yes, it is," he said with a laugh. "But it's also very interesting to follow this man's life. The entire story is told in epistolary form."

"Episto-what?"

"Epistolary. It means letters. Like the ones you mail. The story unfolds through a series of letters written by Werther. I'll lend it to you. I believe you'll enjoy it."

"Okay," she said. "But not today. Today is a happy day. Guess what?"

"What's that, Ophelita?"

Her effervescence was contagious.

"I'm inviting you over to spend the evening with me and my brother."

"Oh, Ophelita, that's very kind of you. But I'd never think to intrude on you and your family. Your brother just moved here. I would imagine he wants to spend as much time with you as possible."

"He doesn't mind. Plus, it's Christmas. You should be with friends as well as family today. I consider you my friend. I owe you so much."

"You owe me nothing," he said.

"I owe you everything."

He grew quiet.

"So you'll come?"

He laughed. She knew she had won.

"I'll come."

"Hurray," she said. "And Javier?"

"Yes?"

"Don't bring that sad book with you, okay?"

"*Sí*, Ophelita. I'll leave the sad book at home."

While Polo watched television, Javier and Ophelia sat at the table and talked. Ophelia had prepared Javier a plate of food and now watched him eat.

He toyed with the turkey, picked at the stuffing, and got a sugar rush from the candied yams. Ophelia studied his face to see if he was enjoying the meal.

"Is it good?" she asked.

He swallowed slowly, choking down a sugar glob.

She waited for his response.

"Ophelita," he said, his voice low. "Can I be honest with you?"

"Yes," she said. "Of course."

"This food is repugnant."

"What does that mean?" she asked.

"It's nasty. *Muy mala*. Terrible, disgusting. You could hang wallpaper with the gunk from the yams."

Polo glanced at his sister.

She sat very still, looking at the plate in front of Javier. Her shoulders began to shake. She burst into laughter.

"I knew it was nasty. I sat right there this afternoon and

watched Polo try to eat that raw bird and dry stuffing, and he wouldn't even say anything. He almost choked on the sweet potatoes. He drank so much water I thought he was going to burst."

Polo laughed. "Then why'd you let me sit there gagging if you knew it was so bad?" he asked.

" 'Cause you ain't have sense enough to say nuthin'," she said.

She threw a quick glance at Javier, aware of her sloppy diction.

He waved his hand at her. "Don't worry about it. It's Christmas. You're allowed at least one day a year to speak as you please."

"*Gracias,*" she said.

"*De nada,*" he replied with a smile.

They sat together in the room that passed for a den. The back window overlooked the campus. They were in armchairs, side by side. The quiet of the night was soothing, despite the disappointing meal and the freezing cold outside.

"I really enjoyed this," Javier said. "You don't know how much it means to know you thought of me. I never would have left my place today otherwise."

Ophelia sat bunched up in her chair, her knees up to her chest. A thick blanket was wrapped around her shoulders.

"I'm glad you came. I didn't know if you would." She was quiet for a moment, measuring her words. "I just wanted to thank you for everything you're doing for me. You've helped me learn so much about myself. In just the little bit of time I've known you, I've begun to open up. That's a big thing for me."

"I'm glad I could help you. That's what every teacher wants. To be able to make a difference."

"Well, you have. I love school. It's giving me something to live for. After my baby died, I didn't think I'd ever have anything to put myself into like that again."

He watched her as she spoke.

"Tuesdays and Thursdays have become so important to me. I spend all week planning what I want to say to you, what I want to ask you, and things we can talk about. But it never happens the way I plan it."

"Really?" he said. "I'm sorry about that. I should not be so controlling when we're together."

"No," she protested, "it's not that at all. Our meetings are always perfect."

"I'm glad," he said. "I really enjoy our times together as well."

She turned toward him. "I wanted to share my Christmas with you because I wanted you to know how much I appreciate you. Two other people have been really kind to me. They helped me get to this school. I never expected to find that type of kindness in my lifetime again."

He reached out and put his hand on her cheek.

"Thank you, Ophelita. You did me a favor, saving me from that sad book. I was very happy when you called."

She blushed at the awkward sensation of his hand against her skin.

He leaned over, nearer, as if to kiss her. As his lips hovered close to her own, Ophelia panicked and shrank away.

"I'm sorry," she said, her eyes downcast.

"It's my fault," he said, moving back. "I had no right to push myself on you like that."

"No, no." She reached out for his hand. "This is still very hard for me. I haven't had much luck with love. I once loved someone with all I had, and when it got down to it, it didn't mean a thing." She sighed. "And the last person I put all my love into, my baby . . . he died."

"That wasn't your fault."

"I know. But that doesn't make it stop hurting."

He listened to her, nodding.

"Right now it's easier for me to love things instead of people," she said. "Like school and books. My writing."

"I understand," he said. "I won't press myself on you like that again."

"No, Javier, really, it wasn't a bad thing. I just need time. Time with people. Time with myself."

"Sure, Ophelita. I understand."

She glanced at him sidelong. "Are you sure?"

"I'm positive," he said with a smile.

"Can we still be friends?" she asked, her voice small and childlike.

"Of course we can. Who knows? Perhaps one day our friendship will blossom into something more. On its own."

"Maybe," she said. "I guess we'll just have to wait and see."

Polo turned off the television and the light in the living room. On his way down the hall, he passed the open door of the den, about to stick his head in and say good night. Ophelia and Javier had their backs to him. He stood in the doorway watching them. His smile was bittersweet. He was pleased for his sister, happy that she seemed to have a new friend. There was an ache in his heart as he was reminded of Coolie.

He decided not to interrupt them. He made his way down the hall into his bedroom. He peeled out of his clothes, knelt down in the darkness, said a silent prayer, and crawled into bed.

CHAPTER TWENTY-FIVE

Before classes began that spring, Polo received a draft notice from Uncle Sam.

"So are you going to go?" Ophelia asked.

She was now making a conscious effort to speak proper English. She was lazy sometimes, but correct diction was becoming a more natural reflection of the way she spoke, no longer a studied and conscious effort.

" 'Course I'm gonna go," he said. "I ain't gon' be no draft dodger. I heard that when they catch you for that shit, they put a whoopin' on your ass for sho'. A nigga like me don't stand a chance."

Ophelia was disturbed but didn't want him to know just how much.

"Canada's right across the way. You could go there."

"I'on know nobody in Canada. What I'm gon' do, just hang out over there till the war's over? I'd go crazy hiding in a place where I'on know nuthin' and nobody. I may as well just take my butt on to Nam."

The two of them sat on the sofa in silence.

"Don't worry about the apartment," he said. "I have a lotta money put away, so there's more than enough to cover the rent while I'm gone."

"But what if you're gone for a long time?" she asked. "What if you end up having to go away until some time next year?"

"Stop speculating. Just be cool, we're okay."

"No, really." Ophelia got up from the couch and began pacing the room. "Maybe I need to think about getting a job. The Deveauxs paid for me to be in the dorm, not in an apartment. If I get a job, maybe I can keep this place."

Polo patted the sofa cushion beside him.

"Sit down, girl. Stop frettin' so much."

She kept pacing. "No, this is serious. I'm going to have to get a job."

"Sit down, Ophelia. I got something to tell you."

She stopped pacing. She could see he was serious. She sat down beside him. Polo held her hands and looked into her eyes.

"Look," he said, "I got some money saved up, so you don't need to be worrying about getting no job."

She opened her mouth. He shook his head.

"No, wait. Just hear me out." He took a deep breath and let it out slow, looking down at the floor as he spoke. "I told you what I used to do. I ain't too proud of it, but I made a lotta cash. I got over forty thousand dollars in the bank. I got another fifty thousand dollars in a savings account."

"Forty thousand dollars?"

"Yeah. And another fifty collecting interest." He glanced up at her. "Close your mouth," he said.

"But Polo," she replied, shaking her head in disbelief. "That sounds like all the money in the world."

"Well, it ain't. You wouldn't believe how much money is out there to be had. I got my piece and split."

"I can't believe it," she said.

"Believe it. And stop all this talk about getting a job."

She clasped his hands tighter.

"That's a lot of money, Polo."

"Yeah, it is," he said. "I thought about buying a house one time, but I wasn't sure this was where I wanted to live. We might leave this place once we both finish school.

"Anyway, I'm gon' leave you a chunk of it. I'll give you the bank papers for all ninety thousand, but you can take twenty thousand of it and use it for yourself. At least till I come back."

"What am I going to do with twenty thousand dollars?" she asked.

"I didn't mean spend it all at one time. Maybe you won't have to before I get back." He looked down at his sister's hands in his. "I just wanted you to know that you don't have to worry 'bout money. Just focus your mind on graduating from school."

"Okay."

"Good," he said. "And make sure to send Mama some every now and then. Act like it's coming from a real job. Don't send too much at once, or she'll suspect something bad. That's the one decent thing I did learn from Lay."

"Learning how to lie to Mama is a decent thing?"

"Better that than she know her son was a dope dealer. Don't you think?"

Ophelia studied the man beside her on the sofa. Polo's still waters ran far deeper than she gave him credit for. She realized now, as she sat next to him, that she had never given her youngest brother very much thought at all. The image of him in the barn smoking with Coolie flitted across her mind.

"Are you going to write and tell Mama?" she asked.

"Yeah. I'ma write her tonight."

He grew sullen. He released her hand and leaned back against the couch.

"I wish there was some way I could let Coolie know. I been thinking 'bout her so much these days. I left her there with Lay. I feel pretty bad about that, you know."

"I could tell her," Ophelia said. "I could even go see her if you want."

"No, Ophelia," he said. "I done told you, don't go nowhere near Detroit or Lay. He don't mean no good to nobody. I guess Coolie just couldn't see that."

Ophelia pressed her lips together. Polo's expression was just as firm.

"I know you don't wanna believe me. I know you just can't get it through your head that your precious brother could ever hurt somebody. But listen to me." His voice had a bitter edge to it. "Lay don't care 'bout nobody but hisself. And if you get anywhere near him, he'll find a way to exploit you. Just like he did me. And just like he's doing to Coolie right now."

Ophelia's expression was unchanged.

He sucked his tongue at her, shaking his head as he got up from the sofa. He headed for the front door.

"Just do yourself a favor," Polo said. "Stay away from him."

He left the apartment.

Ophelia sat on the sofa, listening to Polo's footsteps as he walked down the sidewalk. She heard him open the door of the Mustang, crank the ignition, and drive away.

"Lay's still my brother," she said. "He'd never hurt me. No matter what."

Ophelia was alone in the apartment the afternoon she picked up the phone and dialed the number. It rang several times before the familiar voice answered, filling her with the same rush of feelings it always had.

"Hello?"

"Hi. How are you?"

There was silence on the other end.

"Hello?" she asked. "Are you there?"

"I'm here," the voice answered.

"Are you okay? I haven't heard from you in such a long time. I think about you every day."

"You shouldn't. It's best that we just leave things the way they are. I told you that before."

"That's much easier said than done, don't you think?" she asked. "We shared a life together. We share the same blood." Her voice grew softer. "We shared a child."

Lay breathed into the phone, his face twisted in an anguished expression.

"What did you call me for?" he asked. "Can't nuthin' good ever come outta this. The baby died. It was for the best."

"You can't even say his name." She closed her eyes and leaned her head against the wall. "Why can't you say it? Why can't you just say his name?"

" 'Cause it don't make no difference, that's why. He's dead. I left that world behind when I moved away. I got another life now. You need to grow up and get ahold of yours."

Tears fell from her eyes as she listened to his words.

"We're still family, Lay," she said. "I thought we at least cared about each other because we was family."

He didn't respond.

The tears stung her cheeks with their salty heat.

"Why are you doing this?" she said. "You used to say I was your best friend. We used to talk about everything. What did I do to you to make you shut me out like this?"

"You didn't do nuthin'. I don't need you no more."

The remark pierced her ear, driving straight to her heart.

"She told you to do this, didn't she?" Ophelia asked. "How can you let her split us up? Why does she have so much control over you?"

"Ain't no 'us,' Ophelia," he said in a cold tone. "So there wasn't no 'us' to be splittin' up. When you gon' get that through your thick head?"

"You don't mean that."

Lay rubbed his left hand across his face as he stood holding the phone. His leg was shaking as he listened to his sister cry. He was angry and impatient.

"Ophelia, listen to me, and you listen good," he said. "You need to go on with your life. I'm not the same person I used to be. I left the old Lay and all that country bullshit in Downtown when I moved away. I don't ever intend to look down that dead-end road again."

"But what about when you used to write us letters and send money when you first went to Detroit?" she asked. "You were still the same person then."

"Wasn't no big thing for me to send y'all money. Ain't no big thing for me to send it now. But don't trouble me. The last thing I need is my love-struck sister trying to come back into my life with a buncha bullshit."

"I'm not just your love-struck sister, Lay," she said. "I'm a human being. I know what happened with us wasn't right, and we can't go back and relive that. But I am your flesh and blood. You might not want to be connected to me, but you are. You can't just cut me loose like this."

"I can," he said, "and I'm about to. I don't want no part of none of that whole scene no mo'."

She held the phone to her ear. He listened on his end to the sound of her breathing.

"Why can't you just accept this for what it is?" Lay asked. "I don't want you in my life no more. Plain and simple."

"So you're gon' do me like you did Polo?" said Ophelia, slipping into her old, familiar speech pattern. "Just turn your back on me and treat me like I ain't nuthin' to you?"

"Polo's a grown man. But I guess he ain't grown enough, crying that I done turned on him. He ran outta here. Looks like life in the city was too much for his sorry ass. His girl hung on all right, though. Coolie's making it happen in the Motor City."

Ophelia was horrified as she listened to her brother discuss Polo and Coolie as though they were strangers.

"How can you be so mean?" she whispered. "You were never like this before."

She turned around and leaned her back against the wall, the phone pressed tight into her ear.

"Maybe I always was," he said. "Maybe you just didn't want to see it."

Ophelia cried into the phone.

"I'm hanging up," he said, his nostrils twitching.

"Why? I just want to talk to you. I just want to hear your voice."

"Well, you heard it," he said. "Now I gotta go."

"Lay," she cried. "Lay, why are you doing this? I know you still care about me. I can hear it in your voice. Please. Don't hang up the phone. We need each other. You and me and Polo."

He wrestled with his rage.

"I gotta go, Ophelia," he repeated, his voice cracking. "Do yourself a favor. Don't call me no more."

Before she could respond, the phone was dead.

Ophelia slunk to the floor, her back against the wall, the receiver still in her hand. Her chest heaved and the tears fell, but her body wouldn't give up a sound.

Lay slammed the phone onto the hook so hard that it cracked. His eyes were red with fury. He grabbed the entire phone, wrapping the cord around his wrist in deliberate winding motions, and jerked it from the wall.

Coolie was just exiting her room when she saw him.

Lay huffed as he swung the phone by the cord, hurling it against the wall, tears streaming down his face. Coolie could hear him mumbling through the din of smashing pieces of plastic and metal. He kept swinging the phone against the wall in a crazed rage until there was nothing but a scattered array of cracked parts around the room.

He turned, exhausted, to see her standing in the hall near the living room, watching him. She flinched, expecting him to direct his anger at her.

Lay glared at the girl, frightening her with the intensity of his pain.

"Why the hell did she have to call here?" he said. "Huh? Why the hell did she have to call?"

He slid down against the wall, his head in his hands, as Coolie watched his usual controlled demeanor break down into a miserable display of tears.

Polo got into the car a few days later to run errands. The time was nearing for him to report to Uncle Sam.

Walter watched the Mustang pull away. He slumped in his car as it passed. Polo never even turned his head.

Walter wanted to know that she was all right. He'd been spending his time at the Cherokee Motel, basking in his new-found freedom. Sukie's dark shadow had hovered over him for more than twenty years. The past weeks without her influence was a necessary step in his new direction. He was getting his head together. Now he wanted to make sure Ophelia was okay.

He'd been around campus, watching, waiting to catch a glimpse of her. He needed to know she was safe. It was important for him to stay connected to her.

He had followed her and Polo from campus two days before to see where they lived. He wanted a closer look. Just so he'd have an idea of how she was living.

He opened the door of his car. The sun was bright, but the air was biting cold.

He closed the door of the dark green Chevy and walked toward her apartment. Just as he crossed the parking lot, a yellow Volkswagen pulled up in front.

A tall, striking Latin man stepped out. He glanced at Walter, who froze in place, made an about-face, and walked back to his car.

The man stood for a moment, puzzled, then walked up to the apartment. He rang the doorbell. By the time Ophelia let him in, Walter was safe within the confines of his car.

"Buenos días, mi amigo," she said. "Did I get it right?"

Javier kissed her on the cheek.

"Right on the money," he said. "Ophelita, were you expecting some company?"

"No. Why?"

The puzzled look returned to his face.

"What's wrong, Javier?" she asked.

"I don't know. I just saw a man who looked like he was coming to your door. When I pulled up, he stood there like he was scared, then he ran away."

"He ran?"

"Well, he didn't run, but he sure left in a hurry."

Ophelia peered out of the window.

"What'd he look like?"

He shrugged.

"I don't know. He was a black man. Maybe he was in his forties. He seemed frightened. And lost."

"Hmm. There's no one out there," she said.

Javier peeked over her shoulder. "That's strange."

He scanned the parking lot.

The big dark green Chevy was gone.

"So what are you going to do now that Polo has to go away?" Javier asked.

Ophelia leaned back on the sofa, her legs tucked beneath her.

"I don't know. I'm just going to have to get through school without him, I suppose."

"Are you going to keep this apartment? You said he was going to pay for everything. If he leaves, you won't be able to afford it."

Ophelia weighed whether she should tell him about the forty thousand dollars. She decided that it was best if she didn't.

"I'll work it out," she said. "I can just go back to the dorm if it comes down to it. I probably won't be able to get a single room at this point, but I don't mind if I have to get a roommate."

Javier rubbed his chin.

"You don't mind roommates?" he asked.

"Not at all. I grew up with two brothers, remember?"

Her words felt empty as she said them. She still couldn't accept how Lay had treated her, even though she knew in her heart it was best she take Polo's advice and forget him altogether.

Javier touched her hand.

"Ophelita, my friend, I have a proposition that you might like to hear."

"Ophelia called me," Lay said into the phone.

"And?"

Lay's expression was stone.

"And I told her not to call me no mo'. I told her I wasn't gon' have nuthin' else to do with her."

"Are you telling me the truth?" she asked. " 'Cause you know I'll know if you're telling me a lie."

"Yeah, Susu," he said. "What I'ma lie 'bout it for?"

His eyes misted over with anger. His focus was fixed on the images flashing across the television screen.

"This is for the best," she said, " 'though it's still not finished."

"Well, it is for me. I hope you're happy. You got what you wanted."

"I didn't get everything."

"I'm sure you will."

The same day Uncle Sam took Polo away, a teary-eyed Ophelia kissed him good-bye, then moved in with Javier.

He had a little house he had bought the year before. It was just big enough for two people. There was a garden that Javier said bloomed throughout the spring and summer. It was barren now, but the walls were licked with running vines that crisscrossed around the house.

Polo's belongings were put away in storage. He gave Ophelia the Mustang to keep until his return.

By the end of the first week, Ophelia had settled into her new bedroom and the new environment. She rushed home after school to study, cook dinner for herself and Javier, and write in her journal. On the prettiest days, she worked in the garden.

In the distance, Walter watched her, the big dark green Chevy nestled in the shadows of the trees that lined the cozy street. This place was different. He had to be sure this man would take care of her.

And soon enough, when he felt stronger, he would make himself known.

PART X

1945–1969

SECRETS

*He that communicates his secret
to another makes himself
that other's slave.*

—Baltasar Gracián

Grace and Big Daddy had been living in their restored home for almost five months.

Walter left right before the house was finished. All the complicated work had been done. Big Daddy completed the rest by himself.

He had been digging around in Grace's belongings for months, desperate for a clue to Walter's outburst the day it was announced Ophelia would be going to college. He found nothing, which further fed his suspicions.

When Walter left, Sukie shut herself up in the house, and neither Grace nor Big Daddy ever saw her come out of it again.

Sukie had been hearing the baby's cries upon the wind all along. She knew they had almost driven Ophelia mad, and she had taken great joy in the girl's unraveling. Now that she was alone, though, the cries haunted her without respite. The gurglings and murmuring ruled her nights. The anguished screams hung above her as she moved about the house in the day. All the incantations, crushed bones, and voodooisms she could muster would not free her from the torment.

With Walter there, she had found the power to tune them out. When he left, he took with him the wellspring from which she drew her strength, and she fell victim to the cries and bedevilment of the wind.

Not even Lay, who had always been so steadfast, would help her. He had his own affairs now, he said, no time for her insignificant country games. Under her guidance, he had become a very powerful man. She had believed he would remain loyal in return, the one piece of terra firma upon which she could always stand. Now he made it clear to her that he would no longer be distracted. He stopped writing letters and taking her calls. Her standing with him was now as shaky as everything else in her world.

As she realized that all her tools of defense were waning, Sukie began to feel her very essence drain away.

Grace's demeanor had undergone a drastic change. She stayed in the bedroom most of the time, dark and despondent. Big Daddy watched her youthful face show its age within a matter of weeks.

Her skin took on a leathery texture and an unnatural hue. The beautiful hair began to turn a shocking white, strand by strand. After her children left and her brother disappeared, Grace shut herself off from everyone.

She was asleep in the bedroom, when Big Daddy found out the truth. He had been sitting in the dim light of the living room, listening close as darkness settled heavy over everything, inside and out. He could hear the wild winter wind whipping through the trees, across the porch, over the roof and windows, the shutters clanging against the house. The chill penetrated the walls and began a slow creep across his body.

He leaped from the couch, grabbed an old lantern from the kitchen, lit it, and rushed out into the gusty, frigid night air and blackness, across the path that connected the two homes.

His breath came in quick puffs of condensing mist as he tramped his way over. Big Daddy stood on his brother-in-law's porch and looked back at his own house. It was dark except for the faint light peeking through the living room curtains.

He knocked on the door. The forceful wind whipped through the legs of his work pants, chilling his ankles. His feet remained planted.

When no one answered, he tapped on the window. Through the curtain, he could see a light on in the back of the house, toward the kitchen.

Against the wind, he walked around the side of the house to the kitchen door. He could see the silhouette of Sukie sitting at the table. Her burnt-orange hair was piled high atop her head, and he could see her hunched over something. It appeared to be a bowl. Through the door, he could hear a low moan, like the sound of singing. The wind whistled around him.

"Sukie."

She did not move.

"Sukie. Open the door. It's Big Daddy. I wanna talk to you."

"Go 'way," she said, her voice muffled as it came through the door. "You just want me to let that howlin' baby in here. I hear it whipping all around you. Y'all just came over here to taunt me some more."

She moaned again, still bent over the table. Through the sheer gauze kitchen curtain, Big Daddy could see a mist rising between the bowl and Sukie's face.

"Sukie, please," he said, his voice booming through the door. "I need to talk to you 'bout what you said that night. I need to understand some things."

She stopped moaning.

"I wanna know what you meant when you said they thought you didn't know but you did. I wanna know what it is you know. I wanna know why you slapped my wife that night."

Sukie laughed. "Why you wait so long to ask me? Any decent husband woulda demanded a explanation right then and there."

Big Daddy stood outside the door, his hands stinging from the cold.

"Can I come in?" he said. "I just wanna talk to you. It's cold out here. I just wanna sit down with you for a minute."

Sukie moaned.

"Sukie, please. Listen to me. I just wanna know why it was Walter got so upset that night 'bout Ophelia going to school. He ain't never had nothin' to do with how we raised our kids. I think you know something, and I wanna know what it is."

"Funny," she said, "he didn't care none when Lay and Polo went away, don't you think?"

"What you mean?"

"Just what I said. Funny Ophelia the only one he seemed to care was leaving."

Big Daddy's hands began to tingle. An unfamiliar feeling began to creep up through his chest.

"Why do you think it's funny, Sukie?" he asked. "She's the only niece he got. Sometimes men feel more protective of girls than they do boys."

Sukie continued to moan, ignoring his words.

"I think he was just being careful," Big Daddy explained. "He prob'ly thought Michigan was too far away. That's a big jump for a girl who ain't known nuthin' but this all her life."

"Shouldn't that be your worry and not his?"

"He was just concerned about her," he said. "That's the kind of man he is."

"Shut up," she cried. "You stupid, just like your wife and Walter."

She rose from the table and came to the door but didn't open it. She peered through the glass at him as he stood in the dark on the steps of the back porch. The flickering glow of the lantern created an eerie silhouette of his massive frame. She could hear the howling wind whip around him, shaking the door. She grabbed her ears.

"You ever wonder where the daddy was who got your wife pregnant 'fore you married her?" she asked, her hands clamped on both sides of her head.

Big Daddy's fingertips were hot. He thought it was from holding the lantern.

"She never said where he was," he replied, "and I ain't never wanted to know."

"That's a lie. You been wanting to know all the time. You was just too stupid to ask."

He cleared his throat. His neck felt hot. "So who you saying the daddy is?"

"I ain't got to say. You already know."

His hands were tingling with the prick of a thousand hot pins.

"Quit playing with me, Sukie," he said, " 'fore I come up in that house and snatch you out. What you tryna say?"

"Your wife ain't never been outta Downtown. She ain't never hardly left her mama's house before her mama burnt it down."

"So?"

"So . . . that don't leave too many people to father no baby. It wasn't her daddy. He been dead since she was little."

"I know 'bout her daddy." His voice was thick with anger. "I didn't ask you her life story. I'm just asking you 'bout one thing."

"Well, it wasn't but one 'nother man hanging 'round once her daddy was dead."

The blood was rushing in Big Daddy's ears. He stood outside on the doorstep, his hands throbbing from the heated prickling sensation in his fingertips and the racing of his pulse. The sharp wind beat against his legs and chest.

"You ever wonder why they mama burnt the house down?" Sukie asked. "Wasn't no bigger than a tater when they found her. You ever wonder 'bout that?"

He listened, his eyes wet with stinging tears.

"They mama caught 'em. She seen it when it happened. 'Cause sho'nuf, nine months after she burnt up, Grace had that gal, Ophelia. And Walter can't have no mo' babies. Everything he get close to since then just ball up and die."

Big Daddy couldn't keep still.

"Is that why you came to the house and seduce me that time?" he asked. "So you could get back at my wife? So you could tear our family apart?"

"Your family?" Sukie said with a laugh. "What kinda family you call yourself having? It ain't nuthin' but a sham." The wind whipped and howled as Sukie taunted him. "You knew that gal was pregnant with her brother's baby, and you married her anyway. You's a fool."

Steam formed as the heat from Big Daddy's breath met the cold air and rushed from his nostrils. He stamped his feet on the porch in an attempt to contain his rage.

"You the evil thing, Sukie," he said. "You been cloudin' over everything good since you set foot here. Until you go away, ain't nuthin' gon' ever be right."

Sukie laughed. "This is my domain. Can't nuthin' make me go, 'cept me and the Lord Himself."

"Maybe that's why He sent me over," he said. "So His will could be done."

He dropped the lantern at the foot of the steps, then rushed toward his house. The wind pushed him along, aiding his haste. Kerosene gathered by the steps of Sukie's house in a pool of dust and dried mud.

Just inside the kitchen door, Sukie watched him, shaking her head and sucking her tongue.

"You's a fool, Big Daddy," Sukie said. "You's a damn fool."

Grace was in bed reading. She had been knitting, but her hands had grown tired. She had set the basket of yarn aside in exchange for an old favorite. The leather-bound copy of *Hamlet* was inches from her face. Her vision had grown dim over the years, and the words were beginning to blend together.

She heard the door slam. She assumed Big Daddy had been outside working in the yard. But it was a chilly night, windy and dark, and she wondered why he was putting such a strain on himself to work so late under such unpleasant conditions.

He left her alone often. She felt sad for him because she knew he wasn't sure how to deal with her. She didn't blame him. She no longer knew how to deal with herself.

She heard his heavy, hollow footfalls as they approached the bedroom. She was reading the scene that fascinated her most: the one where Hamlet prepared to steal upon his uncle and avenge his father's death. She was amazed by the power of Shakespeare's turnabout—had Hamlet killed Claudius as he was kneeling in prayer, he would have become the sinful murderer and his evil uncle would have received God's grace.

Big Daddy flung the door open, tears streaming down his

face. The door slammed against the wall and came apart from its upper hinge. It dangled beside him, threatening to fall.

Grace lowered the book.

"Why didn't you tell me?" he demanded.

She stared at him in silence.

"Why didn't you tell me?" He rushed to the side of the bed, grabbing her by the shoulders and shaking her.

Her body went limp in his hands. He continued to shake her, his breath thick. His eyes were closed. Hot tears dropped onto the bed.

"How could you do that to me, Grace? How could you let me raise Ophelia and not tell me she was Walter's child? How could you do that to me?"

Grace let him shake her, her graying hair flying free from the bevy of pins that held it in place.

Big Daddy opened his eyes and flung her down on the bed, searching the room for something to hurt her. He wanted something to hurt her deep. Something to hurt her the way that she had hurt him.

He saw the knitting needles.

He grabbed one, lunging for Grace, who had fallen back against the bed. He stabbed into her chest, the force behind his girth so strong that the needle broke through bone with ease. He drew it back and came down on her again. Tears clouded his vision.

"How could you do that to me?" he cried. "You cursed me. You cursed my house. How could you do that to me, Grace? How could you do that to me?"

He kept stabbing, stabbing, stabbing at her, until her chest disappeared under a puddle of blood.

Grace's torso heaved twice, then sank as she heaved a final breath. Surrender was easy. She had been half gone for months.

Big Daddy's hand that clutched the needle froze in midair. He stared at Grace, bloody, gored, her long, silky gray hair strewn across the pillows and the bed.

He studied her face. It took on an angelic beauty, the leathery texture of the last few months slipping away. The skin was supple. There were no lines. A soft smile had formed at the corners of Grace's mouth. Someone had finally set her free.

He roared, crying, cursing, falling to his knees upon the bed, plunging the needle deep into his stomach.

"Oh, God," he cried as he punctured his flesh. "Please forgive me for what I've done to her. She's always been good to me. Oh please, Lord Jesus, please forgive me for this."

With every word, he plunged the needle into his flesh. He kept plunging and tearing at his body until the pain was too great to bear.

He fell upon his wife, losing consciousness in a bloody, sticky mess. His breathing became erratic, then began to fade, his body covered with the dark red stuff.

At the precise moment life fled the shell of Big Daddy, Sukie moaned to herself, hunched over the misty bowl.

She raised it to her lips and drank the tea.

Outside, the flame from the wick of the shattered lantern flickered in the rustling wind, connecting the dots of the scattered kerosene. The fire gathered in the pool of fluid at the bottom of the steps and fanned bright as the night wind urged it on.

Sukie was still drinking the tea when it raced up the steps of the back porch and began to dance around the frame of the door.

She rose from the table, emptied the remaining contents of the bowl into the sink, and turned off the kitchen light. Smoke began to seep beneath the bottom of the back door, the odor of burning wood thinned by the fury of the wind.

Sukie made her way through the darkness of the living room and trudged up the stairs. When she walked into her bedroom, she shut the door behind her. She stood still for a moment, listening. The wind whipped against the window, whistling a high-pitched cry. She could hear a soft rapping. She knew she could no longer escape. She walked to the window and lifted it up, inviting the baby in.

She smiled as she began to undress.

By the time Sukie settled into bed, the fire had engulfed the desiccated wood of the back door and was racing down the kitchen walls.

She picked up the receiver of the black phone on the night-stand and dialed. She waited for an answer, smiling at the sound of his voice.

"We gon' all be dead by morning," she whispered into the phone.

"What you want now, Susu?" he said. "I told you I ain't got no time for this."

"Well, now, don't you worry yourself none," she said. "It ain't nuthin' big. I just thought you'd wanna know."

She placed the phone back in its cradle and pulled the covers over her, up to her chin.

Sukie hummed as smoke began to overtake the room. She breathed a heavy sigh and closed her eyes, the cries of the howling baby Hamlet swirling around her head.

The fire raged throughout the house, embers flying upon the wind into the night sky.

A few of the embers reached the Boten house next door, igniting the new wood.

The fire began at the steps of the front door, urged on by the wind. It cracked and sizzled in a battle against the recent construction, proving its power to destroy both the old and the new. By the time it reached the back of the house, overtaking the bloodied, tangled bodies of Grace and Big Daddy, Sukie's place was ablaze in a brilliant display.

Sukie rocked, covered in flames, cradling the crying baby. Smoke filled her lungs as the heat seared her entire body. She hung on to consciousness with all her strength.

She clung to the baby. At last she had a child of her own. Now that she had him, she didn't want to let go.

She hummed as she rocked. The baby's screams would not be soothed.

"I gotta get you some water," she said, her voice choked with smoke, her lips ragged and raw. She pushed her body, struggling against her own burnt flesh in an effort to save herself and the child. She fell from the bed into fire, still clutching the baby tight.

Sukie attempted to roll across the floor. There was nothing left within her now but the desire to live for her very own baby. There was just enough strength for her to turn one revolution. She lay facedown on the flaming floor, the pressure of her burning body crushing the baby in her arms. The cries ceased as baby Hamlet slipped free and faded into the wind.

Sukie let out a howl that Caesar Bucksport heard in the distance as he was reaching into his cooler for another peach Nehi.

He leaned up.

"Y'all heard that?" he asked.

No one paid attention to him.

He shrugged and popped the cap on the soda.

As Sukie's spirit fled, an incredible explosion lit up the cold night sky. The entire foundation of Downtown was shaken. Folks in the Lucky Star Liquor Joint were knocked in every direction. Those who were dancing fell to the floor. Drinks dropped out of hands and food spilled from mouths. The odor of sulfur and cinnamon permeated the air.

Hysteria swept through the club as people gasped, coughed, and cowered on the floor, thinking it was the end of the world.

"I told y'all I heard something," Caesar said.

The town would soon discover the origin of the noise.

Upon Sukie's spiritual exit, her house exploded with such great force that a black crater so deep it later became a lake was all that remained.

It was as if the earth had swallowed her whole.

Folks said the devil himself had yawned open the ground and reached his fiery hands up to snatch her home.

Lay came down alone for the funeral. He made all the arrangements.

"I want the service to be as brief as possible," he told the funeral director when he first arrived in town. "There ain't no bodies, so ain't no need for folks to be standing around too long."

"You want to put up markers?" the man said. "Maybe get 'em each a tombstone and a grave? That's what folks sometimes do, whether there's a body or not."

"Now why would I wanna do that?"

The man's brows rose in surprise.

"Oh, all right," Lay said, reaching into the pocket of his expensive dark blue suit and peeling off three hundred-dollar bills. "Get 'em graves, get 'em whatever. Just get it over with so I can go home."

The funeral director provided three urns in memoriam for Grace, Big Daddy, and Sukie. The empty urns were placed in the graves.

A great number of people attended the funeral. Most of the town was present, as well as a few who came from surrounding areas. Spectators, speculators, and genuine friends. Canada and Piedmont sat up front holding hands, their faces flushed and their eyes red-rimmed in remembrance of their friends. Some folks came just to see Lay, who drove up in a brand-new Cadillac Eldorado, flashing hundred-dollar bills in the stores around town.

"I used to see that there Cadillac all the time," Rita Mae Slackey whispered to Glossy Davis at the funeral. "At least once or twice a month I'd see it heading down that back road. I ain't know it was him." She sucked her teeth. "I shole didn't know it was him."

Lay steered clear of the folks at the funeral. He made sure to stay far away from the Deveauxs.

He didn't linger in Downtown long. There wasn't any reason to. Grace and Big Daddy died intestate. Since he was the only member of his family in attendance, there was no one to contest the property rights. No one else knew how to contact Polo and Ophelia. Lay took immediate ownership of the land. He sold lock and stock to Andrew Woodson the same day. Andrew was desperate to get his hands on the property and was willing to pay a fetching sum. Far more money than Lay knew the cursed ground was worth.

Having cut all the loose ends of his ties to the town, Lay prepared to head back to Detroit. He stopped by the Lucky Star for a bottle of brandy on his way out.

"How things going up there in the big city?" Caesar asked, following Lay out to his car.

"Just fine," Lay said. "That's why I'm in such a rush to get back to it."

He slammed the door, fired up the V-8 engine of the Cadillac, and sped down the hill, leaving Caesar standing in a cloud of dust, his mouth wide open.

CHAPTER TWENTY-SEVEN

Walter got an apartment not very far from Ophelia and Javier. Every day he parked the car in the shadows of the trees and watched his daughter come and go. Sometimes he fell asleep in the car, waiting for her return.

He deliberated over and over in his mind how the day would be when he finally spoke to her.

After three weeks, his money began to run low.

He took a job at a café not far from campus.

The Wildflower attracted all kinds of patrons. The hippie crowd. Druggies. Right-wing pro-Vietnam supporters and flagrant left-wing potential draft dodgers. Walter became the host of this motley crew. He finessed himself into the job, calling on some of the charm of his youth that had been so successful in attracting the local women in Tennessee.

It wasn't Walter's charm that got him the job. The owner, as radical a hippie as they came, saw an opportunity to make a social statement. What better instrument to show the need for forward thinking than an almost fifty-year-old southern throwback? Walter was a token, the unexpected mascot of a forming generation.

He worked evening hours from nine until three in the morning. The Wildflower was a typical campus haunt, a place for cheap food and libations, as well as a venue for amateur singers, musicians, and assorted performance artists. Walter was surprised to realize an appreciation for folk songs, rock and roll, Bob Dylan, poetry readings, and Krishna music. His excitement for work grew as he reveled in all the new things he encountered.

Without noticing it, his focus began a slow shift from the burning desire to contact his daughter. He was embarking upon a discovery of himself.

In the midst of his nights at the Wildflower, he was undergoing a spiritual awakening.

Mornings from six to nine were Walter's time for himself. He began to read books, plays, the dozens of radical papers that sprouted up around the café, touting the horror of war and extolling the virtues of free expression.

Walter wanted some of that free expression for himself. He had spent years under Sukie's dark shadow. He wanted, more than anything, to liberate himself from the burdensome strain of those years.

He chose to change everything about himself, from the way he dressed to the way he walked. He had seen the hip young men come into the café, garbed in psychedelic colors, bell-bottoms, flowing silk shirts. Walter admired it all–their struts, their confidence, their language. The boys oozed charisma, and he knew that he wanted to be a part of that powerful energy.

He bought a full-length mirror and began to effect his transformation. He slipped on skintight pants and airy shirts, leaving buttons open for tufts of graying hair to jut from his chest. He tied vibrant scarves around his head and practiced his gait in front of the mirror. He wanted to be confident but not cocky. When he did meet up with his daughter again, he thought, she would see a new man, someone bold and vivacious. Someone she couldn't help but love, because Walter, for the first time, was beginning to fall in love with himself.

He watched the performance artists at the Wildflower. They were actors. So were the poetry readers and mimes. They immersed themselves in whatever role they were playing at the moment, so much that they seemed to believe it for the time they were in the limelight. Walter knew that was the kind of discipline he needed to transform himself. Someone at the café, one of the poets, had told him something about a man being as he thought. Walter knew what he wanted to be. In a very short time, he began to think that way.

Each night a group of students from the drama department gathered at the Wildflower. They rehearsed for upcoming productions, tested new material on the always receptive audience, and sometimes played critic for those brave enough to go onstage.

Walter got to know them all. He maneuvered his way into their conversations, invited himself to sit with them, and sometimes offered them drinks on the house.

They liked him. They found him as refreshing and displaced as the hippie owner intended them to. Walter was a conversation piece, and they were often amused by his interest in the material they were doing.

The same four drama students frequented the café. Kari, a flaxen-haired, chain-smoking girl with an innocent face and a mature body. She wore the same garb every day: jeans, a cut-off T-shirt, a peace-sign headband, and love beads that hung way past her knees. Evan was a slender young black boy, nineteen, with thick brows and a clean-shaven face. David was an Irish boy with long red hair and a loud mouth, and Layla was the youngest, an eighteen-year-old with wide blue eyes and a soft voice. Walter loved hanging out with them.

As he became more comfortable in their presence and with watching them perform onstage, he told Layla and Evan one night of his growing fascination with acting and other forms of free expression.

"How long have you been interested in this?" Layla asked.

"Ever since I started working here," Walter said. "I didn't grow up around this stuff. It's like a whole new world for me."

"Well," said Evan, taking a drink of his beer, "if this is something you're really interested in, we'd love to help."

Layla agreed. "Yeah. We could give you pointers. Teach you some of the basic stuff. Enough to whet your appetite some more. You're gonna have to take it from there."

"When do you want to start?" Evan asked.

"Tomorrow?" Walter said with hesitation. "Maybe somewhere around lunchtime?"

"Tomorrow's cool," Evan replied, draining the bottle.

"Oh no. I can't," said Layla. "I've got lunch with my dad."

Evan pushed up from the table on his way to get another beer and slapped Walter on the shoulder. "Well, boss," he said, "I guess that means it's just you and me."

At noon the next day, there was a gentle knock on Walter's door. He wore a pair of jeans and a blue turtleneck sweater. He checked himself in the mirror, then rushed into the living room and opened the door.

"Hey, Evan."

"What's up," the boy said as he invited himself in.

"I got snacks and refreshments," Walter said, closing the door behind him.

Evan looked around at the apartment. Walter had tacked assorted posters on the wall. Van Gogh's *Starry Night*. A poster of the movie *A Raisin in the Sun*. The place was a mishmash of quickie decorating.

"I'm not that hungry. I'm still sluggish from imbibing all night."

"What does that mean?"

"Drinking."

"Oh."

Evan leaned close to Sidney Poitier's face on the *Raisin* poster. He ran his finger across the paper. It felt new. Walter offered him a beer.

Evan refused the drink. "Thanks. I had enough last night."

He walked over to the couch and sat down. He was still studying the walls when Walter followed him and sat on the arm of the chair.

"I still can't believe I'm doing this," Walter said. "I feel so silly, like a foolish old man."

"You'll be all right," said Evan. "We all felt like that in the beginning."

"Like foolish old men?"

"Well, no. I don't know. Maybe Kari did," Evan said, laughing. "Anyway, let's get started. The first thing we need to work on is your form. You got a book?"

"A book on form?"

"No. A book. Any book. Preferably a heavy one."

Walter got up from the arm of the chair and began rummaging around the apartment. When he came across the phone book, he came bounding back into the living room, carrying it like a prize.

"All right," Evan said. "This isn't that firm, but it will do. Now, do you have a mirror?"

Walter went into the room again and returned with the full-length mirror he practiced in front of every morning.

"Perfect. We're going to learn carriage and balance. Put the book on your head, and try to walk as straight as possible without the book falling off."

Walter put the book on his head and began to walk. He hadn't taken two steps before the book went crashing to the ground.

"No, no, no," said Evan. "You must walk slowly, deliberately, with one foot in front of the other in order to hone your balance. Watch me."

Evan picked up the book, perched it on his head, and strutted across the room and back. The phone book remained in place.

"Man," Walter said. "I wanna learn how to walk like that. You look like you ain't scared of nuthin'." He knew that was the way he wanted to walk up to his daughter. Bold, with the authority being her father would afford. "Let me try it," he said.

Evan handed him the book. "Walk toward the mirror this time. That way you can correct your carriage as you go."

Walter perched the book on his head again. He took three steps, and the book crashed to the floor.

He stooped to get it. Evan came up behind him, took the book from his hand, and placed it back on his head.

"Stand still. Give your body a chance to adjust to the additional weight."

Walter stood in place. He watched Evan's face in the mirror as the young man instructed him.

"Now. Straighten your back. You're slumped over. That's why the book keeps falling off."

Evan pressed his hand into the small of Walter's back.

In the mirror, Evan watched Walter watching him.

"Make sure your neck is perfectly erect."

He placed his hand around the nape of Walter's neck.

The two men watched each other in the mirror.

Evan's fingers lingered, then fluttered against the man's skin. Walter didn't move.

Evan began to stroke his neck, his fingers moving up and down with confidence. His other hand pressed deeper into the small of Walter's back.

Their gaze remained locked in the mirror.

Walter leaned his head back and closed his eyes.

CHAPTER TWENTY-EIGHT

Javier held Ophelia close as hot tears dropped onto his bare shoulders.

"Caesar says they've been dead for more than three months now," she said. "All of them. Mama, Big Daddy, and Sukie. He said Lay put the funeral together, and everybody wanted to know why me and Polo weren't there. I wrote Mama a couple of letters, and I was concerned when she didn't write me back. I wasn't worried. She didn't always write back as quick as I did."

Javier rocked her as her words came, erratic, halting, and choked by uncontrollable spasms of sobs and gasps.

"They all just burnt up. I can't get the image out of my head of my mama and daddy burning up like that." She clung to his shoulder. "Just like my baby."

The tears were running over his shoulders in rivers, down into the small of his back, where they gathered in the elastic band of his pajama bottoms.

"Big Daddy worshiped her. He loved my mama so much."

Ophelia pushed away from Javier and got out of the bed. She walked toward the window and looked out into the garden.

"I know Sukie had something to do with it."

"But she was killed," Javier said. "She wouldn't deliberately be the cause of her own death, would she? It had to be an accident."

Ophelia shook her head. "Nothing that involves that woman is an accident."

"To say she started it, though. That's pretty harsh, don't you think?"

"You had to know her to know what I mean," she said. "Sukie was evil. That's just something I know in my heart." She stood at the window watching the sun dance across the grass. "My uncle was afraid of her. Imagine that. Being afraid of your own wife."

Javier watched her at the window with her back to him.

"I guess she must have loved him once." Her hair moved as she shook her head. "She was so full of hate for him and my mama. It just twisted itself up into something ugly."

"Why did she hate them?"

Ophelia's eyes narrowed as they focused on a hydrangea bush. The vibrant flowers danced in a kaleidoscope of color through the veneer of tears, which no longer fell, but were still very much alive.

"I don't know. Uncle Walter and Mama had a strange relationship. They hardly ever said two words to each other, but I know my mama was crazy about him." She touched the window. "I liked him, too. But you know what?" She turned back to Javier, her eyes fixed and penetrating. "I don't think he ever liked me back."

Javier leaned back in the bed, propped on his elbows. "Then why did you like him?"

Ophelia's gaze hardened. Her eyes were now dry.

"Because I felt close to him. I just felt like I understood him, and that he needed someone to understand him really bad."

She walked over to the bed and climbed into the center. She pulled her knees up to her chin, wrapped her arms around them, and rocked herself calm.

"So how do you know he didn't like you?" Javier asked.

"I just know it. Whenever I tried to say something to him, he would walk away. He never made eye contact with me. And when Sukie was around, he wouldn't say anything. She watched his every move, especially around Mama and me. I felt so sorry for him."

"Was she jealous?"

"I don't know what she was." She rubbed her eyes.

"Didn't Polo say he left Sukie?" he asked.

She nodded, looking away.

"I guess he couldn't take it anymore and finally got away from her," she said. "I'm glad he did."

Javier moved up to where Ophelia sat on the bed. She turned away.

"I still can't believe Lay wouldn't contact me to let me know what happened. He said he didn't want anything else to do with me, but these were our parents. If I hadn't called Caesar Bucksport, I never would have known they were dead. Mama and Big Daddy didn't have a phone. They never wanted one."

Javier rubbed her back. She leaned her head down on her raised knees so he couldn't see the fresh tears that fell.

"I should have been more concerned. I never should have left them at all."

"Don't be ridiculous," Javier whispered. "Your mother wanted this for you. She saw a chance for you to have a better life. You're not responsible for what happened. There was no way you could know."

"Lay could have told me," she said.

"You said he told you he didn't want anything else to do with you. Why would he say that? Why wouldn't he want to have anything to do with you anymore?"

She looked up at him, the tears streaming. She wanted to tell him everything.

"I don't know."

She rocked faster, her arms still tight around her knees.

"I feel like everything is slipping away from me," she said. "First my baby, then Polo goes away, and now Mama and Big Daddy. And my own brother lives right here in the same state as I do and won't even see me. My own brother. I guess he never really loved me at all."

He watched her as she rocked, frantic, her words choked. He wanted to tell her. Not now, he thought. Not now. She'd only pull away.

"Polo loves you," he said.

"He's gone now, too. Everything I ever love either leaves, dies, or just plain doesn't love me back."

Javier put his arms around her shoulders to stop the rocking. He lifted her chin and searched her eyes.

"You are not alone," he said. "I'm right here with you. And I have no plans of dying soon. Unless you plan on killing me off for being such a messy housekeeper."

"Thank you. That makes me feel a little better."

"I'm not saying it to make you feel better," he said.

"Then why are you saying it?"

"Because I mean it," he replied. He realized that perhaps now was the time. He glanced down at the bed, clearing his throat. When he found her eyes again, his expression was bold.

"Ophelita, sometimes I'm so excited at the thought of seeing you, I can barely get through my day. All I think about is coming home."

"Javier, don't," she said, dropping her head.

"Don't what?" he asked. "Don't tell you that I love yo
Don't tell you I admire the way you get through pain and stil
keep going? Don't tell you that right now I want to kiss you so
bad—"

She looked up. "Javier, no."

He leaned into her and kissed her lips. It was a gentle, breezy
gesture that made her heart flutter with pleasure and fear. She
closed her eyes and relished the moment, afraid for it to end.
Afraid of it beginning.

When he pulled away, she was weak. Before she could
take another breath, he pressed his lips to hers again. This time,
the kiss was overwhelming. Ophelia leaned into him, intoxicated.

He pressed her back onto the bed. As he kissed her neck and
the tops of her breasts, her eyes were open, staring at the ceiling.
The white of the paint was blurred by a haze of tears.

Over and over in her head, she reminded herself that this
was Javier. That she didn't have to be afraid. That he was a
friend.

She closed her eyes again and let him take her away, just for
a moment, from all the fears, deaths, and betrayals that had
checkered her past.

She had been avoiding him for days, and Javier was uneasy.

The morning after, things seemed fine. Ophelia was some-
what shy, almost skittish, at first. Once she realized his affec-
tions were genuine, she began to relax and let him into her
space.

They made love again, many times more, over the course of
the following weeks. For Javier, it was a beautiful intimacy he
wanted to continue, and while she didn't care to speak on it, he
had thought her feelings mirrored his own. Many times, she had
initiated touch. Her behavior now astounded him.

When he returned in the evenings, Ophelia was locked in
her room. Dinner was on the stove, but she didn't eat with him.
She would remain closeted away for the rest of the night. He

't sleeping. He could hear her moving about. His
answered. So did notes he slid beneath her bed-

—ne out of the room until she heard him leave in
—mornings. When the disconnection became too painful for
him to bear, he took control of the matter himself.

He arrived home unexpected, two hours earlier than usual.
Ophelia was still cooking dinner. She never heard the car as it
pulled into the driveway.

"What's going on with you?" he said.

He was standing behind her in the kitchen. Her back grew
rigid.

"Have I done something? Have I said something wrong?"

Ophelia had been cutting potatoes. She leaned against
the counter without responding. He moved closer, until
she could feel the warmth of his breath across the back of her
neck.

"Ophelia?"

She kept cutting.

"Ophelia."

He grabbed her by the shoulders and turned her around to
face him.

"What's wrong with you?" he asked.

Her hands, ashen with potato stains, were shaking. She was
still holding the knife.

"Are you not going to answer me? Why have you been
avoiding me?"

She gazed back at him, her eyes lifeless and empty.

"I'm pregnant."

"What?"

"Don't worry," she said, her expression unchanged. "I won't
stick you with it. I'll get out of here as soon as I can find another
place to stay." She wiped her hands on her apron and dropped
the knife into the front pocket. "The baby probably won't live,
anyway." She turned back to face the counter.

Javier grabbed her by the shoulders and spun her around, his

breath heavy, his eyes dark. Ophelia was frightened by the
they flashed.

"What's the matter with you?" he said. "Nothing's going to
happen to the baby. You don't have to move away. Why are you
doing this to me? To us?"

"I'm doing you a favor."

He tightened his grip on her shoulders, pulling her in to him.

"Well, I don't need you doing me any favors." His eyes were
bloodshot. "You crazy *negrita*. I want the baby. I want you
both."

Ophelia shook her head as she tried to push him away. "This
thing with us . . . Javier, this thing with us . . . it isn't good. Nothing positive can come out of it."

"But don't you see?" he whispered. "Something positive already has."

"No," she said, breaking free. She tried to leave the kitchen,
but he pulled her back, his chest pressed against the curve of her
spine.

"I'm not going to let you go. You can't walk away from us before we even have a chance."

Ophelia's left cheek twitched with fear. Her eyes were stinging from the salt of her tears.

"How do I know that you're not going to leave me?"

"I won't," he said, the words rushing into her hair. "I've never
lied to you, Ophelita. That's not who I am."

The two stood in the middle of the kitchen, her breath coming in short heaves that made her feel faint.

"Say you'll stay with me." He held her tight against him. "Say
you won't take our baby and go away."

He touched her belly with soft, fluttering motions.

"I love you, Ophelita. I know you know this. This baby, our
baby, is a new beginning for both of us."

She turned to face him, searching his eyes for a hint of deceit.
"But what if–"

He covered her mouth with his own. When he pulled away,
she let herself sink into his embrace.

ill be strong and healthy," he said, his fingers

e of her neck. "And we will be here together to

at him.

ur her."

He cradled her head against his bosom.

She kept watching his face, waiting for a shadow of change.

In her heart she began to believe that she would never see one.

CHAPTER TWENTY-NINE

Just after one o'clock, Coolie crossed the busy intersection, glancing over her shoulder as she walked. The blare of a honking horn and screeching tires made her jump. She looked around, her shoulders hunched in fear.

"Get your bony ass out the way," yelled the angry man behind the wheel.

He leaned out of the window. His brow was furrowed, his hair a tight-matted Afro. His shirt was off, exposing a wide expanse of muscled dark brown skin. Aretha Franklin's "Baby, I Love You" was blaring from the speakers of his car.

Coolie stood frozen in the street, staring at him.

"Move, bitch!"

She ran across the street and onto the crowded sidewalk. She stood there a moment, checking around for any sign of Lay or his associates. The sound of her heartbeat was thunder. She was terrified by what she was daring to do. But Coolie wasn't sure which thing she feared most: being caught by Lay or the thought of not taking this new step in her life. Both things were threats to her very existence.

Loiterers and junkies leaned against the storefronts and buildings, hurling catcalls and begging for money. She recognized a few of them. Lay dealt to a lot of people who were doped out and hanging around on the streets. He never had to deal with them himself. His runners did that. But they all knew him. And they knew she was one of his girls. She moved to the edge of the sidewalk, trying to avoid being noticed.

Music poured from high up, out of one of the open windows in an apartment building. It was still Aretha Franklin's "Baby, I Love You." The song seemed to be blasting from everywhere.

Coolie rushed, her heels clacking hard on the concrete, trying to make her way through the throngs of people on their way back to work, back home to catch the stories, or on their way to the grocery store.

"Sssp. Sssp-ssp."

She hastened her pace, ignoring the call.

"Sssp. C'mon, baby," the gruff voice pressed.

A lanky boy dressed in dirty white pants and an oily T-shirt fell in step with her.

"Ain't no doubt about it, baby, I love you," he sang in time to the music filling the air.

Coolie kept her eyes straight ahead, her heels loud on the sidewalk.

"What's your name, baby?" he whispered, touching her on the arm. "You shole look good walking 'long here by yourself like this."

She leaned away from him, scooting around an old man with a cane, making his way in front of her.

"What's your name, girl?"

The boy touched her on the backside.

"Lee me 'lone," she said, waving his hand away with hers, still not slowing down.

The boy stepped in front of her.

"C'mon, slim, what's up?"

Coolie faked a move to her left, then went the other way.

"Oh, you tryna be slick with a brother, huh?" he said with a laugh. "Gimme some play, girl. Let me take you to eat. Show you a good time."

Coolie rolled her eyes at him and walked faster.

He kept up with her, relentless, down the block and around the corner. A little ways down the street was the Soul Serenade, a restaurant that used to be a favorite of Polo's. The greasy scent of hot fried chicken washed over them in a warm breeze.

"Umm-umh. That shole smell good," the boy said. "Don't you wanna step in there and get a plate of that hot chicken? Slap some greens on the side with some black-eyed peas and a big hunk of cornbread? That'll put a little meat on your bones."

He reached out to touch her side, but she swayed out of the way.

Coolie was trying to outwalk him. His pace was almost as fast as hers. She could hear the grease crackling with frying meat when they reached the door of the restaurant. She was very hungry, but she didn't dare stop for fear of seeing someone she knew. The spicy aroma of well-seasoned collard greens whisked up her nostrils, and her mouth begin to water.

"Smell that hot sauce in them greens?" the boy teased. "Ooo-weee." He twisted up his face as though he could taste them himself.

She tightened her jaw, trying to tune out the delicious smell of the food. It was almost impossible to ignore the enticing cloud that hung thick over the sidewalk in front of the door she passed.

"C'mon, girl," he said, pulling her by the arm toward the entrance.

"Quit it," she said, trying to get away.

He held on to her, grinning as though she was complicit in his game.

"Let me go." Her arm was pinched in his grip. "Quit 'fore I call the police."

"C'mon, slim," he said, still tugging, "ain't nobody tryna hurt you. I'm just tryna show you a good time."

"I don't want no good time," she replied, angry, jerking her arm free.

They were just past the door of the Soul Serenade, and Coolie was still tussling with the ragged boy. A group of men emerged from the restaurant.

They stood outside the door, lingering with small talk. One of them noticed Coolie and the boy.

"Look at that fool down there trying to pick up that girl," he said.

"I'on see why niggas be acting so dumb," said one of the others. "They know damn well they ain't gon' get no play picking up a woman that way on the street."

He pointed.

"Look at her. She damn near running from his ass."

They watched the scroungy boy bantering with the girl. One of the men, younger than the rest, squinted, trying to get a better glimpse of the two.

"Hey," he said. "I know that girl."

The other men burst into laughs and agitated talk. No one believed he knew her. He was far too countrified.

"Yeah right, bruh. You wish you knew her."

"Nuh-uh," the younger man insisted. "I done had her before."

"Nigga, please," they replied in unison.

"I did," he said. He called out to the boy chasing after Coolie. "Hey, man. Hey."

He kept calling until the boy turned around.

"Leave that 'lone, man," he told the boy, waving his hand.

The boy walked backward, facing them, still trying to keep up with Coolie. "What?"

"Don't chase after that, bruh," the man said with a grin. One of his front teeth was missing. "That ain't nothin' but a two-dollar hooker."

Coolie looked back over her shoulder at the man. She recognized him at once.

"You a hooker?" the boy following her asked.

"Leave me the fuck alone," she said and took off running. When she reached the end of the block, she turned the corner and leaned against the side of the building, catching her breath. After a few minutes, she looked around and began walking again.

"We shoulda known that girl was a prostitute," one of the

men said. "Ain't nobody walkin' 'round just giving pussy to your country ass."

The other men laughed again.

"Fuck y'all," Booty said. "I tell you what, though. That bitch can suck a mean dick."

The men sputtered and choked, laughing at his outlandish remarks. They clutched their bellies and shook their heads as they walked away and left him standing alone outside the restaurant door.

"Y'all wait up," he called and ran off after them to catch up.

Coolie walked on a few more blocks, her feet sore and tight in the fake leather heels. When she reached the door, she stood outside for a moment, afraid to go in. At the same time, she knew that if she didn't, her life would continue to spiral down into nothingness. She grabbed the doorknob and opened it, chin up, full of determination.

The thin, light brown woman behind the desk took one look at her and frowned, her sharp nose scrunched up in a knotty bunch of wrinkles.

"May I help you?" she said, sniffing.

"I wanna sign up for the typing school," Coolie said, ignoring the way the woman appraised her.

From the back, Coolie could hear the clackety, rhythmic sounds of keys striking paper. She listened, comforted by the freedom of what seemed to be hundreds of typewriters in a symphony of noise. She wanted to escape into that din and get so lost in it that no one would ever find her again.

"All the classes are full," the woman said.

Coolie's jaw tightened in surprise at this unexpected turn.

"I called here just a little while ago. Y'all told me it was a buncha spots open."

The woman stared at her, wondering what this junkified hooker really wanted.

"Look, honey," she said, "this class is for people who wanna try to go somewhere with their lives. We ain't got time for nobody tryna come in here and bullshit us around."

Coolie's face twitched with anger, and her vision misted over with a cloud of tears. She had never anticipated the possibility of rejection. It had never been a part of the equation at all.

"That's what I'm tryna do," she replied, biting her lip. "I'm tryna find me a way to get me some skills so I don't have to do this no more. I done sold my soul to the devil and I'm tired of it. This free class is the only chance I got."

The woman looked the girl up and down, studying the track marks on her arms, her emaciated frame. Her skin was a shroud that hung over her bones as though it resented them. The girl didn't look comfortable in her body. Like she was rotting from the outside in.

Coolie stood firm under her gaze, her expression fixed.

"How do I know that if we give you a seat in this class, you won't waste it and not show up?"

"I'll show up every day," Coolie said, meeting the woman's eyes. The two held each other's gaze. The woman softened.

"Look, gal," she said, "just 'cause this class is free don't mean it ain't worth something to somebody. If you doing this just to hide from your pimp for a few hours, ain't no way we want you coming around here."

"That's not what I'm doin'," replied Coolie. "I'm tryna make something better for myself. All I'm asking for is a chance to do it."

The woman grabbed Coolie's arm, examining the track marks.

"You still on heroin?" she asked.

"Yes ma'am. But I'm tryna get off. I know I should go to a center to get help for it, but I can't do that. If I do, my man gon' find out."

"Is he on drugs?"

"No ma'am. He just wanna make sure I stay this way. He told me he owned me. That I can't never get away from him." Coolie breathed in and out in movements so sharp that the woman could see the faint outline of her ribs against the thin veneer of one of the old chemises Lay had once bought her. "My man told me that if I ever try to leave him, he'll kill me hisself."

"Well, you're going to have to get help," said the woman. "You can't get off heroin by yourself. It's a physically addictive drug. Somebody gotta help you do it."

"I can't go to no center," Coolie replied. "I can't go. I'ma just have to fight it by myself. I ain't been taking as many hits. It hurts when I don't, but I know I got to get out this mess my life done turned into."

She stood in front of the woman, her lips pressed together. "I'ma do what I gotta do," she said. "I'ma do what I gotta do."

The sound of keys striking paper enveloped the silence between them. The woman's face was still stern, but she felt sorry for the girl. There was enough determination evident in Coolie to consider letting her in.

"Classes are every day from one o'clock to three. Can you handle that?"

"Oh my goodness, yes ma'am," Coolie said, clapping her hands over her mouth with excitement. "You mean I can get in?"

The woman nodded.

"I shole 'preciate this," Coolie said, taking the woman's hand in her own, then pulling away. "You don't know it, but you helping me save my life."

"Oh, I know it all right," the woman replied, her tone sharp. "You better not let me down by not showing up."

"Oh no, ma'am," the girl said, intoxicated by the clackety-clack-clack of the typewriter keys. "This time tomorrow I'ma be right in there making noise with everybody else."

She turned and walked out of the door, her step much livelier than when she walked in. Coolie was so elated, she didn't even bother to look around to see if anyone she knew saw her exit the place.

The woman watched her leaving, smiling to herself at the

vivid flicker of hope she saw shining so bright in the desperate
girl's eyes.

"Place your fingers in position," the instructor said. "A-S-D-F,
J-K-L-semicolon."

Coolie put her fingers down on the keys, excited at the touch
of the plastic against the pads of her fingers. She felt empowered and covert, proud of the fact that she was doing something
to better herself without anybody's help.

Just wait, she thought, wait till Lay see I can do something
'sides tricking and horse. He gon' be surprised. Everybody gon'
be surprised.

"A-S-D-F," the instructor said, standing alongside her. "Your
left hand should be on the letters A-S-D-F."

Coolie looked down at her fingers and shifted them over
one key.

"Good," the instructor said, smiling. "Now," he addressed the
class, "type these letters over and over again for the next twenty
minutes."

Coolie began pecking, her fingers pressing hard upon the
keys. She lifted each finger up high as she punched a letter.

"Don't raise your fingers like that," the instructor said, paying particular attention to the scraggly girl. He pressed her
hands closer to the keys. She was too embarrassed to look up at
him.

"Keep them low with your palms close to the edge of the
typewriter," he said. "That should make it much easier and will
increase your speed."

Coolie began again. Her eyes followed the dance of the keys
against the black and red ribbon and paper. She couldn't help
smiling to herself as she listened to the sounds of her typing getting lost in the bigger sounds of the group.

"A-S-D-F, J-K-L-semicolon," she repeated to herself as she
typed.

By the end of class that day, she could type the words "sad,"
"lad," and "flask." She left clutching her sheet of paper, staring at

the random letters typed on the page. Before she turned the corner headed toward the apartment, she folded it small and tight into a square and stuffed it down into her purse.

At the end of two weeks, she could type her name. Not fast, but she could find the letters without much difficulty. She spent most of her day picturing the locations of the keys in her head. Q above A above Z. T by Y. R by T. She had a hard time with the numbers. They were positioned high on the typewriter, and when she reached for them, she always lost her hand position.

When she was alone in the apartment, before and after class and the late nights spent tricking, she would turn on the little transistor radio next to her bed and sing along with the music while she practiced her hand positions. The school had let her borrow one of their old and tattered typing books, and she would lie in the bed with her hands on the pictures of the typewriter keys.

"A-S-D-F, J-K-L-semicolon," she recited, her eyes closed while her fingers were in place on the page.

The sweet croonings of David Ruffin and the Temptations telling her "Get Ready" pumped from the radio beside her. Coolie bobbed her head in time to the music, her eyes squeezed tight as she practiced her strokes.

"Fee-fi-fo-fum," she sang. "Look out, baby, 'cause here I come."

When the music and the mood most moved her, she would jump from the bed and dance around the room, her body flailing to the Motown magic.

One afternoon she was prancing around the room in one of her many wigs, dancing to the music. This wig was a favorite, purchased because it was just like one she'd seen on her idol, Diana Ross, although it was no longer as lustrous as it had once been. She was alone in the house, in her bedroom, taking a break from practicing her typing.

"Stop! In the name of love," she sang, moving her arms in

swimming motions like she had seen Diana do on television the day before.

"Before you break my heart."

She stopped cold, catching a glimpse of herself in the mirror.

Coolie faced her reflection. Her face was gaunt, and her once peachy skin looked as though it had aged years overnight. The circles under her eyes looked almost like blows she had taken in the face. Her hip bones were visible as they jutted through her dress. She unzipped the sheath and stepped out of it, studying her body. It was the first time she had paid attention to her appearance in months.

"Oh my God," she whispered, shocked at her own emaciation. "Look at me."

She scanned the outline of her ribs. Her stomach was so concave that her navel had all but disappeared, a slight dot against the narrow leathery measure of skin. Her thighs were troubled sticks with splotches and bruises splattered across the inner regions, war wounds of her profession.

She burst into tears, bringing her hands to her face to block the view of the sad image before her.

"I look like something dead," she cried.

She rushed over to her bed and collapsed on the mattress, sobbing into the covers. The typing book lay open on the bed. The feel of it against her elbow reminded her of her focus.

"I gotta get outta this," she said, sitting up. She wiped her face with the back of her hand.

"I can't let him keep me down like this. I can't let him do it."

She reached for the book, her fingers positioned back in place on the page.

"A-S-D-F," she said, choking back a sob. "J-K-L-semicolon."

Beside her, the transistor piped out its rhythmic beats.

Over her chanting, the voice of Smokey Robinson sang encouraging words: "If you got the notion, I second that emotion."

Coolie left the apartment at dusk to have time to turn enough tricks and still get a decent amount of rest before going to typing school. She worked deep into the night, but not until dawn, the way she had done before. She couldn't afford to cut back on hooking; all she could do was make a small adjustment in her hours. She needed the money to give Lay so he wouldn't suspect anything unusual about her behavior. He didn't challenge the shift in her schedule as long as the money remained consistent.

She kept taking heroin in order to deal with it all. One hit before class, just enough to give her a high that would get her through. Coolie had mastered the art of firm concentration. Through her heroin haze, she never took her eyes off the prize of flight. She took another hit at night to help her deal with Lay.

Those two hits were the only ones. She was trying to quit. It was hard. Much harder than she had realized.

Coolie was high in the wake of her first typing test. She typed ten words per minute with only twelve errors. It was worthy of celebration.

She held her graded test clasped in her hand as she raced up to the apartment.

Lay was slouched on the sofa watching television when she rushed in.

"Oh." She hadn't expected him to be there.

"Oh?" he said, his eyebrows raised.

"I mean, hey. How long you been home?"

"Since when you start questioning me?"

She clutched the paper tight in her hand.

"I just asked," she said. "I'ma go take a shower."

She made a move toward her bedroom.

As she passed Lay, he reached out and grabbed her wrist. The one attached to the hand that held the typing test.

"What's wrong with you?" he asked, watching her face.

"Nothing." The tone of her voice was high, unnatural.

"Why you acting all weird? You stoned?"

"A little," she said.

"Oh."

He snatched the paper from her hand. "What's this?"

"What?"

"This, fool," he said, waving the paper. "You don't know what you holding in your own hand?"

He opened the paper. He looked up at her, his eyes dark and angry. "What the hell is this?"

"I'on know." She shrugged. "I picked it up off the street. I was tryna read it."

He stared at her, searching her face. Coolie's left cheek twitched. He focused on the cheek, waiting for it to twitch again. He looked down at the paper.

"What the hell you want with somebody's school test? You know your dumb ass can't read worth a shit."

Coolie was convinced Lay could hear the aggravated thumping of her heart. She knew he wouldn't hesitate to kill her.

She reached one of her arms above her head, stretched, and yawned.

"I'on know. I couldn't make out what it said, anyway." She yawned again. "I'm so tired. I forgot I even had it in my hand. You want it?"

"You stupid," he said with a laugh as he released her hand. "Trying to read somebody's test, like you got some sense."

He looked at the paper again.

"The least you could do is pick somebody smart. Look at all the mistakes this got on it."

Lay balled up the paper and threw it on the floor.

"I'm finna take my shower," she said. She hurried off down the hall.

"Coolie."

"Huh?"

"Where my money for the day?"

He had returned his attention to the television. He didn't look up as he held his hand outstretched in her direction.

Coolie walked toward him. She opened her purse, her hands trembling as she reached inside. She pulled out four twenty-dollar bills and placed them in his palm.

Lay examined the contents. He counted it, then cut his eyes at her.

"I ain't even gonna say nuthin'."

"It wasn't that many people buying today."

He crumpled the bills and threw them on the coffee table.

"You coulda kept this shit. You better make it up tonight, or you and me gon' have to have us a 'Come to Jesus' meeting."

"Okay," she said, and hurried off before he had the chance to ask her anything more.

When she got to her room, she shut the door and sat down on the bed. Her legs were shaking.

"ThankyouLordthankyouLordthankyou."

The tests at school identified students by number and not by name. Her number had been in the top right corner of the paper. The number seven meant nothing to Lay.

For Coolie, lucky seven had just saved her life.

When the typing class ended three months later, Coolie was typing thirty-five words a minute with no errors.

"I guess you did it," said Mattie, the woman who had first admitted her to the class.

"I did," Coolie said with a grin.

Mattie nodded, appraising the girl.

"You still ain't off that stuff yet, is you?"

"No ma'am. But I'm trying. I passed this class. I wasn't sure I could do it, but I know how to type now. Doing this helped me get a little confidence back."

"I see."

"All I needed was something to help me feel like I was living again," said Coolie. "Right now, Miss Mattie, I swear, I feel like I can do 'most anything. Like kick them drugs and get away from my man."

"I know you can," said Mattie. "You made it this far. I'ma tell you, when you walked in here the first time, I ain't think it was no way you could do it."

She put her arm around Coolie. "But you proved me wrong. Shole did."

"Well, at least you gave me a chance," Coolie said. "Ain't nobody done that for me in a while. I 'preciate it."

Coolie went to hug the thin woman, awkward at first. Mattie patted her on the back.

"I'm proud of you. You can do anything you want with your life. Don't you forget it. Don't let no pimp or nobody else tell you you can't."

Coolie smiled and hugged Mattie tight.

She walked down the street, the same street the boy had followed her down just months before. Coolie felt empowered as she passed the Soul Serenade, the fragrant aroma of fresh-baked sweet potato pies dominating the air. From an upstairs apartment, the sounds of Aretha came spilling over her in a wave.

Coolie smiled, humming along to the music. She crossed off the first item on her mental checklist. Typing. Next up was number two, the heroin. After that was number three.

Freedom.

The last stop after that would be finding her man. The real one. Polo.

She began to sing aloud, her gait animated and strong.

"You make me feel like a natural woman. Woman."

CHAPTER THIRTY

Polo lay sluggish in the dark and the underbrush, the cold feel of the damp grass and the burning sensation inside his boots preventing him from succumbing to sleep.

Insects gnawed away at his skin, but he was so tired that he didn't even fight them back. Invisible, insidious mites had already eaten away at his ankles, leaving a raging rash that rushed down the tops of his feet in a fury toward his toes. The itching was so unbearable that he scratched and scratched until the rash bubbled up in little pustules that burst at the slightest friction. They caused his socks to stick to his feet inside the boots.

As a boy, Polo had been meticulous, insecure, and overcompensating, always conscious of his appearance. He had grown into just such a man. But this was war, so he could not afford to concentrate on how pitiful his feet looked, with the lint from the socks clinging in clotted patches to the oozing pustules. He took his boots off every chance he got to scratch his feet and pick away the lint, but such chances were few. He had begun wearing the ankle socks he brought with him overseas, and though they weren't regulation, they were less painful than the big thick socks that almost pulled the skin off his feet when he tried to remove them.

It was rainy and dank in the brush. The sight of Polo's ravaged feet tormented him. As he crawled across the terrain with the rest of the men, he knew he should be concerned with just trying to stay alive. But little things, like how his feet looked and what Coolie, Ophelia, Lay, or his mama would think if they saw his legs, kept him awake at night. While everyone else worried about survival, Polo became obsessed with his feet. Those thoughts led him to thoughts of home.

A few feet away from him, one of the soldiers had a radio on. The music played low, but Polo was close enough to hear Jimi Hendrix's sad voice singing "Hey Joe." The song made his head hurt. He listened in the darkness, his eyes and mind wide with pain.

"Hey Joe, where you goin' with that gun in your hand?" the song wailed.

The words washed over him.

"Goin' out to shoot my old lady. You know I caught her messin' 'round with another man," Jimi whined, his guitar echoing his misery.

As Polo lay there, images of Coolie loomed heavy. Not the Coolie he fled. Not the one he had seen kneeling between the legs of the man, her head bobbing. That was not the Coolie he thought of at all. He had long since blocked that memory.

The Coolie he remembered was the gentle, considerate, feisty girl he'd loved in Downtown. The one whose face was flushed from heat and terror the night they tried to put out the fire baby Hamlet died in. The one who almost gagged on the first joint she ever smoked that night in the barn. The one who said she would love him no matter what and go anywhere with him. The one who became angry and frightened at the thought of him leaving her behind to go anywhere, even to the store.

He wondered if she was scared now. In the shadows of his selective memory, he imagined that his Coolie was lost without him. That she was scared and desperate somewhere back in that big city. And that he had failed her. He had broken his word—he promised to never leave her, but that was what he had done.

As he lay curled up in the brush, his body tired, his feet on fire, guilt pressed down upon him with unbearable ferocity. Tears welled up in his eyes as he forced himself to think of the Coolie he abandoned. The one in sweaters, always cold, full of attitude and disdain. Trying to be something she was not. Being consumed by the elements around her.

With great effort, he commanded himself to remember the image of her head between the man's legs. He saw himself raping her, then rushing out of the apartment with his suitcases, leaving her to the fate of those consuming elements, knowing full well she was not equipped to contend with them.

He felt ashamed for letting his pride control him. For not taking her out of that apartment with him, away from Lay, the drugs, the stray men and the mean streets. He felt even worse for not going back to get her when he had the chance.

He had written her a letter once, after he fled Detroit and was shipped off. In it, he told her everything. How he felt. How much he loved her. How hurt he was. How sorry he was for treating her the way he did. But every time he tried to mail it, something stopped him. He would think about her between the legs of the man, or he would imagine she had done similar things with his brother, and he would become angry. Later, he was always sorry he hadn't mailed the letter. It was in his bag back at the camp. More than anything, Polo wished right now Coolie had that letter in her hands.

In the dark and dampness of the brush, Polo began to cry and pray. He prayed for forgiveness of his sins. For selling drugs, for leaving Coolie, for taking her to Detroit in the first place.

He prayed for forgiveness of the greatest sin of all, one called hubris. Ophelia had told him about it. She said it was excessive pride and arrogance. She reminded him that pride was one of the seven deadly sins, and that he had let his keep him from the woman he loved.

In the darkness, he prayed and prayed and prayed. His heart pounded with every word he sent forth to the heavens. As the seconds turned into minutes, and the minutes passed into the night, he began to feel the pressure lift, as though forgiveness was enfolding him. The pounding in his heart lessened, and the image of Coolie became strong and bright. Full of hope. Full of redemption.

A few hours before dawn, his mood had lifted. He felt renewed and at peace.

As he drifted to sleep, happiness and horror passed each other, like night and day watchmen changing shifts. Polo heard the rustling in the brush and turned his head in the direction of the sound. He felt something round roll up against him. His eyes focused on the grenade. With split-second recognition, the joy in his heart was replaced by a sinking sorrow as he realized that it was the last thing he would ever see. The muscles in his face quivered. Three seconds later, the grenade blew him and the six men around him into oblivion.

His body exploded into a mosaic of tattered flesh. His arms, fingers, shredded torso, and assorted organs took flight and seeded the area in a fantastic display that would make him forever a part of the Vietnamese landscape.

One of his legs, with the boot still attached, landed in an enormous ant bed some eight hundred yards away. By midmorning, the ants had crawled inside the shoe and devoured most of the flesh.

All that remained deep within the boot was the white bone jutting from the rash-ridden ankle.

Intact was the sticky ankle sock, still matted to Polo's pustular foot.

CHAPTER THIRTY-ONE

Evan was curled around Walter Martin in a deep slumber. His head rested against the older man's back. His snoring was a mild rumble, a noise that reverberated against Walter's soft skin. Evan dreamed he was having dinner with the women who raised him, his mother and her three sisters. He began to salivate as he tasted the cornbread and smothered chicken. Drool spilled from the corner of his mouth onto Walter's back.

In the burgeoning light of dawn, Walter was wide awake. Their arms were entwined. He hugged Evan closer to his body.

He thought of the night before, when Evan worked with him on his acting and confidence techniques. Walter shared with him his desire to begin a relationship with his daughter. He was careful not to divulge anything about Grace or their history.

In the months that had passed, he had become outgoing, even aggressive. Evan helped him get a small role in a play off-campus. Walter felt a freedom he had never known was possible.

Homosexuality opened for him yet another world. From the first moment Evan touched him, Walter was ignited by a desire stronger than anything he had ever experienced. In all of his conquests of women in Tennessee, even in his most passionate moments with Sukie, he knew of nothing, save his innocent beginnings with Grace, that was comparable to what he felt with Evan.

He wasn't sure if it was Evan or the novelty of sex with another man that brought about these feelings. What he did know was that he could unleash himself for the first time in his life to explore and ask and do as he chose. He could touch Evan any way he desired, and Evan responded. When Evan pounded against him, Walter was sometimes so overwhelmed by the intensity of feeling that he cried.

He segued into this new lifestyle with relative ease. Evan's friends knew that he had begun a relationship with the older man. They welcomed Walter into their clique, exposing him to the mind-widening powers of marijuana, acid, Quaaludes, and exotic opium teas. Walter didn't indulge very often. He preferred to keep his senses unimpaired. He did enjoy wine. It helped him relax and kept him uninhibited.

Walter knew that once he established a relationship with Ophelia, he couldn't let her know about his love for men. It would be too much for her, something too different from what she was accustomed to from him. He wondered what she would think of it. He wondered what his father would think. Benny, he was sure, wouldn't be surprised. If Benny had been alive, Walter would have been too ashamed to even indulge in the thought or appreciate the experience.

But Benny wasn't alive, and Walter wasn't ashamed to indulge in the high of sex. Coupling with Evan seemed taboo. It gave Walter an addictive rush. They kissed in the open at the Wildflower. The café and the liberal college setting provided the ideal environment for Walter's renaissance.

Evan didn't know it, but Walter was so intoxicated by the carnal euphoria of gay sex that he began to pick up other boys from the Wildflower. He did some of them in the bathroom. One of them, a John Lennon look-alike, gave him the most explosive blow job he'd ever had.

As he lay in the bed now, watching the sunlight seep along the edge of the windowpane and grow in intensity, he remembered the zeal of his and Evan's lovemaking the night before. He stirred, tightening his grip on the boy's arms.

Behind him, he felt Evan moving. Along his lower back, Walter could feel the familiar jerky motions of the boy's penis as it came to life. Evan's fingers made soft butterfly motions against the older man's belly.

In the growing dawn, Walter began to smile in anticipation as Evan, like the sun, began his morning ascent.

CHAPTER THIRTY-TWO

Coolie looked over her shoulder as she stood outside the apartment building. Seeing no one, she stuffed part of the money in her bra. She reached beneath her skirt and put some of it in the seat of her underwear. The rest she shoved into her purse.

An old man across the street watched her from his apartment window, sucking his tongue in pity at the degenerate whore.

She opened the door to the building and rode the elevator upstairs to the apartment. When she exited the elevator and rounded the corner, Lay's men were standing in the hallway. She could hear the sounds of loud music and people talking as she neared the door. She checked her bosom again to make sure the money was not sticking out of the top of her bra, then she smoothed her blouse down in front so the outline of the bills could not be seen. Her ribs were more visible than anything else. She missed the plump fullness of good health that Polo used to love about her. She knew that, given a little time, she was going to get it back.

Coolie turned the doorknob. The erratic, deafening squeals of Jimi Hendrix's guitar stylings poured out, filling the hallway. "Purple Haze" was blaring from the stereo inside the apartment. Coolie's ears began to hurt the moment she walked in the room.

The thugs in the hall were used to her coming and going. They didn't acknowledge her entry. No one stopped talking or even turned around when she walked in. It was difficult to hear over the music. People were sitting on the sofas, snorting lines of cocaine and licking LSD from paper. Some of them were shooting heroin. The pungent smell of marijuana was thick in the air.

Lay sat in the midst of them, talking loud, drinking brandy, wearing a brown leather vest trimmed in fringe and a pair of brown leather bell-bottoms. He didn't notice Coolie at all.

She slipped past them into her bedroom. She pushed the door closed, rushed over to the dresser, then reached down between her legs and removed the money from her underwear. Coolie opened the bottom drawer and pulled out a black stocking stuffed full of money. She shoved the new money in, then slid the stocking into a bunch of other stockings she kept wadded together. She closed the drawer.

Coolie went over to the bed, placed her purse on top, knelt down, and slid her fingers between the mattress and box spring.

"What the fuck do you think you're doing?"

Lay's voice was even.

Coolie's fingers hadn't touched the nylon stocking pressed under the mattress. She turned around, her face twisted in mock frustration, and saw him standing inches behind her.

"Looking for my stash," she stammered. "Have you seen it?"

She stood up, rubbing her arm as if she were jonesing.

He studied her, his expression fixed. "How the fuck do I know where it is? Why don't you just come out front and get high with everybody else?"

She sat down on the edge of the bed.

"Because I'm tired, Lay. I been out there tricking all day. I just wanna cool out and relax. I don't feel like being 'round no whole buncha people."

He snatched the purse up from the bed.

"Since you been tricking all day, bitch, where's my money?"

He opened the purse, reached in, and pulled out several folded bills. He looked down at them, then shook the bills in front of her face.

"Is this all you have after working all day?"

He counted the money.

"Twenty, forty, sixty, seventy-five dollars? This is all you made today?"

Coolie's arms were crossed in front of her. She looked down at the floor.

When she didn't respond, he reached over and slapped her hard on the face. The blow was so forceful it spun her head to the side and made her jaw throb and begin to swell.

"Bitch. This doesn't even take care of your habit. You got to come better than this. Something's gotta give."

He flung the purse to the floor.

"You better get your ass out there and do double duty. I'm getting sick of this shit."

A beautiful young girl with a rainbow Afro, a Stars-and-Stripes halter, and skintight hip-hugger jeans stuck her head in the doorway.

"Lay, baby," she said, "you coming?"

"Yeah," he replied, not even turning to look at her. He was still staring at Coolie. His eyes narrowed and his voice was steel when he spoke.

"I wanna see some more money, and I wanna see it quick. I don't care who you suck, fuck, or buck to get it. But you better get it. Or you got to go."

"C'mon, Lay," said the girl with the Afro.

"Yeah. I'm coming."

He turned and walked away. When he got to the doorway, he turned toward Coolie again.

"Gimme them squares I saw in your purse."

Coolie bent down, her jaw still throbbing, and picked up the purse. She pulled out the cigarettes and walked them over to him.

He took one out and waited for her to light it. When she did, he took a long drag and blew the smoke in her face. The girl with the Afro laughed. He turned to her.

"Don't laugh at my bitch," he said. "This is gon' be your ass in a coupla weeks."

The girl laughed again and pulled him back into the living room.

Coolie closed the door when they left, rushed over to the bed, and pulled the nylon stocking out from under the mattress. The pain in her jaw was excruciating. She snatched the money from her bra, put it in the stocking, and put the stocking back.

She opened her purse, rooted around in the bottom, and found a joint. She lit it, took a few pulls, and put the rest in an ashtray on the night table. Then she leaned back on the bed, closed her eyes, and took several deep breaths. Her craving for heroin was fierce, but she resisted. She continued to get the drug from Lay so that he wouldn't be suspicious, but she had begun the harrowing process of weaning herself away. Each time he gave her a ration, she flushed it down the toilet. It was the hardest thing she'd ever done in her life. It hurt more than the day she lost Polo.

She once found herself in tears as she clung to the edge of the toilet, trying to scoop the substance out before it whooshed away into the bowels of the city.

She spent many a night cold and racked with spasms, praying for sleep. She kept her radio on and rocked herself into a slumber listening to Gladys Knight, Otis Redding, and Wilson Pickett. Way past the midnight hour.

Sometimes she opted for silence, wanting nothing but thoughts to take her down.

Sometimes Coolie reached beneath her bed and pulled out the little typewriter she bought at the pawnshop for twenty-five dollars. She would turn up the radio and practice typing articles from *Jet* magazine. She had worked hard to earn her skill. She wasn't about to do anything to let it get away.

All these distractions helped her make it through the nights without drugs. Getting through the day was her greatest challenge. What was hardest for Coolie was doing the johns without horse, but she had a goal that kept her focused. With the money from tricking, her possibilities began to broaden. She relied on less addictive drugs like marijuana to get her through. Coolie began to reinvent herself one minute at a time.

It took awhile after Lay hit her for the pain in her jaw to subside. She lay in the darkness, staring up at the ceiling. After a few minutes, she seemed to be asleep.

She wasn't.

Coolie was plotting. Thinking.

Planning her escape.

CHAPTER THIRTY-THREE

Ophelia was lying on the sofa reading Dostoyevsky's *Crime and Punishment*. She was lost in the book, engrossed in the character's torment. She made notes in the margins and turned down the corners of pages for further discussion with Javier.

It was a sunny afternoon. She had been home from school since twelve, eaten lunch, and taken a brief nap. It didn't take much to tire her, and her mornings were becoming more taxing each day. Her classes were spread all over campus, and the long walks in between were exhausting. Her belly was prominent beneath her clothes.

The house was cozy, and the fragrance of blooming flowers invaded the room through the open windows. Summer was in full thrust, but a cool breeze wafted in, refreshing her. She rubbed her stomach and smiled. The baby was due in September.

She no longer heard the cries on the wind. They'd ceased months earlier, she realized one day. Somewhere around the time of her parents' death.

Ophelia reached down and grabbed the glass of lemonade on the floor beside the sofa. Just as she brought it to her lips, she heard the sound of a car door slamming. Before she had a chance to get excited at its being Javier, another door slammed. She sat up and tried to look through the window. From where she was sitting, the view of the driveway and the curb in front of the house were blocked.

She pushed herself off the couch with great effort and made her way to the window. She pulled the curtains back and peered out. Two uniformed army officers, one white, one black, were moving away from the very plain white car parked along the curb and making their way up the walk. The black one carried a small bundle. Ophelia's chest felt tight.

The men were at the door, about to ring the bell. They saw her peering at them and were startled, as if they'd been caught.

When Javier arrived a few hours later, Ophelia was no longer in tears.

He walked into the house, excited to see the woman he had just married on the quiet in a small chapel around the corner. In his right hand was a bunch of posies picked from beside the door.

He found her sitting on the floor, her back against the sofa, head down, rocking back and forth. Javier dropped the nosegay and ran to her.

"Honey, what's wrong?" he asked. He fell to his knees and put his arms around her. "Are you okay? Is it something with the baby?"

Ophelia kept rocking.

"Ophelita. Are you okay? Please tell me."

Javier lifted her head. Her face was tear-streaked, but her eyes were dry. She seemed dazed. He could feel slight tremors go through her body.

"Is it the baby?" he said. "Do you need to go to the hospital?"

When she didn't answer, he tried to open her arms to check for blood. Ophelia balled her body up tight and began to rock with urgency. He checked her pulse and felt her forehead. She wasn't sweating or faint.

He sat on the floor beside her and held her close to him. Her rocking was so pronounced, it was stronger than his grip around her. He found himself rocking along with her. He could feel her trembling as though it originated from his own body.

Javier had learned much about Ophelia during the time they'd been together. He knew there were sides of her that would take him awhile to reach, but he was patient. He had seen her upset before, and he found that the best way to calm her was to hold her, whisper, and assure her of his love.

He moved close to her ear.

"Sweetheart, I'm here. Nothing can hurt you. Tell me what's wrong. I love you and I want to help."

She kept rocking.

"It's going to be okay," he said. "I'm right here. Whatever happened, it's going to be okay."

The rocking began to slow.

"Should I call a doctor?" he whispered. "Is there a problem with the baby?"

Javier stroked her hair as they rocked in sync.

Ophelia's shaking began to subside, her limbs relaxed, and she unfolded her body. She wrapped her arms around her husband and nestled her head against his chest. He kissed the top of her hair.

"It's okay, baby. We can fix whatever it is. Is your body hurting?"

She shook her head.

"Do you think the baby's okay?" His voice was very soft.

She nodded.

He kissed her hair again and pulled her tight against his body. He held her that way for a while, letting the silence settle around them like a comforting blanket.

"What happened today, Ophelita?" he asked.

She was resting against his chest. She looked up at him, her eyes clear and sad.

"Polo is dead."

"I see," Javier said. He was careful not to say anything further that might aggravate her emotions. There would always be time for questions later.

CHAPTER THIRTY-FOUR

When Coolie had left earlier to work the streets, Lay was in front of the television. She knew his ritual by rote. Every morning, he was up watching the *Today* show. He would sit with his breakfast—eggs, bacon and toast—sometimes talking to the television. He drank black coffee, then went to the gym and sparred a few rounds with the local boxer. That was his favorite part of the morning. The fight.

He knew the boxer wouldn't hurt him. Lay's reputation preceded him. In turn, he had the chance to land several powerful blows. His gunmen always accompanied him to the gym, where they were required to watch.

The boxer was young. He had just turned twenty-one. He asked his trainer to find a way to get him out of the morning warmups with Lay, but there was nothing that his trainer could do. He knew his life would be on the line if he interfered.

"Just block your face," his trainer said. "Lay Boten puts a lot of money into this gym."

Then the trainer walked away, removing himself from conflict and further scrutiny.

No one was in the apartment when Coolie returned. She checked the hallway. It was empty. It was the only time of the day they didn't hover around.

Coolie called Lay's name when she walked into the apartment, a precaution just in case he was inside. She always prepared herself for the unpredictable. She knew it was better to expect him to be there than to rely on him not to be.

She gave the place a thorough check. He was not in the kitchen or any of the bathrooms. She went to his bedroom door and knocked several times. She figured if he was inside, she would say she needed another fix. She could deal with the ensuing ass-whipping that he would give her for begging for more dope.

It was a risk she was willing to take.

She pressed her ear to the door. She heard nothing inside. She relaxed. Lay wasn't home.

Coolie ran into her bedroom. She snatched the fat stocking from the drawer, then went over to the bed and pulled out the one from under the mattress. All of the money was still there.

She didn't bother to count it, pack any of her clothes, or take anything else from the room. All she had was the money and her purse. In the purse, she kept a switchblade. She never used it. She wasn't sure she knew how.

Coolie didn't want to waste time. Lay would be at the gym for an hour or so, if he'd gone there at all. She was almost at the front door when she remembered her typewriter. She ran back to the room and pulled it from under the bed.

She didn't look back as she left the apartment, headed down the stairs, and dashed out of the building. Her mouth was fixed in a grim smile as she walked down the boulevard, not looking to the left or the right.

From across the street, the old man watched her, checking out her harried gait and the black case in her hand. He sucked his tongue and shook his head. He knew the degenerate whore was trying to break away.

Coolie was on a bus back to Downtown by nightfall. She dozed in fits, battling nightmares of Lay catching up with her and beating her to death. She would awaken with a start, ill at ease, until she realized he didn't know where she was. Coolie was smart enough to know that, given time, Lay just might catch up with her.

It would take him a couple of days to notice she was missing. He would scour the city. He didn't think she was bold enough to leave Detroit, and he didn't know she had weaned herself off the heroin. Since she left everything but the money, that would throw him off for an even longer period of time.

When no reports of bodies came up, or none of his gunmen gave him word that she'd been found drunk and drugged out in some alley, that's when Lay would understand. That's when he would begin a serious hunt.

For now, she had the advantage. The runner's edge. She knew she'd better use it well.

Coolie planned to. She figured Polo had gone back to Downtown when he left her, and she was determined to find him. She knew that somewhere in his heart, he must still have love for her. She knew she still loved him. Enough to risk her life to get him back.

All she wanted was a chance to apologize.

She knew Downtown would be the best place to start.

CHAPTER THIRTY-FIVE

Walter sat in his car, parked in the shadow of the trees.

It had been some time since he had seen his daughter. He watched her during the different stages of her pregnancy, proud that he soon would be a grandfather. Walter knew it was best to wait until Ophelia delivered. There was no way he could approach her and say all the things on his mind. He would wait. He just wanted to see her. With everything else going on in his life, he needed to see her and know she was well.

Within moments he saw her step out onto the porch to gather the mail. She wore a yellow sundress, her belly forming a tent in front.

Ophelia turned in his direction, placing her left hand over her eyes to shield the brightness of the noonday sun. Walter slouched low in the car. Ophelia leaned forward, straining to see. Then she went back into the house with the mail.

Walter waited a sufficient amount of time before he started the car. He was relieved. Ophelia's man seemed to be taking good care of her.

He rode past the house, glancing its way as he passed. He could see the back of Ophelia's head just inside the window. His smile was bittersweet as he drove away.

• • •

His relationship with Evan had grown into an intense bond. For the first time, Walter had someone who nurtured and encouraged him, a partner with whom he could share his feelings aloud. He and Evan were in love.

As their relationship deepened, Walter felt the need to know more about himself and his attraction for Evan. His father's words of contempt had come to fruition. He was a faggot, it was something he couldn't deny.

That Benny had seemed so confident about his destiny nagged at him. Walter wondered if there was something else at work. Something beyond the desires of the flesh.

More like something that lived in the blood.

Walter sat on the sofa, searching through a stack of documents. As he sifted through a small cedar box of mementos, he came across a small picture of his mother. Standing beside her was his father. Benny's expression was stern.

The picture angered Walter. He would never forget the beating his father delivered, nor the legacy of a whole lifetime of shame.

Walter didn't want to live with the rage anymore. His life had entered so many positive phases. He wanted to face all his demons and put them to bed.

He hunted through the pictures and papers until he found the address. His mother had given it to him when he was fifteen. She said it was important to know where his people were, even if he had no desire to see them.

He packed a bag, taking enough clothes to last a few days. He explained things to Evan. Walter decided it was time for some answers.

He was going to take a trip.

The big black woman he remembered from his father's funeral was now old and addled. She didn't have much to say about Benny, other than the fact that he was "mighty mean."

Walter's uncle was now taking care of his mother. Hailey, at sixty-five, was still vibrant and animated. He had a rich, resonant, musical laugh.

He gave Walter all the information he needed.

Hailey embraced Walter in a warm hug at the door.

"I knew one day you'd turn up again," he said. "When I saw you at the funeral, you were just the cutest little thing. I know your daddy must have made your life hell, being as cute as you were. Bet you was glad when he died, wasn't you? What was that, damn near thirty-seven years ago?"

Walter didn't know how to respond. He'd never been given permission to admit how he felt about the death of his father.

Hailey led him into the house and sat him down at the kitchen table.

"Mama's in the back. I'll take you to see her in a minute. I ain't gon' lie to you and tell you she'll be happy to see you. She don't recognize shit these days but breakfast, dinner, and suppertime. She shole know when that is. Let one of her meals be late. She'll slap the piles down on you."

Hailey laughed. Walter smiled, not quite sure of what the piles were to begin with.

Hailey stood at the stove. He was stirring the contents of a pot. The aroma filled the room and toyed with Walter's nose and stomach.

Hailey wore a flowery dress with short sleeves and had an apron tied around his waist. His feet were stuck in a pair of pink house slippers. A pair of nylons covered the square muscles of his calves.

"So go on," Hailey said. "I know you're here to ask me stuff."

"Yeah, I am."

"Of course you are. This has been brewing for years."

Walter rubbed his hands against his legs. "I wanna know if you always dressed like this," he said.

"Shole did. From when I was a little boy. I knew what I was right away. It was your daddy who had trouble accepting things."

"What do you mean?" Walter asked.

"Me and Benny was raised 'round a whole lotta women.

From the very beginning, wasn't no menfolks around for us to even speak of. Just a whole buncha aunts and sisters and cousins and shit."

A cigarette was burning in an ashtray on the counter. Hailey picked it up and took a drag from it, then put it back in the ashtray.

"Now me," he said, "I always liked women better. They just got a better sense of understanding and compassion than men do. Got more heart." He shook his head. "Men can be so cold. I never explored my feminine side at first. I just knew I felt close to women. It was your daddy who helped me explore it. It was almost by accident for me."

"What did my father do?" Walter said.

"Mama used to make us bathe together when we was boys." Hailey picked up the cigarette again and took a pull. He blew it out into the air. "Your daddy was a li'l bit older than me. He used to play with me in the tub funny, you know what I mean?"

He squinted as he looked at Walter.

Walter nodded.

"Well, it felt funny the first time he did it. Then it got to feeling good, and he would do it all the time. 'Bout the third or fourth time, he started beating me up real bad afterwards. He told me that if I said something to anybody, he'd kill me. Benny was mean like that. He was the one who liked doing it so much, but he didn't want nobody to know that it was him."

"Then why are you like this?" Walter asked.

"Because, chile. I got to where all I knew was men. Your daddy did that to me until the day he left home." He puffed the cigarette. "He left when he was around sixteen. Got to where he was raping me, he did it so much. Made my life hell. Wasn't no pleasure in it at all for me." Hailey turned back to the stove and stirred the contents of the pot. "I was all fucked up in the head. I started dressing like this before he left, when I was about twelve or so. Couldn't nobody stop me. All the beatings in the world from Benny couldn't keep me from being what I am. Benny just couldn't face what he was, too."

"Benny liked boys?"

Hailey laughed as he slapped the counter.

"Obviously, honey. I may not look like it no mo', but I shole am a boy. A man. I got proof. More proof than your daddy had, with that one nut of his."

Walter stood.

"My daddy had one nut?"

Hailey took another drag of the cigarette, blowing the smoke into the air.

"Of course. Everybody knew that. That was his nickname his whole life. Nut. He couldn't stand it, but that's all he heard at every turn. Beat the shit outta me for saying it. Evil mother-fucker. All of us was surprised to find out he had a wife and kids. How anybody could stand to live with him, let alone a woman, is beyond my understanding."

Hailey wiped his brow.

"Whew. Shole is hot in here. You drink moonshine? I got a big ol' jug out here in the back. C'mon."

When Walter returned, Evan was studying.

Walter came up behind him, planting a soft kiss upon the boy's neck.

"What's that for?"

"For helping to free me," Walter said. "If it wasn't for you and me, there's a whole lot I wouldn't know about myself."

Evan looked up at him.

"You all right, chief?" he asked. "That sounded kind of heavy."

"Not really," Walter said with a smile. "Matter of fact, right now it feels pretty light."

CHAPTER THIRTY-SIX

"Well, just look at you, Miss Coolie," Caesar Bucksport said, his long yellow teeth bared in a grin. "We thought you had long cleared outta these parts."

He took a swig of his cold peach Nehi and pulled out a chair.

"Have a sit-down, girl. It's so good to see you. Look like you done dropped a few pounds."

Coolie slid into the chair. He took a seat across from her, the striped shirt tight across his potbelly.

"So what brings you back down here? I thought you hit the road with Polo and wasn't never coming back."

Coolie looked around the Lucky Star Liquor Joint, studying the walls, the tables, and the hapless patrons sitting at the bar, drinking themselves blind in the middle of the day.

"Hey, girl." Caesar poked her in the arm, vying for her attention. Coolie focused on him, her eyes beginning with the greasy processed pompadour.

"So what brings you back here?" he repeated. "You come to see your folks? Did Polo come witcha? You know his mama and daddy died in a fire. Miss Sukie dead, too. Got burnt up in her house. House fried so bad they couldn't even find her body in it. Nuthin' but ashes and a big ol' crater. That house must have a curse on it, 'cause this the second time it done happened. Ain't no accident for a house to burn up every time you build it. The earth just keep on swallin' it up. Look like somebody tryna tell them folks something. Shole hope dey's listenin'. Hope they ain't crazy 'nuf to try to build it again."

Caesar didn't even pause for a breath.

"Yep," he said. "Sukie sho'nuf is dead. Dead as dirt. That woman was the devil. You know that, don'tcha? Sukie was so damn wicked, that hole in the ground over there look like she bust hell wide open on her way out."

He rambled on without respite, not even waiting for Coolie to answer. She glanced down at his white Stacy Adams. The shoes were spotless, even though they rested on a dirt floor.

"So what you come back for, gal? Where's Polo?"

Caesar stopped to take another gulp of soda, a whiff of peaches whooshing Coolie's way. She leaned back.

"I don't know where he is," she said. "I thought he might be here."

"You don't know where he is? Good Lord, gal, you left here with him. Don't tell me he got separated from you in Dee-troit. That's a great big ol' city. What'd he do, find another gal? You know how them Botens is. Ain't none of 'em screwed on too tight. You shole did get po', gal. You want something to eat?"

Before Coolie had the chance to respond, Caesar had bounded out of his chair and was dashing toward the kitchen.

"Cair-line. Cair-line. Whip up a plate back there for this gal. She so po', I can see clean through to the other side of her."

Caroline Hixton leaned her head out of the kitchen window. She cocked a critical eye at Coolie, examining her. She had already been studying the girl on the sly, but Caesar's request gave her permission.

"What you want, girl, some of everything?" she asked.

"No ma'am," Coolie said. "I'm really not hungry."

Caesar waved his hand.

"Look at how scrawny she is. Gi' that girl a whole plate. Dee-troit done put a whooping on her ass."

Caroline nodded her head as she spooned, scooped, sliced, and picked out food for Coolie. She handed a heaping dish to Caesar.

"She shole looks bad," she said to him, shaking her head. "Give her one of them sodas out the deep freezer."

Caesar pulled a Pepsi from the big red Coca-Cola cooler. While he had it open, he reached in and grabbed another peach Nehi. He strutted back over to the table and placed the dish before the girl.

The plate was piled with steaming food. There were collard greens with smoked neckbones, cornbread, macaroni and cheese, potato salad, baked ham, and fried chicken. Coolie didn't think she was hungry, but as the warm scents wafted upward, she began to pick at the chicken, taste the potato salad, then to eat the rest of the food as though she was famished.

Caesar cut his eyes at Caroline, who was still shaking her head as she watched the girl devour the meal.

"Drink some soda, chile, 'fore you choke," Caroline said.

Coolie kept eating, desperate, as though running a race. It wasn't that she was starved. She just hadn't eaten a square meal in such a long time. Nor had she had the appetite. As she pillaged her way through the food in front of her, she realized that she had forgotten how well Caroline cooked, and why so many men, and a good share of women, came to the Lucky Star and sometimes didn't want to go home.

"Slow down, gal," Caesar said. "Here." He pushed the Pepsi toward her. "Wash it down."

Coolie picked up the Pepsi and drank in big, long, gasping gulps. The soda was very cold. The acid rushed to her nose and made it hard for her to breathe between swallows. When she finished, she was panting. She resumed shoveling the food into her mouth.

Caroline came out of the kitchen and sat down at the table with Coolie and Caesar.

"Baby, does your mama know you back in town?" Caroline asked.

Coolie shook her head, her mouth stuffed. She forced the food down before she attempted to speak.

"No ma'am, she don't."

"Well, what exactly have you been doing with yourself?" Caroline asked.

Coolie wasn't surprised by their interest. Caesar and Caroline ran two of the biggest rumor mills in town.

Coolie didn't care about her reputation. She knew she no longer had anything to speak of, save the money in her bag and the clothes on her back. She didn't care what Caesar and Caroline knew or found out about her. She just wanted someone to lead her to Polo.

"I been working as a prostitute in Detroit. I got strung out real bad while I was doing it."

Caroline sucked in her breath and clutched her chest.

"Lawd hammercy," Caesar said.

Their reactions had no effect on her.

"That's why I lost so much weight," Coolie said. "I got up there and me and Polo stayed with Lay. Things got crazy. Lay was into stuff we didn't know nuthin' about, making fast money offa gettin' folks hooked on dope. I ended up all mixed up in his mess."

Caroline cut her eyes at Caesar, who was now suckling the Nehi bottle like a tit.

"So where is Polo now?" Caroline asked.

"Like I told Caesar, I don't know. I thought maybe he came back here. He left me with Lay last year when he caught me with another man. I don't even remember how it happened. I was so messed up on dope, I ain't know too much of nothing."

Caesar kept sucking, his eyes glued to Coolie.

"Who was it he caught you with?" Caroline said. "Somebody new you took to seeing?"

Coolie was full. She leaned back in the chair, her stomach distended for the first time in almost a year.

"Miss Caroline, I don't even know who it was. All I know is I was sucking his . . . in the bed with him when Polo came home."

Coolie leaned forward and put her head in her hands.

"I just want my man back," she said. "That's all I want."

Caesar pried his mouth away from the Nehi.

"Well, last time I talked to Big Daddy," he said, "it musta been a month or so 'fore they was found dead, he said Polo had gone up to college where Ophelia was. I just assumed you was up there with them."

Coolie looked up with bright eyes.

"You think he still up there?" she asked.

"Well, I wouldn't know that for sure, but I'd say that if he went to stay with his sister, he prob'ly still up there."

Coolie got up from the table.

"Then I'm gon' go up there and find him," she said.

Caroline grabbed her by the arm.

"Honey, you can't go up there tonight. Ain't no more buses coming through here. You might as well just take your time and rest for a minute."

"Yeah," Caesar said. "Go on over to your mama's house and spend a little time with them 'fore you leave again."

"I told y'all I can't let them see me like this," Coolie said. "It would kill my mama to see me. It's still hard for me now, even though I don't shoot up no more. A lotta times I get the shakes real bad and feel like I'm gon' die."

She looked down, her voice cracking.

"I just can't let my mama see me like this."

Caroline stood and put her arm around the girl.

"Listen, baby, why don't you come spend the night at my house. I got an extra bed, you'll have a nice cool place to sleep, and tomorrow you can figure out what you gon' do."

Coolie looked up. Her eyes were wet.

"Thank you, Caroline," she said, wiping the tears before they had a chance to drop. "I appreciate your being so nice to me. I done got to where I ain't used to kind folks no more. People in Detroit is mighty mean."

The two of them walked toward the door.

"That's all right, sugar. Everything's gon' be just fine. We'll go fix that bed up for you, and you can get yourself a good night's sleep. You got money to go back to Michigan?"

"Yes ma'am."

"All right," said Caroline.

She turned to Caesar, who was standing beside the table watching the two of them walk away.

"We'll see you later, Caesar. I'm gon' go help this girl get herself situated. Po' thang, all she need is a little love."

Caroline rubbed Coolie's back. Coolie smiled at her, grateful for the kind words and hospitality.

The two of them left the Lucky Star and made their way down the winding dirt road.

Caesar watched them.

He drank the last swallow of Nehi and put the empty bottle

in with some two hundred others that were soon to be returned for the deposit.

And for more peach Nehis.

Coolie was in a deep sleep, her angular body stretched across the cool sheets, a pillow clutched between her arms. Caroline had placed a fan beside the bed. The feathery breeze stroked Coolie's face and cradled her into the most restful slumber she'd had since she left Downtown with Polo.

Before she went to bed, she and Caroline sat up and talked for a while. Caroline had a lot of questions, most of them about how determined Coolie was to find Polo. She was also very curious about prostitution. Caroline asked her if she liked turning tricks and commented on how disgusting it must have been for the girl to have so many filthy men crawl on top of her and do their business.

"It was just work," Coolie said. "It paid for my habit and it helped me get away."

"The men that sleep with prostitutes are nasty," Caroline replied. "You'll be lucky if you ain't ruined for life."

Just before she fell asleep, when she was sure Caroline had gone back to her room, Coolie pulled the stockings from her purse and counted the money for the very first time.

She had over four thousand dollars, most of it in twenties and hundreds. She had found those easier to steal than the fives and tens. Lay thought she was just turning cheap tricks. Coolie had been doing round-the-worlds and upping her fee. She was astonished by just how much she'd made. She wrapped the money back in the stockings, tucked them into her purse, and fell asleep.

As she lay there, she dreamed of finding Polo. In her dream, he held her tight and wouldn't stop kissing her.

"Baby, I'm so glad to see you," he said. "I'm sorry about everything, and I swear 'fore God, I won't ever run off from you again."

Coolie smiled in her sleep and squeezed the pillow tighter in the darkness of the night.

The next morning, Coolie was gone before Caroline even awoke. She'd caught the first bus headed to Michigan.

She couldn't wait to get to Polo and tell him how sorry she was for everything that had come between them.

PART XI

1969

LOVE

*Even as love crowns you so shall he
crucify you. Even as he is for your
growth so is he for your pruning.*

—KAHLIL GIBRAN

CHAPTER THIRTY-SEVEN

The sun was shining bright when Walter pulled away from the curb. The big dark green Chevy turned the corner and weaved through the neighborhood. The afternoon glare flashed off the rearview mirror, blocking Walter's ability to see.

His quiet surveys of his daughter had become more frequent. He worried about Ophelia as she entered the last stages of her pregnancy.

In the earlier part of the morning, he would see her leave for school. She didn't come out again once she went inside. Her belly was enormous.

Walter had grown to like Ophelia's boyfriend, even from a distance. He watched the way they treated each other. Ophelia often greeted him at the door. He always held her hand as he guided her in and out of the house.

Funny, Walter thought, how he didn't feel threatened about approaching her anymore. He already knew what he would say to her if she saw him.

As he drove away, he realized how much she reminded him of Grace. As he gripped the steering wheel, his sister's image flooded his mind. He allowed himself to think about her. He wondered what she was doing back in Downtown. He had left town without even saying goodbye, and he hadn't looked back since.

Grace and Ophelia were the two people in the world Walter cared about most.

It was too late for Grace, but he wouldn't make that mistake with Ophelia.

Now that she was grown, he could tell her everything. She would forgive him for how he treated her all those years. He knew that once he explained everything, she would understand why he did what he did.

They would begin again. He would acknowledge his daughter and be a part of her life.

He smiled as he thought of how it would be. The glare of the sun caused his eyes to moisten. At least he thought it was the sun. He couldn't see well as he looked into the rearview mirror with caution, then switched lanes.

When he reached the main highway, he turned right at the light and blended into traffic.

A few car lengths behind him, Javier's yellow Volkswagen blended into the traffic, too.

CHAPTER THIRTY-EIGHT

Coolie stood in line at the registrar's office. Since it was September, the room was filled with students who wanted to add classes after the semester had already begun, withdraw because of unforeseeable reasons, challenge flags on their records, or get transcript information.

The students were dressed in jeans and T-shirts, tie-dyed tank tops with running shorts, button-downs with chinos and loafers. They carried assorted books and book bags and were very youthful and fresh in appearance and demeanor, even those with long hair. These kids looked to be in their natural habitat. Coolie did not.

She was thin and frazzled. Though she was in the same age group as most of the people around her, Coolie's face seemed hardened and old.

She wore a short, bright red, close-fitting skirt, a black halter, and some slides. The clothes were disheveled and her hair was a tangle of unkempt curls. Coolie had not bought anything new.

She had checked in to a hotel and bathed every night, washing her clothes in the sink. Even though she was clean, her clothes had become dingy, and she wasn't always successful in getting stains out of them. As a result, they developed a faint gamy scent that now stole upon the people standing in line around her. Several glances gravitated her way. The old Coolie from Downtown would have been embarrassed. Strung-out Coolie didn't care. She was trying to find her man.

When she reached the front of the line, the woman behind the counter stared at her. She knew there was no way someone as bedraggled and seedy as Coolie could be a student. Coolie's unkempt hair and haggard appearance were an affront to the woman's sensibilities. Her name tag revealed her to be Mrs. Richards. She scanned the girl's body. When her eyes met Coolie's tired, determined face, Mrs. Richards' expression of disapproval twisted into a scowl.

"How can I help you?" she said.

"I'm tryna find one of y'all students," she said with a broad smile.

"We don't issue unauthorized information about registered students," Mrs. Richards replied. "Unless you are a family member, a member of some local, state, or federal agency, or an attorney who can produce accurate identification and a subpoena, we will not release any information whatsoever."

Mrs. Richards' disgust with Coolie was evident. Some of the students in line behind the girl leaned around to get a better glimpse of the young woman. All activity in the registrar's office seemed to cease and focus on Coolie and Mrs. Richards.

"Are you a member of a government agency?" Mrs. Richards said with sarcasm. "Are you an attorney?"

"I'm a family member," Coolie said.

Mrs. Richards sucked her tongue. "Who are you trying to locate?"

"Polonius Boten."

Mrs. Richards wrote the name down on a white index card.

"And what is his relationship to you?"

"He's my husband," she said.

Mrs. Richards leaned forward and peered at Coolie's left hand. Finding it bare, she shook her head at the girl.

"May I see some identification?"

"I didn't bring any identification with me," Coolie replied.

"Please, ma'am, it's really important that I find him. There's a very bad family situation, and I need to let him know about it."

Mrs. Richards, eyeing Coolie again, doubted with strong conviction that there was a family emergency. This girl was a junkie, a prostitute, or both, and she was determined to make trouble for some self-respecting student trying to better himself.

"What's his major?" she asked.

"Major?" Coolie said. "What is that?"

Mrs. Richards huffed. "I don't know what you're trying to pull, young lady, and I use that term very loosely, but anybody who can't produce identification for herself or provide her husband's pertinent data is certainly not going to be getting any information from us. I suggest you move along and let the people with valid needs get on with their business."

She waved Coolie away. "Next," she called.

Coolie stood a few moments, staring at the woman, not believing she had been dismissed without any direction, assistance, or offer of hope.

A young white girl with acne-covered skin and washed-out hair walked up beside Coolie and glanced at her, then directed her attention to Mrs. Richards.

"How may I help you, hon?" Mrs. Richards said with a smile.

Coolie walked away. She exited at the door just opposite the front of the line.

Ophelia leaned around. She was standing at the back of the line. Her feet were tired and her back was aching. She had set her book bag on the floor.

The line began to move again. She was relieved. She needed to drop the fall classes she had registered for. Her baby was due any day. Ophelia hadn't wanted to take a break from school and thought she would need just a couple of weeks off after the baby arrived. As the delivery date grew near, her discomfort made it difficult for her to concentrate, and she began to skip a lot of classes. She also realized she'd want to be with her baby as much as possible after the birth. When Javier recommended she withdraw until spring, she agreed.

Ophelia waddled forward as the line moved up. She watched the skinny, tired-looking woman open the glass door at the front of the room.

"I wonder what she wanted," she said to the lanky boy in line in front of her.

"I don't know," he replied, "but she held up the line a long time. I wasted the whole afternoon. They close in five minutes."

"What?" Ophelia said. "I stood in line all this time for nothing?"

"Well, so did I," he said, "and so did a whole bunch of other people ahead of us. Sometimes they'll keep seeing people out of pity."

The boy peered around at Mrs. Richards' face.

"I don't think today is going to be one of those days."

"So now what do I do?" Ophelia asked. She had never withdrawn from a class before.

"Tomorrow's the last day to do anything," he said. "Just try to come back early, and you should get through."

Ophelia sighed as she picked up her bag from the floor.

"Guess I'll see you tomorrow," she said.

"No way," he said. "All this has made me decide to keep my classes."

Ophelia smiled as she headed out of the door into the bright afternoon sun and down the sidewalk to where the Mustang was parked.

CHAPTER THIRTY-NINE

"That bitch ran out on my ass."

Lay kicked the wall, making a hole the size of a basketball. The girl with the rainbow Afro shrank against the couch. His gunmen watched in silence. One of them came over and touched him on the shoulder.

"Calm down, man. She can't be gone too far. Everybody in the city knows her ass."

Lay looked at the man's hand on his shoulder.

"Y'all motherfuckers the reason she got away," he said. "Y'all s'posed to know her every move. Just let her run the fucking off."

He punched the man in the face, knocking him to the floor, then leaped upon his chest and pummeled him with his fists. The other thugs stood and watched, terrified to act for fear Lay's fury would be directed at them.

He beat the man until his face was a bloody brown mush. When Lay stood, he was exhausted. The man lay unconscious on the floor.

Lay pulled a gun from the holster beneath his arm. He shot the man five times. Once in the stomach, once in the heart. Three times in the face.

"Motherfucker," he grumbled at the body. "I bet you the one who let my bitch get away."

He pointed the gun at the others.

"Which one of y'all punks wanna be next?" he said.

The men backed away.

"I didn't think so," Lay said. "I tell you what. Y'all asses better comb this city till you find her. Comb it till ain't a square inch left unsearched. You hear me?"

The men nodded.

"Then get the fuck outta here and start combing."

The thugs left the apartment in haste.

Lay flopped down on the sofa, the gun still in his hand. The girl leaned toward him and began to rub his neck. He didn't pull away.

"I got an idea where that bitch at," he said. "She think she slick, but she can't trick the tricker."

"Where you think she went?" Afro girl asked.

"She done took her ass up to where Polo is," he said. "I know she did. But she can't get away from me. I own her. She owe me too much to slip away without a mess."

Afro girl watched him, unnerved by the way his top lip trembled as he spoke. She kept stroking his neck.

"I'll kill her before I let him have her back," he said. "And I know how to find her. Mama gave me the address where him and Ophelia stay 'fore her and Big Daddy died."

The girl rubbed his back and chest.

"I'll damn shole use that address now to stop Coolie's ass."

The girl kissed his shoulders and chest, her tongue fluttering across his skin.

"She better hope I don't find her," Lay said. "I believe I'm gon' kill her just for having the gall to run off."

The girl took one of his nipples in her mouth.

"I'll use her ass as an example."

The girl climbed over him, straddling his chest.

She came into his focus as she slithered down his torso.

"Get off me, bitch," he said, knocking her to the floor. "I got some killing to do."

Lay stepped over her and the dead man lying in the middle of the floor. He went into his bedroom, slamming the door behind him. He went to the dresser, snatching open the top drawer. He rooted around for the letter with Ophelia and Polo's address.

When he came out of the room, he glared at the girl with the Afro.

He grabbed his keys from the coffee table and exited the apartment.

"Clean that up in there," he said to the gunmen that patrolled the hall. "And I want that bitch out when I'm gone." He held his car keys out to the guy at the end. "Bring my Eldorado around," he said. "I've got to make a trip to Lansing."

"They don't live in that apartment anymore," the landlady said.

She thought the young black man in her office was very attractive, clean-cut and mannerable. His Cadillac looked new.

"Do you have any idea where my brother and sister went off to, ma'am?" he asked. "I've got some troubling news about our folks to share with them. I need to get in touch with them as soon as possible."

The old woman felt sorry for him. He seemed so concerned. She had no idea where her children were and wished they cared for her as much this young man seemed to care for his parents.

"Well, the boy, Polonius, went off to Vietnam," she said.

"Is that right?" Lay said, his expression serious.

"Why yes," the old woman replied. She was pleased to be able to offer him some useful information. "And I believe the young lady, Ophelia, left me a forwarding address to where she was going. I think I've got it right here."

She opened a box of index cards and rifled through them.

"Here it is. She only lives a few miles from here."

She scribbled the address on a piece of paper.

"There you are, young man," she said, smiling, handing him the paper. "I hope you find them and that things are okay with your folks."

He took the address from her.

"Thank you, ma'am," he said. "I'm sure everything will be just fine now, thanks to your help."

The old woman walked outside with him. Lay glanced at her sidelong, his smile still polite.

She stood beside his car and waved. This was a good boy, she thought. A nice, caring family boy. She was glad she could help. Perhaps someday her children would come looking for her.

Lay climbed into the car, whistling as he closed the door. He revved the engine, triumphant, and peeled out of the parking lot.

PART XII

1969

REVELATION

*All your life you live so close to truth,
it becomes a permanent blur in the
corner of your eye, and when
something nudges it into outline it is
like being ambushed by a grotesque.*

—TOM STOPPARD

CHAPTER FORTY

Javier sat in the car and watched the man as he stepped out of the dark green Chevy and went into the apartment. He wanted to be sure this was the man's home.

He waited thirty minutes. When he felt sure the man would not be coming out again, Javier exited his car, tiptoed over to the side of the apartment, and looked in the window.

The drapes were open. Javier could see the man sitting on the couch. It was him, this closer look confirmed it. The same man he had seen approach Ophelia's old apartment months before. The same man whose car had become such a nagging presence. Javier was determined to learn who this stranger could be.

He walked around to the front door and rang the bell. He slipped his hand in the front pocket of his jeans.

The man's face appeared at the window. His eyes met Javier's. The sound of the door being unlocked was followed by the slow creak of its being pulled open.

The man stood in the doorway, a bleak look on his face. He dropped his head.

"Excuse me, sir," Javier said. "Who the hell are you and why have you been following my wife?"

CHAPTER FORTY-ONE

Ophelia lay in bed. Javier was out much later than usual.

Perhaps in a meeting, she thought, or advising a student. She was surprised he hadn't called.

Ophelia was exhausted from having walked the campus and stood in line all afternoon with no success. She rubbed her belly. The baby had descended into her abdomen, and the pressure against her bladder was constant. She would think she had to pee, but every time she or the baby shifted, the feeling would be gone.

She stared at the ceiling, weaving in and out of sleep. Ophelia thought about life as the baby squirmed inside of her. She thought about her uncle Walter.

She wanted to talk to him, but she had not seen him since the day she noticed him parked down the street. When Javier said he saw a man who fit the same description outside her old apartment, she didn't tell him it was Walter. Javier knew nothing about her uncle watching the house from down the street. She figured he must want to see to her real bad to be as persistent as he was. She'd been waiting for him ever since.

Ophelia remembered the last time she saw him in Downtown. She was standing in her window watching him trying to start the car. As she had watched him, she cried.

She knew why she cried for him that night. He seemed trapped and displaced, the same way she'd felt for so many years. That feeling kept her anxious, hungry with the need to know more. First she sought it in annoying questions she'd ask her mother. The details of things never seemed to gibe.

Once she asked her mother the date she and Big Daddy were married. Grace told her, and later Ophelia did the math.

"But that's too close to my birthday," she said. "Did y'all get married after Big Daddy got you pregnant with me?"

"Shush, chile," Grace said. "Don't be so foolish. It's rude for chillun to be meddling in grown folks' affairs."

The girl sat across from her mother at the kitchen table. Her eyes were sullen. She buried her head in her arms on the table.

Grace reached out to her, stroking her hair. "I'm sorry, Ophelia. I didn't mean to fuss like that."

The girl's head remained down.

"All that matters is that Big Daddy did right by me," her mother said. "So don't you go concerning yourself about it."

Ophelia had taken her mother's words as confirmation that they'd had sex before the marriage.

She lay there now, thinking about how Walter had shied away from her for all those years. She used to long to see him laugh the way Big Daddy did. She had no memory of even seeing him smile.

She never believed he disliked her, at least not the way Sukie did. And now he was trying to reach out to her.

During her childhood, when the Martins made her feel so different, Lay was the one person who indulged her questions. As the baby squirmed against her bladder, she thought of Lay and how close they had been. Polo's words resounded in her head.

"Lay don't care 'bout nobody but hisself. And if you get anywhere near him, he'll find a way to exploit you. Just like he did me."

Ophelia hadn't wanted to believe Polo at first. She didn't until Lay told her that he was cutting her loose. She reflected on all the time they'd spent together. She thought about the times in the barn. And she thought about the baby.

As she waited for Javier, dusk descending around her, for the first time in her life she accepted that what happened between her and her brother wasn't right. He had deceived her, and she'd meant nothing to him.

She had her own family now. She ran her hand across her belly.

As she drifted to sleep, her thoughts were of Lay. It was the last time she would ever reminisce about him.

"Wake up, honey," Javier whispered.

It was pitch black in the bedroom. Ophelia opened her eyes, struggling to focus. She strained to lean forward, the baby pressing hard against her bladder. She reached for the lamp beside her on the nightstand. Javier sat on the bed next to her. As she brushed against him, she smelled the alcohol on his breath.

She turned on the light.

His eyes were bloodshot and watery. She blinked several times in an attempt to clear her vision. His expression was glazed but intense.

"Where've you been all evening?"

"We need to talk," he said.

"Talk about what, honey?" she asked, searching his face. "What's the matter?"

"Your family's the matter. There's some things going on you haven't told me about. I've been patient with you, I've been here for you. The least you can do is be honest with me about what's going on here."

Ophelia's pulse quickened. She reached out for him, but he shrank away.

"Javier, what are you talking about? You've been drinking. I haven't known you to drink before."

He angled the lamp shade so he could see her face.

"I've only had a few drinks. I'm not drunk. I'm as coherent as I've ever been, but I needed some time to think. Things aren't making sense to me, and I don't like it when things don't make sense."

She leaned back against the pillows.

"I don't understand what you're talking about."

"Oh yes, Ophelia. I think that you do."

She shivered. She could count the times he had called her Ophelia since they'd first started dating. He always said it as a strong assurance to comfort her. Now he was saying it in what appeared to be anger and distrust.

"I need to know details about your family," he said. "You haven't shared very much with me, and I think it's time I learned the whole story. Go ahead and start talking. I have all night."

"Start where?" she asked. "I don't know what you want to know. Are you concerned about something specific?"

"No. I want the whole thing. But why don't I help you get started. Tell me about your relationship with your brother Laertes. No, wait, why don't you talk about the father of your first baby. Why your aunt didn't like your mother. Just tell me something, Ophelia. These are all things I think about in the middle of the night. Things I've waited for you to tell me at your leisure that never seem to come."

Ophelia was silent.

"Come on," he said. "I'm tired of waiting. I don't care where you start. Just start somewhere."

He adjusted the lamp shade again so that the light shone even brighter in her face.

"Why now?" she asked. "We've been married for months. How come it never mattered before?"

"It has always mattered. There's just never been a good time to talk."

"And now you suddenly need to?" she said.

"Yes. I have to know these things now. Start talking."

"All right, Javier," she said, tears dropping onto her cheeks. "I'll tell you whatever it is you want to know."

It was deep into the night before Ophelia stopped talking. Javier was silent. He lay beside her on the bed, his focus on nothing, his mind blank.

She told him everything, not caring about the consequences. She gave him everything he wanted to know.

"What are you thinking?" she asked.

She could hear his breath coming in whispers, almost as if he was sleeping. She glanced down at him. His eyes were wide as they stared up at the ceiling.

"Javier?"

She touched his arm. He stirred, turning his gaze to her. The expression in his eyes was unnerving.

"I know this is a lot for a person to hear in one sitting," she said. "And I know it was wrong for me to do what I did with my brother."

She played with her hands.

"But I can't lie, Javier. No matter how wrong it was, all I know was that I loved him. He said what we were doing wasn't bad, and even though I felt it wasn't right, I trusted him. He was the only one who cared enough to listen to me. He cared about what I thought, and I felt validated as a person. When he left, all I had was my baby. That was the only thing that made me feel validated."

Javier's eyes remained on hers.

"When my baby died, it was like everything shut down. There was no one else I could relate to. I couldn't talk to anybody. So I just retreated into myself. Then I met you."

She stopped talking, waiting for a response. All she could hear was the whispery breathing beside her.

"I'll understand if this is too much for you to handle," she said. "I never expected to find someone in my life like you. I never expected it at all. You came and made me happy and loved me. That's been the greatest feeling of my life. I don't want to lose you."

Tears dropped onto her wringing hands. "But I'll understand if you want to go."

His eyes glistened. He wrapped his arms around her stomach.

"I don't want to go," he whispered.

Her tears dropped onto his face and arms.

"Don't cry, Ophelita. I have no intentions of leaving you, and I never did. I thought you understood that by now."

"But you were so angry tonight," she said.

He shook his head.

"No, baby. I wasn't angry with you. I was angry because I felt like I couldn't help you. So much was going on around me that I felt excluded from. There are some things you just don't talk about. I've known from the start there was more to you than you were willing to say."

"I didn't know how," she said. "I swear to God, I didn't know how."

Javier kissed her face.

"I didn't mean to upset you," he said. "I shouldn't have done this now, with you so close to term. I would never do anything to hurt you or our baby."

"No, no, you didn't hurt me," Ophelia said.

"But can you imagine how I felt? I can't ever help you if I don't know what I'm dealing with."

He kissed the top of her head, thinking of how he could tell her about Walter. He knew he couldn't do it now. There was no way she would be able to handle anything more.

He and Walter had talked for several hours. There was so much the man wanted to tell Ophelia. The first bombshell would be enough to rattle her. Javier wanted to be present when Walter broke the news.

"What are you doing tomorrow?" he asked.

"I have to go back on campus," she said, wiping her face. "I still need to withdraw from my classes."

"I thought you did that today."

"I was still in line when they closed."

"Okay . . . hmm. What time are you going over there?"

She reached for a tissue on the nightstand next to the bed.

"I'm going early in the morning. Tomorrow's the last day I can do it."

"All right. What if I meet you here around noon? I have something I want you to see."

"Okay. What is it?"

"Don't worry about that, you just get some sleep. You need to rest, and there's not much left of the night."

He kissed her lips. It was a delicate gesture that assured her of his love.

"I'm so sorry you've had so much pain in your life," he said. "You deserved so much better."

He reached over her and turned off the light. He spooned around her, his hand on the baby.

"*Te amo,* Ophelita," he whispered to her.

"I love you, too," she whispered back.

"*Siempre?*" he asked.

"Always."

CHAPTER FORTY-TWO

Sukie was in the kitchen cooking a great pot of stew. She and Walter had been in Downtown just four days since their arrival from New Orleans. She smiled as she stirred the pot, dropping chunks of pork and beef into the swirling water. She needed more tomatoes for the stew. She opened the kitchen door and went out back to pick a few from the garden.

"Why did you run off without telling us?" she heard the voice ask. *"You leave here without a word to anybody, and next thing you know, you show up with a wife."*

The voice was gentle but persistent. Sukie stopped and listened.

"I don't wanna talk about this, Grace. Just go back home to Big Daddy. I don't wanna ever talk about this no mo'."

"But we gotta talk about it, Walter. You're my brother. I love you." There was a pause. *"I got a baby by you. We can't act like it ain't happen. You can dance around me and my daughter all you want, but you know Ophelia's your baby. You know she is."*

"She's Big Daddy's baby now. He done raised her since she came out the womb."

"But you know she's yours. Don't forget that when you look at her. She's yours, just as sure as she's mine."

Sukie's blood churned as she listened to the exchange.

"Grace, go back home. I got a wife now. Pretty soon we gon' start our own family."

"I'm happy for you, Walter," Grace said. *"I really am. But who is she? Is this what you want? You seem so scared when you're around her, like she might hurt you or something. Is she in the family way? Tell me what it is. Something ain't right with y'all. I'll help you if I can."*

Grace was stopped by the appearance of Sukie from around the side of the house. She materialized next to them as if from thin air. Walter's face tightened.

Sukie placed her hand on his elbow and looked Grace in the eye.

"We don't need your help, thank you, ma'am. Ain't nothin' wrong with me or my husband."

Walter remained silent.

"And as for your daughter, I don't wanna ever hear no talk 'bout that again. Don't think I don't know. I suspected somethin' was funny, but now I done heard it from your own sick mouths."

She turned to Walter.

"I better not see you so much as look at that child, let alone claim it, you hear me?"

Walter looked down at his feet.

"You hear me?" Sukie said.

He nodded.

Grace held up her hand. "Sukie, listen, I think you're misunderstanding me. I wanna be your friend."

Sukie pointed her finger in Grace's face. "I'ma tell you this one time, and that's it: stay away from my husband. Unless you want me to stir up some shit with your own."

Grace said nothing.

"Y'all shoulda killed that child soon as she was born," Sukie said. "It ain't natural. She ain't gon' bring nuthin' but bad luck to anybody she get near."

"Don't you hurt my daughter," Grace said, her tone harsh. "She's an innocent child. Walter, don't let her talk about our baby like this."

Walter was helpless.

"He ain't gon' contest me," Sukie said. "Long as you stay away from my husband, you ain't got to worry 'bout your baby none. But I better not ever hear nobody talkin' 'bout her being Walter's child."

She jerked Walter by the arm and disappeared around the side of the house.

CHAPTER FORTY-THREE

It was still early when Ophelia began the long trudge back to her car. She'd been in the line at the registrar's office for over an hour, then she spent another twenty minutes explaining why she needed to drop all her classes. She thought her distended belly seemed obvious reason enough.

The sun was positioning itself toward its apex when she passed a girl in ill-fitting jeans and a Michigan State T-shirt sitting on a bench near the parking lot, a black bag by her leg. She never would have noticed her, except Ophelia's back hurt and she was winded. She stopped to rest.

Ophelia leaned against the bench. Her brow was sweating. She sat down, closed her eyes, and took a few deep breaths.

She felt a hand on her shoulder.

"Ophelia?" the girl said.

Ophelia, thinking it was someone who'd had a class with her, looked up with tired eyes. She took a good look at the girl's face.

"Coolie?"

Coolie grinned.

"Oh my God," Ophelia exclaimed. "It *is* you." She reached out and hugged her.

Coolie was grateful to be received by a kind and familiar face. She held tight to Ophelia's embrace.

"Look at you," she said, letting her go. "You're finna have another baby."

Ophelia smiled. She scanned Coolie's face, amazed at how much it had aged since she had last seen her. Gone was the rosy fullness of good health, and her trademark head of ringlets was now a disheveled and dusty tuft of wool.

Ophelia remembered all the things Polo told her that Lay had gotten Coolie involved in. The girl looked as though she had been ravaged by dope. Her arms were scarred with track marks. Ophelia then realized that Coolie was the same woman she had seen leaving the registrar's office the day before. Ophelia had thought the woman was a streetwalker begging for food.

Coolie was aware of Ophelia's scrutiny. She didn't care. It didn't make a difference.

"I'm so glad to see you, Ophelia. I can't tell you how glad I am. I been through so much shit, you wouldn't believe it."

Ophelia took the girl's hand in her own. She was both pleased and saddened to see her.

"What are you doing here?" Ophelia.

"I'm looking for Polo. I know he came up here. That's what Caesar Bucksport told me. He said y'all was staying together. I came up here to find him. It's a blessing I ran into you. I went to that office yesterday tryna find out how to get to Polo, and that white bitch behind the desk treated me like dirt. I went out and got these cheap clothes and tried to dress a little more fit for school. Guess I drew too much attention in my other getup."

Ophelia stared at Coolie. She didn't know how to tell her. Her heart was aching for the girl.

"What's wrong, Ophelia?" Coolie said. "Why you looking at me like that?"

Before Ophelia could answer, Coolie waved her hand.

"Oh, I know why. Don't worry. I ain't spend all my money buying these clothes. I ain't as po' as I look. I got almost four thousand dollars."

Ophelia shook her head.

"Polo's dead, Coolie."

Coolie's smile took a moment to fade. She didn't register what Ophelia had said until the sound of the words connected with the sight of her tears.

"What?"

"He's dead," Ophelia repeated, reaching out for Coolie's hand.

"No, he's not," she said. "He's here with you. Caesar said so."

"Coolie, I'm sorry. He got drafted and died in the war."

"He can't be dead," Coolie cried. "He can't be dead. What I'm gon' do? Polo is all I know, Ophelia."

Ophelia struggled to get up from the bench. She pulled Coolie by the hand.

"Come with me, honey," she said. "I have something I want to show you."

Coolie, blinded by tears, followed Ophelia to the car, slid into the passenger seat, and lapsed into a stupor that lasted the entire ride from campus to Ophelia's house.

"Where did you get this?" Coolie asked.

They were sitting on the bed amid a bundle of papers.

"When the army people came and told me about his death,

they brought me all that was left of his belongings. The letter was in there."

Coolie turned it over in her hands, stroking it as if it were Polo himself. She rubbed the envelope against her cheek.

Ophelia watched her. Coolie kept touching and staring at the letter.

"Look," she said, pointing, smiling at Ophelia. "That's my name on the outside. He put Boten as my last name. He always used to call me Coolie Boten. Said I was practically his wife, anyway." She sighed. "I guess he forgave me after all."

"Why don't you read the letter and see," Ophelia said.

"You mean you ain't read it already?" Coolie asked.

"It wasn't mine to read."

"So you were just gonna keep it till you found me?"

"Uh-huh."

"S'pose you never found me?"

"Well, we don't have to worry about that now, do we?" Ophelia replied, stroking Coolie's matted hair.

"I guess not," she said.

"So go on," Ophelia said, "open it."

Coolie played with the edges of the letter, then slipped her finger under the flap. Her hands were rough and bony, but her fingers were graceful as she took care with the envelope, opening it slow.

"I'm scared," she said. "It's like I'ma find a piece a him in this letter."

"It's okay."

"Yeah," Coolie said. Her hands were shaking as she pulled the letter from the envelope. She folded it open and looked at it, shuffling the pages. Polo's deliberate scrawl covered the white paper.

"Read it to me, Ophelia. I can't read that good nohow, and you in school. And I think I got somethin' in my eye."

She wiped her face with her hand.

Ophelia took the letter from her without comment. Inside, she felt a similar longing and sadness for her brother.

Coolie sat still beside her, eyes moist, watching her face.
Ophelia opened the letter and read:

Dear Coolie:

*I been turning over in my head again and again what happened
with us. I think the bottom line is that I never should have
gone chasing after Lay in Detroit. I messed up your life and I
messed up my own. You're up there by yourself with my
brother, and believe me, Coolie, he don't care about nobody. He
don't care about nobody but his damn self. I'm over here in this
godforsaken place watching people die left and right around
me. If I had been smart, I would have come back and got you.
When I got drafted I should have just come back, snatched you
up out of that apartment, and gone off to Canada like a lot of
other brothers did. Coolie, I'm so sorry about what happened at
the apartment. I keep thinking about that day over and over.
Ain't no way I should have hit you like that. And I been asking
God to forgive me every night for the other terrible thing I did to
you. God, Coolie, I'm so sorry. I just love you so much that seeing you with somebody else killed me on the inside. It was like
somebody just went and stuck a knife right in the middle of my
heart. I was wrong. I shouldn't have left you like I did. I saw
that you needed me, and I let my stupid pride push me right out
the door. Ophelia and I talked about that. About me and my
stupid pride. Ophelia's smart. She said I should have just told
you I love you and that none of what happened didn't matter to
me. 'Cause it don't. If I could have anything right now, I'd be
with you like we used to be. Just me and you, back in Downtown, in the barn tussling. Those were the happiest days of my
life, Coolie. When it was just you and me and all we had was
us and our love. I think about all that now. I pray for you every
night and hope you get away from Lay. I wish I had been man
enough to save you from him. I pray that if I get out of this hell-
hole, I can come back and you'll forgive me. Maybe we can go
off somewhere far away from Detroit and start all over again*

from scratch. What happened to our lives in Detroit don't mat-
ter no more.

All that matters is that I still love you, Coolie Boten. I just
hope and pray that somehow or another you still love me.

Plant me now,
Polo

When Ophelia finished reading, both she and Coolie were crying.

Coolie lay back on the bed.

"Dig you later, babe," she whispered.

"What was that?" Ophelia asked.

"He signed the letter 'Plant me now.' That's how we used to
always say goodbye to each other. Whichever one of us was
leaving would say it, and the other one would say 'dig you later.'
It was like our own little way of saying 'I love you.' "

"I see."

"I took me a typing class," Coolie said.

"Coolie, that's great."

"Yeah. I did it. I wanted to get away from Lay so bad. I took
that class so I'd have something to get me out of that dark world
he had me hemmed up in."

Ophelia watched her.

"Polo would have been proud of me."

"I know he would have," Ophelia said.

"You think so?" Coolie asked.

"I know so," Ophelia said. "Why don't you get some sleep."
She covered the girl with an afghan.

"I guess he really loved me, huh?" Coolie asked.

Ophelia smiled back at her.

"I guess he really did."

"She's in the bedroom," Ophelia said to Javier. "I gave her a
sleeping pill. You should have seen her, honey. I thought she
was going to have some kind of breakdown when I told her

about Polo. Reading her that letter helped. It made a big difference in things for her."

Javier walked to the bedroom door and looked inside. Coolie was stretched across the bed.

"So what are we going to do?" he asked.

Ophelia shrugged.

"I don't know, Javier. I don't know. But God, did you look at her? We have to help. She's so thin, you can see her bones. I don't know how she got away from Lay, but she did. She made it this far out of sheer determination. We need to do whatever we can."

"I agree," he said. "We can let her stay here for a while. Polo said she had a bad heroin addiction, didn't he? Maybe we can get her into a rehab program."

"I feel a sense of responsibility to her," said Ophelia. "Polo missed that girl so much. It was all he talked about before he went away. He never had a chance to reconcile with her. She came all this way to try to find him. Can you believe that?"

"So many sad things have happened in your family." He sighed. "Hopefully all this pain will end before any more people get hurt."

"Yeah. I don't know how much more of this I can take."

Javier glanced at the clock. It was half past noon.

"How long do you think she'll sleep?" he asked.

"Most of the afternoon, I expect. Maybe even into the night. This hit her pretty hard. The sleeping pill will help."

"Do you think we could leave her for a little bit?" he said. "Remember, I told you there's something I wanted you to see."

Ophelia walked to the door of the bedroom and looked in at the girl. "I think she'll be okay."

"Come on, then," he said. "I've got your purse."

When she turned around, he was standing at the door with her bag and the keys.

He had a look she hadn't seen before as he stood at the door, shifting back and forth. She wondered at his anxiousness.

• • •

When Coolie heard them leave, she picked up the phone and made a call.

"Is he there? I need to talk to him."

"Is this Coolie?" a gruff voice said.

"Yeah. Can you put him on the phone?"

"No. He's out looking for you. Where you at?"

Coolie paused, looking around the night table. She found an unopened bill for Javier.

"Tell him I'm in Lansing, Michigan. Tell him I need him. I want him to come and take me home. He can find me at"—she read the envelope in her hand—"8311 Sycamore Lane."

The man on the phone asked her to repeat it.

She did.

"It won't take him long," the man said. "He's already there looking for you."

"Good. That suits me just fine."

She hung up the phone. Now that her questions about Polo had been answered, she had only one piece of business to finish.

She figured she may as well get on with it so that she could forge ahead.

She looked around for a piece of paper and began to write Ophelia a letter.

CONFRONTATION

*Let everyone witness how many
different cards fortune has up her
sleeve when she wants to ruin a man.*

—BENVENUTO CELLINI

CHAPTER FORTY-FOUR

After making the phone call and writing the letter, Coolie, still sluggish from the sleeping pill, had dozed off to sleep. She awakened with an overpowering need to pee. She sat up in the bed, disoriented. She looked around the room, trying to get her bearings. She saw a picture of Ophelia on the nightstand and remembered the morning's events, the sleeping pill, and the phone call to Detroit. She remembered Polo was dead.

She pushed herself out of bed and stumbled to the bathroom. She sat on the toilet, her jeans bunched in a pile around her ankles. She kicked the door shut. There was a pile of *Jet* magazines stacked along the wall. She reached for one and flipped through it.

She thought about Lay. She knew exactly what she was going to do when he came to get her. She found herself anxious to see him.

When she finished, she felt queasy. Now that she was off heroin, that was always her first reaction to the feeling of hunger.

She pulled up her jeans, washed her hands, and searched the cabinet for something for her nausea. She rooted through bottles of lotion, alcohol, hydrogen peroxide, gauze pads, cotton balls, Q-Tips, and Band-Aids.

She kept a bottle of Pepto-Bismol in her purse. She opened the door of the bathroom and went back into the bedroom. She stopped and looked around. She could see into the living room. The house was quiet.

"I guess they're still not back," she said.

Coolie grabbed her purse from the nightstand beside the bed and rushed back into the bathroom. She didn't bother to pull the door all the way shut.

She sat down on the toilet, opened the bottle, and took a

long swig. She picked up the magazine and flipped the page. There was a picture of the Jackson Five with Berry Gordy. She stared at the photo. Jermaine Jackson looked a lot like Polo.

"I must be going crazy," she said.

She closed the book, picked up her purse, and flicked off the light.

Just as she was about to walk out of the bathroom, someone passed by the cracked door.

About an hour after the yellow Volkswagen pulled out of the yard, the Cadillac rounded the corner of the street. Lay had just called Detroit collect to check on things and see if there was any word about Coolie. The message from her confirmed what he already knew.

Lay drove past the houses, checking each number until he saw Polo's Mustang parked in the driveway.

"Ha. There's his car right there."

Lay dashed across the lawn of the house next to Ophelia's and crouched low along the hedge.

He looked around. The streets were empty. He stood, smoothed his pants, and walked up to the door.

There was no peephole.

He waited, but no one answered.

He rang the doorbell again, then knocked on the door. When nothing happened, he turned the knob.

It was locked.

But the window next to the door was up.

"Ophelia always was stupid," he said.

He reached inside the window, unlocked the door, and climbed in.

Coolie peeked through the cracked door.

She could hear Lay talking to himself as he stood just a foot away.

"Them motherfuckers ain't even in here." He walked around the bedroom. "That's all right. I'll wait on they asses till they come back. When they walk through the door, all cozy and shit, splaa-dat, I'ma fire on that ass."

The sound of his voice made Coolie's nausea worsen.

She opened her purse, reaching in for the switchblade. She didn't know how she could open it without him hearing the noise.

Lay helped her.

"Guess I should reload before they come. I'ma go out like Matt Dillon," he said to himself. He whipped the gun out, pointing it at his reflection in the mirror. He grinned at his image. "Yeah. It's gon' be like the OK Corral up in this motherfucker."

When he cocked the gun, Coolie flipped open the knife.

Lay looked up, then began filling the gun with additional bullets.

He only had a chance to put in two.

"Hey."

He turned around, his mouth open, the chamber still hanging out on the gun in his hand.

"Splaa-dat," she screamed as she rushed toward him with the open knife. She stabbed him in the chest.

Lay fell back to the floor.

"That's for me," she cried. "These are for Polo. He's dead because of you."

She jumped on top of him, her frail body straddling his. She stabbed at the fleshy areas of the torso and arms.

He twitched and kicked against her.

"Bitch," he said. "You can kill me all you want. Your life is fucked. What you gon' do with yourself? Without me, you ain't got shit."

"I don't need you," she said. "You just gave me all the peace I want. Now that I've taken care of you, I can handle my business."

"What kind of business you got?"

"This," Coolie said. With strength that superseded her fragile body, she stabbed him hard, through the breastplate, plunging the knife into his heart.

Lay's chest buckled and began jerking with spasms.

Coolie stood over him and placed the knife against her throat. She pressed deep and pulled it across in a swift, sweeping motion.

Blood spurted out of her jugular into his face.

"Shit," he cried.

She collapsed on top of him. The weight of her fall landed against his struggling heart. He gasped and sputtered, coughing up bubbles of blood.

Lay died on the floor. Coolie's face pressed into his was the last thing he ever saw.

CHAPTER FORTY-FIVE

"Whose place is this?" Ophelia asked.

They sat in the car outside the apartment. She did not see the dark green Chevy parked a short distance away.

"It's a surprise," Javier said. "Do you feel up to a surprise? I think it's something that might be of help to you. But we don't have to go in if you don't want."

She turned in her seat toward him. She couldn't read his face, but she knew she could trust him.

"Sure," she said. "I feel fine."

"This is a big surprise, Ophelita. I don't want you to go in if it's going to upset your condition."

"Shouldn't you have thought of that before you drove me over here?"

"Yes, I should have," he said. "On the way here, I started thinking about the impact it could have on you. Maybe we should just go back. We can always do this later."

Ophelia looked at her husband.

"What's this all about, Javier?"

He was hesitant. "I thought it was important."

"Then come on," she said. "I want to go in. You brought me this far."

They got out of the car and went up to the door.

• • •

Walter was in his bedroom ironing a shirt when he heard a soft knock.

"Did you forget your key, baby?" he asked as walked into the living room to let Evan in.

Ophelia and Javier stood on the front step.

The sight of his daughter overwhelmed Walter. He threw his arms around her neck and began to cry.

Walter was on the sofa, his face in his hands. Ophelia was sitting beside him.

"I wanted to tell you for so long," he said. He couldn't look at her.

"Tell me what?" she asked,

"About us. Me and your mother."

"Uncle Walter, how long have you been living here?"

"Since December."

Javier interrupted him.

"Ophelita, your uncle has something really important he needs to tell you. Something he needs to say to you right now."

Walter looked up at Javier, his eyes wet, grateful for the other man's presence.

"I believe I already know," she said. "I still want to hear it. There's a whole lot of pieces that I can't make fit."

"I don't know how to start," Walter said, his voice thick. "I guess the best way is to tell you I always loved you. That much is true, no matter what else you think."

Ophelia leaned back on the sofa and listened to her uncle unfold the tragedy of his life.

Ophelia was crying when Walter stopped. Her tears were of relief.

"I think I always knew about this," she said. "I knew something wasn't right. Big Daddy raised me, but I guess he never felt I was his own. Lay was always trying to tell me. He said Sukie told him I was some kind of bad seed."

"Sukie and Lay are two of a kind," he said. "She set that fire that killed your baby. Lay knew she was gon' do it before it even happened."

"Dear God," Ophelia said, and she leaned into her palms.

"She tricked me into marrying her," said Walter. "Made me think I killed her mama. I'm not for certain, but I believe Sukie hit her mama in the back of the head. I was so scared, I helped stuff the body in a mattress and Sukie sewed her up in it, and we put it right back on the bed like it always was. That's why I stayed with her all those years. She made me think I was a murderer. She told me she would call down to New Orleans and turn me in if I ever got outta line."

Ophelia reached out and put her hand on his head.

"I'm glad we're clearing all of this up while we're still alive," she said. "I just wish I could have done the same for Mama."

"What do you mean?" Walter asked. "What's wrong with Grace?"

"*Ay, dios mío,*" Javier whispered. "Ophelita, he doesn't know."

"I don't know what?" Walter said, turning to Ophelia. "What's wrong with your mama?"

She gripped his hand. "She's dead."

"Lawd. Lawd. Lawd hammercy," he cried. He pried his hand away from hers and sobbed into his palms.

She wrapped her arms around him.

"Don't cry. I believe Mama's happy now. Be happy for her. She spent most of her life living a lie. She's free now. Be glad for her. She's free."

He nodded, still crying into his hands. "What became of Big Daddy?" he asked, not looking up.

"He passed away, too. They both died in a fire."

Walter wiped his face and looked up at her. "Big Daddy's dead?"

"Yes." She knew she might as well tell him the rest. "So is Sukie."

His sobbing ceased.

"Sukie's dead?" he said.

"Yes."

He stared at the floor. His shoulders began to heave as he rocked back and forth. He was silent for a while, but Ophelia, her arms still around him, could feel the pain rumbling within him.

"She stole my whole life from me," he said, his voice choked. "She took everything from me I ever loved."

"No she didn't," Ophelia said. "We're here. You have us now. You don't have to worry about Sukie anymore."

"I hated her," he said. "I hated her so bad. Y'all ain't got no idea what that woman took me through."

His body trembled as his words turned to howls. Walter sat on the sofa, his head in his hands, the sound of his sobs filling the room.

Ophelia's body rocked with his until his cries began to subside. She stroked his hair.

"So what do I call you now?" she said. Walter seemed so troubled, she didn't want him to suffer any longer.

She saw a tiny smile at the corners of his mouth.

Javier was proud of her. In the face of everything, his wife embraced the change as a welcome part of her life.

"Call me Walter," he said. "I wouldn't expect anything more from you right now. Maybe someday, when you're comfortable enough, then maybe you can call me Pop."

"Pop?" she said with a chuckle.

"Yeah. I always liked how that sounded. It'd be nice to be your pop. You've grown into a beautiful woman."

She hugged him. "Can I ask you a question?"

"Yes. Anything," he said.

"It doesn't look like you live here alone."

Walter looked toward Javier, who shrugged.

"It's kind of awkward for me to explain," Walter said.

"Why?"

Walter was embarrassed. He realized that even though he and Evan were bold in the world of their friends, exposing it to the world of his daughter was more difficult than he had imagined it would be.

"Since I moved here, I've found out a lot about myself.

Things I ran away from, feelings I ignored." He danced around the words. "You see . . ." He cleared his throat. "One of the things I learned about myself when I left Sukie and came here is that I like boys."

He waited for her reaction, but she didn't respond.

"I like boys better than I like girls. And I was surprised at how easy it was for me, especially since my daddy convinced me I was gon' be nuthin' but a faggot anyway. When I was coming up, I went out of my way to prove I was everything but that. Come to find out that's exactly what I am."

He looked down.

"You don't have to be ashamed to tell me," she said. "This is your life now, nobody is else controlling it. Run it the way that you want."

Walter shook his head. "You're something else, Ophelia. You're kind and sweet, just like your mama."

"My mama was a good woman," she said.

"You know, I went back a little while ago and looked up my daddy's people. I went to see my grandma. I hadn't seen her but one time before at my daddy's funeral."

He stood and walked around the room.

"That grandma of mine was still alive. She wasn't too much to talk to after all these years, but my uncle Hailey, Daddy's brother, was another story."

Ophelia sat back on the sofa, taking the pressure off her spine.

"You know what my uncle Hailey told me? He said my daddy, Benny, was funny. He used to beat up on Hailey 'cause he like to dress up like a girl, but my daddy was the main reason he started dressing that way. And my daddy used to sneak around and lay up with boys. He just ain't want nobody to know 'bout it. Ain't that something?"

Walter had stopped pacing and was staring at Javier and Ophelia.

"All that time he had me thinking something was wrong with me. Went to the grave making me think I wasn't normal. Come to find out that I was just like my daddy after all. Now ain't that something?"

Ophelia sniffed the air.

"Do you smell something burning?" she asked.

"Oh Lawd," he cried, jumping up. "I was ironing my shirt."

He ran into the bedroom.

"Walter, is everything all right?" Ophelia said.

"Fine," he said from the bedroom. "The iron fell over. It just scorched my shirt and burned through the ironing board a little. Long as we been talking, it's a wonder the room ain't burn down."

"Okay," she said. "You got anything cold to drink?"

"Yeah. There's some soda and juice in there. Javier, could you please fix her a glass? I need to clean up this mess."

Javier went into the kitchen. He opened the refrigerator. "There's milk in here," he said loud enough for Ophelia to hear. "I'm going to pour you a glass of that."

"No, honey, please. I don't want milk. Could you fix me some soda or something?"

He stuck his head out of the door.

"No soda," he said.

Ophelia pushed herself up from the couch and waddled into the kitchen. She made her way over to Javier as he opened the carton of milk.

"Just a swallow of soda, please, baby. I don't feel like drinking milk right now."

He pretended to frown. He opened the refrigerator and poured a quick splash of Pepsi into the glass.

He smiled as he watched her guzzle it down. She held out the glass for more.

Ophelia was drinking the last of the soda when she felt her water break.

"Uh-oh," she said.

"Come on. Let's go back and sit down. You've had enough to drink. You can barely hold anything in your bladder now as it is."

Javier pushed the kitchen door open to let her out first.

"Why are you standing there like that?" he asked.

"My water just broke."

"You're kidding me, right?"

"No, I'm not," she said.

"Okay, okay, come on. Let's get you out of here."

They left Walter at the house. He agreed to meet them at the hospital. Then Javier, moving faster than he ever had in his life, rushed his wife into the car and sped toward the hospital.

CHAPTER FORTY-SIX

The baby was coming. There was nothing they could do to stop it.

They were two miles from the hospital. Ophelia's contractions were too strong to wait. Javier was forced to pull the Volkswagen over by the side of the road.

"This car is too small," he said. "You can't have it in here."

"I have to," she screamed. "It's coming. You have to do something now."

He grabbed a dusty blanket from the backseat, got out of the car, and came around to her side. He opened the door. Ophelia's head was thrown back as she clutched her stomach and moaned.

"Javier, help me. It's going to come."

He was terrified, watching his wife cry in pain. He threw the blanket on the ground beside him, then knelt on the rocky shoulder of the road. He was careful as he pulled her legs toward him, until they were hanging out of the car. He crouched between them, pulling her panties away.

"What do I do now?" he asked. "Ophelita, I don't know anything about this."

As he said it, the head began to push its way through.

Ophelia moaned, lying back against the stick shift.

"What do I do, pull it?" he asked.

"Yes," she said, panting, "do something. Hurry up."

He grabbed the baby's shoulders, which were already coming through. As Ophelia screamed, the baby squeezed its way out, until Javier realized he was holding the whole thing in his hands.

Two cars had pulled over, and people were watching him deliver the baby.

"Clear its mouth," said a woman standing just behind him. He looked up at her, still in a daze. She wore a nurse's uniform and was holding a first-aid kit.

"Let me help," she said, kneeling beside him, sitting the kit on the ground. She extended her arms. Javier hesitated. "I know what I'm doing," she said. "My shift just ended at the hospital." He handed her the baby.

"What is it?" Ophelia asked, leaning up. Javier looked over at the nurse.

"It's a boy," the woman said.

She opened the kit and began to work on the baby. There were scissors, alcohol, swabs, and gauze. It was all a blur to Javier. Ophelia looked over at her husband, who leaned his head against the car. Tears were running down his cheeks.

"What are we going to name him?" he asked.

"I like Horatio," she said. "Horatio Javier."

He watched the nurse cut the cord on his brand-new son.

"Is that name okay with you?" his wife asked.

"It's just fine, Ophelita."

The nurse wrapped the baby in a white towel and handed him to Ophelia, then turned to Javier.

"You need to get them to the hospital immediately," she said.

PART XIV

1998

EPILOGUE

The richest love is that which submits
to the arbitration of time.

—LAWRENCE DURRELL

CHAPTER FORTY-SEVEN

"So honey, what happened when Ophelia found Coolie?" the woman asked.

"She didn't find her. Javier did. He came home from the hospital after he checked her in, and he found the bodies. He found the letter Coolie wrote to my mother. He read it and broke the news to her the next day."

"Why didn't he tell her right then?"

"Because," Horatio said, "she was in the hospital. She'd just had a baby. He told Walter. He was the one who was able to make a positive ID on Lay."

"So that's your family's story?"

"That's it," he said. "Pretty crazy, huh?"

"Yeah, babe," she replied. "Your people went through some serious changes."

Her head was lying in his lap. The soft brown skin of her brow furrowed as she stared up into the ceiling. Horatio ran his index finger along the creases in her forehead.

"You know what's funny, though," she said.

"What's that?"

"As crazy as your family seems, you guys were just a bunch of people trying to work some things out."

"I guess," he said.

"Think about it. There's crazier stuff on Springer these days. Your great-aunt Sukie would have been a star."

Horatio laughed. He leaned down to kiss her.

"So why'd you feel like you had to tell me all of this?" she said, after their lips grazed.

He leaned back, tracing his finger along the slope of her nose.

"I just asked you to marry me," he said. "I don't want to be like my parents and wait until we're deep on the other side of it before you know everything about what makes me who I am."

She reached up and touched his face, entangling her fingers in the thick curls of his hair.

"Thank you," she said. "For telling me something that you really didn't have to. But it doesn't change how I feel. I'm in this now. You know that, right?"

She pulled his face close to hers again and kissed him.

"I just wanted you to know that my family's got a little baggage."

"Whose doesn't, babe?" she whispered.

"Yeah," he said. "I guess you're right. So are you sure you want to marry me?"

"I don't think I've got any choice."

"What do you mean?"

Her rich brown eyes looked up into his.

"My period's been late for two weeks."

He looked down at his beautiful woman's face and ran his hands across her short, twisted locks. Adina's complexion was a rich pecan-tan, just like the photos he'd seen of his grandmother Grace. She smiled up at him and nodded.

Horatio had never been so happy in his life.

ACKNOWLEDGMENTS

All thanks and praises first to God for the abundance of blessings that surround me every day.

Extra special thanks to:

My mother, *Lillie B. Files.* You are the perfect template for a human being. You taught me everything I know about kindness and love.

My brother, *Arthur James Files, Jr.* For saving me from all those beat-downs as a kid when I pulled so many dreadful pranks on your friends.

My uncle, *Jim Brackett.* For taking such good care of us. Love, love, love.

Melvin Flournoy. For taking such good care of my mom.

My *Boopies,* the *Reco-Fivises.* Brooklyn, Lola, Milo (& Telly)—the cutest pack (okay, herd) of dawgies you ever did see.

Victoria Christopher Murray. Good grief, thanking you could take forever. For starters, how about for: being the person I laugh, cry, and pray with for almost everything, never once making me feel like the lunatic you know I am, being the perfect person to tour with, and completely understanding the very real desperation of needing some Roscoe's or glazed walnut prawns from Eurochow.

Eric Jerome Dickey. Bubby. My Knight in Twisted Humor. You're kind, loving, heroic, handsome, compassionate, allergic, comedic, multitalented, tenacious, ever-writing, optimistic, protective—all the good adjectives of life. You keep me on schedule, on focus, on point. You are the embodiment of how God meant for people to be.

Yvette Hayward. Ettevy, my sister. You're high-strung, high-maintenance, high-intensity, high-pitched. Everything a girl could wish for in a friend (or a pit bull). Thanks for always being so fiercely protective of me and my dawgies' well-being.

Michael Cory Davis. I wish you the best of everything.

Sherri G. Sneed & Shaun Robinson. My partners-in-girlfriend therapy-big business-and-crime. You guys keep me sane. Thanks, Sherri, for being the voice of reason for me in all things business and personal. Thanks, Shaun, for making sure I get out of the house and into the mix of this wacky town we live in. Let's turn Hollywood on its ear. (Hi, Shaun's mom! Thanks for the support!)

Warren Frazier. You're a real treasure. I feel very secure in the thought that you have my best interests at heart.

David Rosenthal. For championing this book from the very beginning, believing in it so strongly, and having such a keen sense of vision about what it would be.

Amanda Murray. For being an exceptional editor and giving me such wonderful feedback.

Cherise Grant. For great guidance and great conversations.

Larry Kirshbaum. One of my favorite people in the whole wide world. Thanks for being such a wonderful friend.

Mary Pittman-Jones. Eureka. I have found you.

Jacquatte Rolle. My sister for life.

Courtney Rolle. The world's cutest goddaughter.

Bryonn R. Bain. I'm *sooooooooo* proud of you. It doesn't make any sense for so much talent in so many forms to be housed in one person. I can't wait until the rest of the world finds out what I already know. Much love to you, Placid, and your family.

Troy, Rejeana, & Jalen ("Jake") Mathis. Y'all be my people. I luh y'all, and am so glad you're in L.A. near me ... okay-bye.

Bryan Keith Ayer. Fifteen years of Beav, and still going. White Parakeeta, anyone?

Theresa Coffer. For being so connected to me.

Bernadette Andrews (and Keith, Ariel, and Crystal). I'm so glad we found each other again. I guess, after this, we don't need any more proof to know we're connected for life and for a reason. I've got much love for you.

Dawnn Lewis. For being such an inspirational friend. Much love to you and Tony (Blades).

Dr. Joseph Marshall, Jr. Do we have the best conversations or what? I feel honored to call you my friend. Much love to you & the family.

The *Brackett Family*–Eric & family, Sharlyn Simon & Shemar, Charles, Ted, Bobby (Percy), Sallye Cooper Brackett, Shunda, Cheric, & Charleston (P-nut) Brackett, Charla & Chauncey Shines, Curtis & Debra Cooper & kids, Daetrick Brackett, Wanda in Orlando.

The *Files Family*–Louis & family, Charlestine (Dot) & Sam Carter & family, Ella Mae, Betty Jean & family, Lura (Niney) & family, Inez Files & family, Cleveland (Benny) in Natchez, the Files clan in Birmingham, Alabama, and any other Files I failed to mention.

The *Davis Family* in Brooklyn, New York–Chez, Sebert, Kishane & Trish, Nicole, and Doris Rattagan (I would never ignore you in a million years; you are a jewel). You guys have been family to me. I have much love for you.

The *Murray and Christopher Families*–my extended peeps. Much love to the Murrays in L.A./Venice Beach (Ray Murray and his entire clan) who make me feel like a part of the family (I love all those family eatfests), and the Christophers (Cecile in L.A., Cia & Hubby in Maryland, Mom & Pops in New York) who are stuck with me for life.

Shirley Ann Mausby & family, Douglas White, Mitch & Shiho Lambert (and P.J. & the baby), Antoine Coffer, Mary & Willie Davis in Atlanta, Willie Mae Baltimore, Annie Pearl Nixon & family, Shara, Walter, & Alicia (Nikki) Dickerson & the rest of the May family, Shirley Brackett & John, Harry C. Douglas, Jr., Rachel Douglas, Pamela O. Douglas, & Willie Mae Douglas & Harry Douglas, Sr., the Capers, Prince, & Fenderson families, my newfound family in Southern California (Patsy Davis & the rest of the families), my Boston family the Essexes (Dawn, Petey, Sandra, Michelle, Addie Belle, Bo, & everybody), all branches of the Rolle family, Lisa "Brownie" Brown & family (hi Kim & Cody!), Suzette Webb & family, R. Malcolm Jones & Shenita & the twins, Dave Aronberg, Esq. (shaking things up in the White House!), Frank Frazier & family, Shonda Cheekes & family, my girl Kiki Henson, Karla Greene, Esq., Dominique Dickey, Pat Houser & family, Brenda Alexander & family, Brenda Williams & family, Frank Jenkins & family, Sherlina Washington & family, the Brown family in Hollywood, FL, Rhonda Ware & family, Mommy German & ed, Vernette & the Mayweather family, Andrea & Patrick, Bruce McCrear & all my Birmingham friends, Keith & JoAnn Davis & family, Eric Warmack & family, Andy & Mary Gregory & family, all my old friends from the KinderCare days, Blake & Terry and the crew in L.A., Carol Ozemhoya, Bo Griffin, Olive Salih & Alison Tomlinson, Pamela Crockett & family, Leroy Baylor, Abdul Giwa, Jr., M.D. & family, Louis & Tonya Oliver, Eric Saunders, Lee Eric Smith, Rod Crouther, Dana, Kristi, Madison & Shelby Lee, Glendon P. Hall & family, Rodney Lee & family, Cyndi Johnson, Dionne, Darryl Ranard Nobles, Marty & Monique Berg & Dinky (Eliane), Lance Powell, Jill Tracey, B. J. Barry, Raj, Traci Cloyd, Alton "Butter" McLean, Cliff & Jenean at KJLH, David & Daniel Salzman & family, Brian Dobbins, my friends in Tabahani Book Circle, Carol Mackey, Rosario Schuler-Ukpabi & her fabulous salons *Oh! My Nappy Hair*, Sherri Winston, Debby Ryan, & Renee Stone & family.

To all those writers who are taking this walk and making waves as they do it: LaJoyce Brookshire & family, Kimberla & Will Roby & family, E. Lynn Harris & Rodrick, R. M. Johnson, Jacquelin Thomas & Bernard (& the kids), Bernice McFadden, Nina Foxx, Glenn R. Townes, Donna Hill, Evelyn Coleman, Brian Egeston, Sheneska Jackson, Zane, Van Whitfield, Colin Channer, Timm McCann, Omar Tyree, Yolanda Joe, Franklin White, Blair S. Walker, Steven Barnes & Tananarive Due, Michael Patrick MacDonald, Carolina Garcia-Aguilera, Trisha Thomas, Patrice Gaines, Michael Baisden, Tawanna Butler, Tracy Thompson, Edwardo Jackson, Victor McGlothin, David Haynes, C. Kelly Robinson, Lisa Saxton, Renee Swindle,

Sharony Andrews, Nanci Thomas, all the other authors, artists, and creative spirits out there striving to make it through.

A special shout-out to my new friends, Mat & Mira Johnson. So much talent in one household . . . you two are going to go far. (*Shameless Plug:* Everyone, buy Mat's book, DROP. It'll blow you away.)

My new friends: Reggie McFadden (you are *heeeelarious*), and Ray K. Morris (& Lisette).

My publicist at Simon & Schuster, *Tracey Guest,* for all her hard work.

All my old friends over at Warner Books: (Taura, Doris, Cheryl, Michelle, and Cassandra), Christine Saunders, and Caryn Karmatz-Rudy.

All the bookstores who show me so much support: Jim & Renee Rogers at Zahra's Books-n-Things, James Fugate at Eso-Won, Blanche Richardson at Marcus Books, Ms. Emma Rodgers at Black Images, Jokae's African-American Books, Perris McKnight at Barnes & Noble (in Richmond, CA), The Florida Connection—Janet Mosley at Tenaj, Jackie Perkins at Montsho, Felecia Wintons at Books for Thought, Naseem & Naseema at Nefertiti, D.C. at Afro-n-Books-n-Things, and Akbar at Pyramid; Julie & Daniel at Waldenbooks (in Florida), Fanta & Mutota in Atlanta, Shondalon Ramin, Sundiata Ramin, Mamu, Malik's Books, Karibu Books, Desiree at Afro-centric in Chicago, Faye & Cassandra at Sisterspace in D.C., Jerry (Tariq) Jones at Afro Awakenings, and anyone else I forgot to mention.

Big love to the *Sorors of Alpha Kappa Alpha Sorority, Inc.,* and all the organizations and book clubs that have been with me from the very beginning.

And most of all, to the Readers: thank you for being so supportive of my work and for the opportunity to create new stories in the hopes of always holding your attention with worthy material.

Please forgive me if I forgot to mention anyone. It's because my head is cluttered, but my heart is in the right place.

Oh yeah:

To Manolo, Jimmy, Bebe, Enzo, etc. For being some of the purdiest thangs a girl could ever slip her feet into.

Love to the world. Till we meet again.
Send shoes. Nice ones. (I wear a size 7.)

ABOUT THE AUTHOR

LOLITA FILES is the best-selling author of four novels: *Scenes from a Sistah, Getting to the Good Part, Blind Ambitions,* and *Child of God.* She lives in Los Angeles, where she is currently developing projects for film and television.